Gracie HART

The Girl Who Came From Rags

EBURY
PRESS

First published by Ebury Press in 2019

3 5 7 9 10 8 6 4 2

Ebury Press, an imprint of Ebury Publishing
20 Vauxhall Bridge Road,
London SW1V 2SA

Ebury Press is part of the Penguin Random House group of companies whose
addresses can be found at global.penguinrandomhouse.com

Penguin
Random House
UK

www.penguin.co.uk

A CIP catalogue record for this book is available from the British Library

ISBN 9781785038099

Typeset in 12/15.5 pt Times LT Std
by Integra Software Services Pvt. Ltd, Pondicherry

Printed and bound in Great Britain by Clays Ltd, Elcograf S.p.A.

Penguin Random House is committed to a sustainable future for
our business, our readers and our planet. This book is made
from Forest Stewardship Council® certified paper.

For old friends and new friends who all bring pleasure to my life.

Chapter 1

Mary-Anne sat in the kitchen of Ma Fletcher's house near Speakers' Corner, and realised she could not quite forgive herself for being so selfish and leaving her benefactor and lifelong friend to die on her own. She should have known that the old woman was seriously ill and that she had just put a brave face on her pain. She had encouraged Mary-Anne to leave her be so that she could attend the Guild Ball with her wealthy William Ellershaw – and now Ma was gone.

She shook her head and smiled, then took a slow sip of her tea. Despite feeling guilt over Ma Fletcher's death, she knew Ma would have appreciated the scene that she and William had caused at the Guild Ball, and would have understood why she had not returned to her bedside. They had caused many a tongue to wag with their obvious passion for one another and now both Ma's plans and her own had come to fruition; the only pity was that Ma was not alive to see it.

Mary-Anne knew she had a lot of things to be thankful for and at this moment she was counting Ma's blessings most of all. Ma had bequeathed all that she had possessed to her, keeping her promise to her. She also now had William in the palm of her hand; she was both wealthy and loved, both things that she had only dreamt of a few months ago. And with her sister Eliza now being engaged to Tom Thackery, her childhood sweetheart, things were beginning to look rosy for the Wild girls from Pit Lane.

Mary-Anne set down her tea and wandered into the hallway; she couldn't help but glance in at the parlour where, behind the curtained partition, the body of Ma Fletcher lay in her coffin. She sighed before walking over and glancing at herself in the mirror by the front door. She should be wearing black for mourning, she thought, as she put on her best hat and wrapped her shawl around her, but black was such a dull colour and it did nothing for her complexion, so she'd not bothered. Ma Fletcher would have understood.

She'd not had time yet to tell her sister of Ma Fletcher's death – she'd not spoken to her since the ball. Instead, she'd had to call for the doctor to register the old girl as dead and then seen that she was laid out and her funeral needs were arranged. Now that all was in place, and the funeral was to take place on Friday, she would go and tell her the news. The news that was going to change Mary-Anne's life and perhaps enable her to help her daughter, Victoria, and her sister Eliza.

She hesitated for a second, wondering whether to check in on the old woman before leaving the house, but then thought better of it. After all, she wasn't going to be going anywhere – she was dead and as cold as the grave – but it was hard for her to register that, after looking after her the last few months and seeing to her every need. A cold shiver ran down her spine as she closed the front door behind her and started walking down from Speakers' Corner to her sister's shop on Boar Lane; she'd news to tell her sister, some bad, but mostly good, now that she would soon be a woman of wealth, if the will of Ma Fletcher's that she had found was true.

In the sewing room at the back of her shop, Eliza sat back in disbelief. 'Ma Fletcher is dead? The poor old woman ... she might have been a nosy old devil but she looked out for us over the years when we were both in need of her. And she's been good to you, Mary-Anne.'

'Aye, well, she'd been getting frailer. She wasn't enjoying her life any more, not like she used to. It's a blessing, really. The funeral will be a quiet affair; she'd no relations left. It's at Saint John's at one on Friday.' Mary-Anne looked across at her sister. 'I presume you'll be coming?'

'Yes, of course, I'll come; I owe her that much. I'll always remember standing on her cart down there on Briggate when Queen Victoria visited Leeds.' Eliza smiled. 'She looked after me and Victoria so well that day ... made sure we wanted for nothing.'

'Aye, well, she's done the same for me n'all,' Mary-Anne told her. 'According to the will I found, she's left me everything, just like she said she would, providing I look after her old cat until its dying day. Every last penny and every brick of the house. I can't quite believe it!'

'I remember you saying she'd promised you that and for all her faults she never went back on her word. God bless her, she's done well for you, and—' Eliza turned and looked at her sister '—I hope you appreciate it.'

'I do, believe me, it gives me the power to do what I want if all is settled according to the will, and I've no cause to doubt it won't be. It'll give me the opportunity to make things better for both you and Victoria too, if you'll give me chance.' Mary-Anne smiled.

'Will it stop you from causing more scandal by chasing William Ellershaw and perhaps let his father die in peace? Can't you forget the wrong that Edmund, his father, did to you and accept that he was just rotten to the core and be thankful that out of evil you were blessed with a beautiful daughter that needs your love?' Eliza glanced at her sister and saw her face clouding over as she thought of Edmund Ellershaw and what he had done to her, taking her innocence when she was little more than a girl.'

'I will never forgive Edmund Ellershaw! And, as for William, one day he will truly be mine; we were meant for one another. You know I love Victoria; she's the reason why I have fought for everything I now possess. She'll understand eventually.' Mary-Anne bowed her head. 'Right, I'm off; I need to finish making the arrangements for Ma's funeral. I also have plans to write to William to tell him to come and visit me at home. *My* home, bless Ma Fletcher; I owe her everything.'

'Victoria would much rather have her mother than all of Ma Fletcher's worldly goods and yours,' Eliza whispered to herself as she watched her sister leave her shop without a backward glance.

Mary-Anne watched as the four pall-bearers, dressed in sombre black, loaded Ma's body into the back of the horse-drawn hearse.

'Wait, just wait a moment; I've something that needs to be buried with her,' Mary-Anne hurriedly remembered, as the undertaker took up the reins of the four black horses, ready to take Ma on her last journey to the church. 'Here, place these in besides her.' Mary-Anne passed the precious knitted baby booties that had once belonged to Ma Fletcher's young son who had been so heartlessly killed by Edmund Ellershaw. 'She'll be at peace with these next to her.' She fought back tears as they were tenderly placed by Ma's side and then she watched as the funeral procession took off. 'God bless you, Ma Fletcher; I know you are due heaven but Edmund Ellershaw will rot in hell if I have my way and I'll do it for both of us!'

Mary-Anne sat down in her chair next to the fire and looked at the scrawny cat that was now her charge. 'Well, you scraggy moggy, you've just got me now. So don't you complain else you'll get a boot up your backside.' Mr Tibbs, as if in defiance, stuck his tail up in the air and made for the warmth of the midday sun that was shining through the kitchen window of Mary-Anne's newly inherited house at Speakers' Corner.

Mary-Anne looked around her and sighed; it was strangely quiet without Ma Fletcher yelling for something she wanted doing or having a spirited difference of opinion. There'd be none of that now the old girl was dead and soon to be buried six foot down in Saint John's cemetery. In a way she was going to miss the old woman; after all, she had been company on dreary evenings and, aside from her sister, the closest thing Mary-Anne had to a friend in this world.

Mary-Anne was not one for making friends easily – partly because of her fierce independence and partly because of her dislike of the frivolous, giggling women that seemed to enjoy being kept in place by their husbands or lovers. Although, when it came to William Ellershaw, she found herself being a hypocrite – with him she was charming and flirtatious but it was all part of a bigger plan to become more than just his lover.

It had started out as revenge – William was merely a means to an end to bring hurt to his father, Edmund, but now she realised she did love the dashing William. The trouble was that, as things stood, loving him was all she could ever do, because he was still married, in name if not in deed. Mary-Anne would have to be content with once again being used by a member of the Ellershaw family when the fancy took him.

At least this time the dalliance was her choice and more pleasure than pain. Whether they had deeper feelings or not for one another they both would have to be content with their lot for now, and, besides, she herself had much more now than she ever dreamt possible a few months ago. In truth, she no longer needed William and his wealth; she could now support herself.

She looked down at the will and deeds that the crow-like solicitor had just given her and felt tears welling up in her eyes again. Ma's solicitor had read out the will with a most begrudging look upon his face; perhaps he had been expecting something for his services from Ma Fletcher. But no, she'd left her, Mary-Anne Vasey, everything ... every last penny, every knick-knack and ornament. Everything in the house, including the house itself, was hers and all for the sake of Ma being grateful for Mary-Anne's help – along with a shared hatred of Edmund Ellershaw.

How Ma had hated Edmund Ellershaw. Well, if she'd gone to heaven, she'd be looking down at him and laughing at the state he was in: an invalid struck dumb and being spoon-fed after suffering from a stroke that Mary-Anne couldn't help but feel he had brought upon himself with his decadent life-style. Mary-Anne grinned to herself; it was perhaps a good job that he was in such a state, because after all the gossip and scandal that had been caused by her and William attending the Guild Ball together, he would have surely made both their lives hell.

Thankfully her darling Victoria and Eliza had begrudgingly accepted their love affair, although Victoria was still uneasy with the thought of the man who was her half-brother courting her mother. But even she had come to realise that there was no stopping it and that no matter what she said or did, it would not have the slightest effect on her mother's pursuit of what she saw as Victoria's rightful wealth and position, which her bastard of a father Edmund Ellershaw had denied her.

Mary-Anne folded the will and put it behind the candlestick on the top of the mantlepiece. 'Well, this won't buy the baby a new bonnet,' she said out loud, looking at Mr Tibbs. 'Let's get rid of that makeshift bed and get ready for our visitor tonight.' She shook her head; Lord help her, she was already talking to the mangy old fleabag like Ma had always done, as if it was a person. She smiled as she set about moving the bedding and the chaise longue that had been Ma Fletcher's bed for so long. Tonight she was going to celebrate; tonight she was going to entertain William Ellershaw as he had never been entertained before. This was her home now; she could do as she pleased and nothing nor nobody would stand in her way.

*

Where was her husband? What was he up to? Or more importantly, who? Questions that Priscilla Ellershaw asked herself while all the time she knew exactly where William was. She tossed and turned in her bed, sobbing and clutching at her pillow as she listened to the minutes ticking away on the gilt dial clock that stood on the walnut chest of drawers in her bedroom.

Minutes had turned into hours, and with every movement of the minute hand, Priscilla had grown more desperate and distressed. She had lain in the dark listening for any sound of her husband returning, and now, by the light of the candle, she could see it was nearly three in the morning. Yet again for the third night on the trot, her husband, William, was not going to return home, let alone frequent her bedroom.

She sobbed quietly into her pillow, distraught by the lack of empathy shown by her husband to her, his forgotten and unloved wife, as finally she got out of bed, picked up the flickering candle, opened her bedroom door and tiptoed along the landing to her husband's bedroom. She glanced down into the magnificent hallway of Levensthorpe Hall. It was silent. The servants were all in their beds but a gas light was still burning, just in case the master did return before daylight.

Like a ghostly apparition, Priscilla made her way into William's bedroom. She glanced around her and picked up a shirt that he had discarded before he'd gone out gallivanting. She picked it up and smelt it, hoping that she could smell the man she loved upon it, but instead the smell of heady stale perfume assaulted her nostrils, a perfume that was not hers. It was the smell of his lover, an aroma that added more hurt and pain to her already broken heart.

She threw the shirt back down upon his bed and went and opened the bedside drawer, the drawer where she knew she could find what she was looking for in her moment of sorrow. Quickly she fled back into her bedroom and sat in front of her dressing-table mirror, looking at her reflection in the glass. No wonder William was bedding another woman: a woman she knew from overhearing her own servants' gossip to be beautiful and elegant with winning wild ways.

She'd made little of the words said to her by friends, warning her of the woman who had taken William's fancy. Just another fling, she had thought, thankful at first that she had taken some of the pressure of performing wifely duties but there was now no avoiding the scandal – they were the talk of Leeds society after that woman had taken Priscilla's rightful place at the Guild Ball.

'Mary-Anne Vasey, may you rot in hell,' she whispered, as she sobbed, unwanted and unloved in front of the mirror. She hated herself, she hated every inch of herself for not being the woman William lusted after; why didn't she have the long auburn hair that Mary-Anne Vasey had and the green eyes that bade her husband to bed her each night? She picked up the scissors that the maid had left on her dressing table and started to hack and cut her long blonde locks off her head, leaving her head with clumps of hair and her scalp nearly showing in places, making her look like a workhouse or lunatic asylum inmate. Tears fell down her cheeks as she finally picked up the pistol that she had known William to always keep loaded in his bedside drawer. Her hands shook as she stared at her reflection, holding the gun to her head, and then she pulled the trigger ...

*

'Who in God's name is yelling and hammering on your front door at this time of night or should I say morning, seeing the sun is about to rise?' William Ellershaw looked down upon the sleepy Mary-Anne, her auburn hair cascading around her pale face as she pulled on his arm to rejoin her in bed and forget the din of whoever was hammering on the front door. 'No, Mary-Anne, whoever it is, they mean business. Now leave me be, you vixen, while I see what it is they're wanting.'

William pulled his white shirt over his dark head and went to the window, opening it to look down on the street and the two men that were demanding his presence.

'Shut your racket, you guttersnipes,' William yelled down at the two men, not recognising them at first. 'What do you mean by all this din? It's enough to waken the dead.' He then realised he was looking down upon the face of his butler and that the young boy with him was the stable lad, and that three of his own horses were tethered to the garden railings, saddled and ready to ride.

'I'm sorry, Mr Ellershaw, we didn't know what else to do. We just hoped that we would find you here, sir,' his butler explained, clearly embarrassed at having to have tracked his master down to the house of his mistress. 'You've got to come home. There's been an accident . . . it's Mrs Ellershaw.'

'What do you mean, an accident? Wait there, I'll come down.' William closed the window behind him and sat on the bed edge pulling on his breeches and boots while Mary-Anne sat upright in bed.

'What do they mean an accident and how did they know you were here?' Mary-Anne looked at the worry on Williams' face.

'I don't know what that wife of mine has been up to, but really, my dear, I think the whole of Leeds could probably guess who I'm with, if not where, nowadays, don't you? Now, I've got to go, but I'll be back as soon as I can.' William lent over and kissed her; whatever Priscilla had done he hoped it was worth dragging him away from his night of pleasure.

'I'll be waiting.' Mary-Anne yawned and hid back under the bedcovers as she heard the mumbled voices from outside and the sound of horses' hooves racing off at a pace along the cobbled road. Silly Priscilla, she thought to herself as she closed her eyes, it was probably something and nothing, concocting some drama designed to draw her husband back to her side. She should have guessed by now: William was no longer hers. She might have his name, the fine house and all the trappings that went with it but it was she – Mary-Anne Wild – who had the heart of William Ellershaw, and he would never love, or ever had loved, her.

*

William rode hard after his butler had explained, in hushed tones, what had befallen poor Priscilla. He entered into the ground of Levensthorpe Hall just as dawn was breaking. The morning's dew was thick on the grass and the Hall itself was shrouded in early morning mist. He jumped from his horse and ran up the Hall's steps quickly, opening the large front doors before running across the hallway and up the stairs to Priscilla's room. This was the last thing that he had wanted for Priscilla. He hadn't loved her but he hadn't meant her any harm; he had just wanted his freedom.

The doctor and his housekeeper were standing by his wife's bedside and they turned as William entered the room.

'Well, you are free to do as you please now, William Ellershaw,' the old doctor said, without a trace of respect for the man who paid his bills. He had been Priscilla's doctor since she was a girl and had watched her steady decline since her wedding with a heavy heart. 'She's released you from your vows. The poor woman must have had enough, and I can't say I blame her; you've been the talk of the town of late.' The doctor closed his bag and looked at the ashen-faced Casanova who stood in front of him. 'She didn't suffer, so that's a blessing; her aim was good. I've made a death certificate out – it's on the table – but I'm going to tell you this, young man: I've looked after Priscilla's family in this house for over thirty years and this is the very last time that I will be setting foot into it. You'll not be seeing my face ever again. You are a scoundrel, sir, a rogue, and if you had any morals at all you would have stopped this gallivanting with those whores of yours a long time ago. And then this poor innocent wretch might still be alive.' The doctor walked to the bedroom door. 'I'll see myself out. You and your father have the same weakness. God help any woman that loves you because you'll break them every time. Good day, sir, and may the devil take you to hell.'

William looked at the cold, still body of Priscilla lying on her bed. She had used the small pistol he kept by his bed and, though her face was still recognisable, it was covered with blood where the shot had entered her temple. She had made sure of her death, holding the gun at close range to her head, determined to take her life.

'I'm sorry, sir. We were all asleep; we'd have stopped her if we could have done.' The housekeeper wept as she watched William take Priscilla's hand.

'It's all right, Peggy, you're not to blame. It was, as the doctor said, my fault. She still loved me and I cared not for her feelings; I should have set her free to a life of her own, rather than expect her to put up with my ways. At least she is at peace now.' William smiled sadly at the housekeeper. 'Go and see to yourself and leave me with her for a short while.' He watched as the housekeeper, still dressed in her nightdress and nightcap, left him in the room with Priscilla.

'Well, my Prissy, you've gained your freedom and I have mine. I hope your soul is at peace, my dear. I doubt mine ever will be. The doctor is right; I do have the same traits as my father but, unlike him, I aim to keep Mary-Anne Vasey as mine, because, unlike him, I love her. So thank you once again, my dear Prissy; I now have everything that I wished for and all because of you.' William looked around him and sighed. The biggest mistake of his life was lying dead in front of him and now he was a free man.

Chapter 2

'Don't even think of getting any sympathy here, William. You drove that poor girl to her grave, just like you have your father. Because he might as well be dead for all the use he is to anyone.' Catherine Ellershaw sniffed into her handkerchief as she looked across at her son who had come to tell her his news.

'Mama, that's being unkind to William. Priscilla was always of a nervous position and Father, well … it's not as if he's led a blameless life.' Grace looked across at her brother and tried to play peacekeeper and defend him from her mother's onslaught.

'Don't waste your breath, Grace. I thought by now you'd realise that I'm the black sheep of the family and that everything is my fault.' William's eyes flashed as he sat in the drawing room of Highfield House and played with his hat brim that was balanced on his knee to hide his nervousness of having to share his news.

'What else do you expect? You make our family a laughing stock, strutting and parading a common whore around at the Guild Ball. No wonder poor Priscilla chose to take her life ... the shame that you have brought to this family! I fear we will never recover from it.' Catherine breathed in and reached for her smelling salts as a fit of vapours came about her.

'She's no whore, Mother. Her name is Mary-Anne Vasey; she's a wealthy woman. In fact, she has more money than you, Mama, if what I hear is true when it comes to my father's business affairs. It is not just me that everyone is talking about; everyone knows that my father has been living on credit for years and that both his pits are worthless. And let's face it, Mother, if you insist on calling her names, Mary-Anne was his *whore* before she was mine. The pits are worth nothing, especially with George in charge of the Rose. He's hardly in charge of himself, let alone a suitable person to be given full rein of overseeing a coal mine; it's a good job Tom Thackeray knows what he's about else it would be more than one death that this family would be responsible for.' William took in his pompous brother George's frills and fancy clothes and swore under his breath.

George stood up. 'I say, you take that back, else I'll give you a good seeing to. I've been doing my best for the pits since my father took ill, which is more than can be said of you.'

'Just sit down, George; you are all bluster and wind. You've never fought anyone in your life and I've no quarrel with you. I've no quarrel with anyone; we all are trying to live our own lives how we wish and not one of you has the

16

right to preach to me over my lifestyle. Well, perhaps you, Grace but … I never did love Priscilla and you all knew that. It was you and Grandfather who forced me into marrying her – for her money and her position – and now that she's gone I aim to do as I please.' William stood up and looked at his family. 'The funeral will be at Woodlesford on Wednesday at two; I've arranged for her to be buried inside our family's tomb, despite her taking her own life. It's amazing how persuasive money can be to the clergy.' William put his hat on his head and made for the doorway.

'Wait, William, I'll see you out.' Grace quickly caught her brother up and walked with him down the hallway to the front door before pulling him aside to talk. 'Are you all right? Even if you didn't care for her, you must be feeling something over the death of Priscilla; you are not that cold-hearted.' Grace looked up at her brother who, to some extent, she'd always known had been used as a pawn to gain her family power and respectability through her grandfather arranging his marriage to Levensthorpe Hall's heiress.

'I'm fine, relieved in a way. We were both leading lives that we were not happy with. Though I just wish she had packed her bags and left me instead of doing what she did. I was going to divorce her, if she had only known. I know the scandal would have been upsetting but she'd have been blameless; after all, it would have been my doing. I know I'm the gossip of society and quite frankly I don't give a damn. However, I knew she never would have agreed to it. I'd have given her the means to support herself if she had asked but Levensthorpe Hall meant everything to her; she would never have left that way.' William picked his gloves and riding crop up from the hallway table and looked at his sister. 'And you? How's your life, still entwined with Eliza Wild and her dressmaking? I thought that you would have had enough by now.'

'Funny that you might say that. I am getting tired of it; Eliza doesn't really need me any more. She's as strong as me and I'd have thought that she's realised by now that she does more of the work and I get more of the glory.' Grace looked hesitant before confiding, 'I've also been taking more of the profits from the business than she has.'

William smirked at her. 'Not so innocent after all, dear sister,' he joked, but at her crestfallen face he added, 'Of course, as well you should; it was your capital that started the venture. What will you do?'

'I thought I might spread my wings and venture to London for a while, see the world and become an independent woman. Besides, if Father's affairs are as bad as you say they are, this may not be my home for much longer. Poor Mother, she always thinks the best of Father and yet she knows what he is like really.' Grace looked down at her feet as William opened the door.

'The old bugger's hanging on out of sheer evil; it's the first time he's been unable to get up to no good in his life. But, believe me, things are bad, Gracie; you tuck what money you have away and leave Mother and George to it. George will be all right – he has Grandfather's inheritance to look forward to, and Mother … well, if it comes to her having to sell everything, she should be left with enough for herself, a home and money to live on, as long as she doesn't aim too high. No fancy house in Roundhay!' William kissed his sister on the cheek as he put on his hat and walked to his horse.

'And what are you going to do now, William?' Grace stood below him as he sat in his horse's saddle.

'I'm going to bloody well enjoy myself while I can and sod everybody else.' William grinned. 'What else would you expect?' He kicked his horse into motion and rode off down the driveway on his way to Mary-Anne's house at Speakers' Corner.

'Oh, my love.' Mary-Anne kissed William on the nape of his neck as he held her tight, having told her his news. 'She'll be at peace now; from what you've told me she always was fragile. Even though I was envious of her, having you as her husband, I still can't help but feel sad that things have come to this.'

While Mary-Anne's face was a picture of loving concern, in truth she felt mixed emotions. William was free but even she was not so heartless as to not pity a woman driven to take her own life. Once, when she had been driven to despair as an unwed girl with a baby in her belly, she had contemplated the same. Yet another secret she would keep from William.

'She was a good soul,' she said, 'too good for this world and for the likes of you and me; we might as well have shot her ourselves, we hurt her so badly with our passion.' Mary-Anne wiped a tear away as William lifted his head from her chest.

'Don't say that! We are not responsible for her death, no matter what the gossips might make of it. It was her hand on the trigger. My mother said the exact same words and blamed me too, not to mention calling you all the names under the sun. I told her I wasn't having any of it, that she had no right to judge, when my father was ten times worse than myself. Besides, what does she know? She's only loved one man and she, like Priscilla, just did the dutiful thing and pretended all was well in her world. When really it was falling down all around her.' William looked at Mary-Anne before sitting back in his chair, holding his head in his hands.

'What do you mean that all your mother's world is falling down around her? I know your father is ill, but surely things are not that bad?' Mary-Anne wiped her eyes and showed interest as she realised that William was worried about his family's well-being as well as the death of his wife.

'I heard the other night that my father is nearly bankrupt! The manager of the bank was drinking in the club but I kept out of his way as I knew that he would want me to honour his debts. Father disowned me and he still owes me from the last time I bailed him out. I've told Grace to take care of herself and follow her heart, seeing that she was spouting about travelling to London or even further afield. She never has been happy towing the line and being expected to eventually marry and become a mother. George will be fine – my grandfather has seen to that – and Mother will survive. It will be the shame of it all, if it does come about, that she won't be able to cope with.' William sighed. 'It never rains but it pours; thank God my business is thriving, and with Priscilla gone, we can look to the future ...'

'How is your father?' Mary-Anne asked, trying to keep her emotions out of her voice. William wasn't to know how much she prayed for his demise. 'I'm surprised that he's in such a financial mess; surely the pit is worth something?'

'Father is alive, just. Not that I care. The pit is only worth something if you are prepared to build it back up again. But worse than that, the stupid fool has mortgaged Highfield House without my mother knowing; he doesn't own a brick of it or should I say the chimney pot might just be paid for!' William breathed in deeply.

'Oh, I see; I didn't realise things were that bad. I knew the pit had been neglected but I didn't realise things were so desperate. Does Eliza know of Gracie's plans and what is to become of the shop? Will Grace still keep it even though she is travelling?' Mary-Anne asked with intent.

'I don't know; I doubt that she will want to be burdened with the responsibility of running it while she travels or decides what she wants to do with her life. No doubt she will speak to Eliza about it shortly. But enough of my family. This is our time now; we are free to do whatsoever we wish. We can do and go wherever we wish without fear of rebuke. I know people will hold me to account for Priscilla's death, but it is as Grace said: she was always nervy and the people who knew her the best will verify this. Mary-Anne, when enough time has passed to satisfy the gossips, will you marry me?' William reached for Mary-Anne's hand and squeezed it tightly. 'I know I will have to look as if I am in mourning for a short while, but I'm not going to let you slip through my fingers again. Damn it, I love you, woman, and this time I'm going to get it right.' William looked at Mary-Anne and waited for an answer. He noticed she looked surprised and hoped that he had not sprung the question of marriage on her too soon.

'Priscilla isn't even buried yet, William. There's been enough scandal without us marrying so soon after she's taken her own life. It would not do anything for your standing in the community; the scandal of our affair is still running rife. But saying that, when the time is right it would be an honour to become your wife and so my answer is yes, I will marry you, William Ellershaw. God help us both; we are already the talk of the district and we might as well give them something to talk about! If your father could still talk he'd curse us from here to hell and back.' Mary-Anne's eyes filled with tears as she looked across at the dark-haired William. When they had first met all those years ago, Mary-Anne had been in awe of him but he'd initially looked at her as just an easy conquest for a pit owner's son, and her feelings had soured, but she knew he now loved her without reserve and, although her affair with him had initially been out of spite, she too loved him truly and totally. However, she also knew that her marriage to him would benefit her daughter, Victoria, and before she married her William, there would have to be an understanding between them both.

'Then that's settled, my dear; once the dust has settled and I have mourned for a decent length of time, we will marry. Regardless of any criticism and dissent from either family. I need you, Mary-Anne, and the day can't come quick enough for when I put a ring on your finger.' William leaned forward and kissed her with passion while running his hand up the inside of her leg. 'Now that I'm free of the burden that has been dragging me down, let us celebrate. I want your love and your desire.' His fingers touched Mary-Anne's intimate places, and then he led her up the stairs to the bedroom.

'I'm yours, William. I'll always be yours; there's no need to be so hasty. We are both at last free to do what we want,' Mary-Anne whispered as he laid her on the bed and quickly undid the buttons of his breeches, pulling her skirts up around her waist.

'I know, but now we have no one to answer to other than ourselves.' William looked down into Mary-Anne's eyes as he made love to her; at last, he was free.

*

'I thought I'd catch you here by yourself.' Mary-Anne walked into the designing room of Ellershaw and Wild, and looked out of the window down onto the busy walkway of Briggate that ran through the centre of Leeds. 'Well! Have you heard the news or has it not spread this far afield yet?' She gave Eliza a half-smile.

'Yes, I've heard; it's tragic news. I must say I feel sorry for poor Priscilla; to take your life, you must be desperate.' Eliza shook her head and frowned at her sister who looked like the cat who had just got the cream. 'It's nothing to smile about, our Mary-Anne; that poor woman took her life because of your and William's carrying on. He should be hung for the way he treated her and you should have more shame.'

'Stop being so condescending, Eliza; they were never happy and she was such a weak thing. He knew that when he married her. Let's face it, he married her for her money and estate, not at all like his next marriage is going to be.' Mary-Anne smiled even wider and waited for Eliza's reply.

'What marriage? He's not planning a wedding already, the cad!'

'Eliza, he's asked me to be his bride … not just yet, of course, but yes, we are to be wed. He'd marry me tomorrow if he could but I've told him to show a little respect to poor Priscilla, and, besides, I want to work this marriage to Victoria's advantage.' Mary-Anne couldn't hide her excitement.

Eliza sighed. 'Oh, Mary-Anne, you are really too shallow in feelings to be my sister, and you are always plotting your next move. Why can't you be content with your life?'

'Well, you could at least give me your congratulations, but I should have known better; you never have been impressed by William. You prefer a steady man, like the one who takes on everybody else's problems but doesn't get a move on putting that ring on your finger like he promised you.' Mary-Anne sat down in a chair opposite her sister and played with a piece of ribbon that was lying on the cutting table.

'Now, that's not fair,' Eliza retorted. 'Tom has not had the time and he doesn't have your William's fortune to just buy me a ring. Besides, I don't want to forgo my place in the running and half owning of this shop, nor the home that I now own and the money I have saved. Once married he would have it all and I'd be back at square one. So, it's me who is making him wait.'

'Well, my dear sister, I can solve both problems for you, as it happens. Now that I've come into money, I'm here to repay you for all the years of service you have given in the raising of my beautiful Victoria. After all, you will need your own funds if what William tells me is true.'

'What do you mean? What has William said?' Eliza looked worried.

'He says that Grace has decided to flee the family home and travel, like these new women are doing nowadays. Heavens know why … I'll just be content to be looked after and have servants at my beck and call. I've travelled enough when I was led astray by John Vasey.' Mary-Anne shook her head. 'He says that the family home at Highfield House is very precarious and that he's heard that his father is deeply in debt. A debt that he himself is not prepared to bail him out from this time. Therefore your precious Tom might be out of work shortly, so it's a good job you haven't married him yet.'

Eliza sat down quickly. 'Oh, my Lord, Tom knew things were bad, but not that bad. What will become of all those men if the pit closes?'

'Never mind the pit; that is not your concern but this shop is. Grace will want to sell up. That is why I propose to give you the money to buy Grace Ellershaw's half out before she disappears over the horizon. Then you will be a business-woman in your own right and no longer need her as a silent partner. I'll then take Victoria back in with me and we will both be settled at Levensthorpe Hall.'

'You can't do that,' Eliza gasped. 'The shop is worth a considerable sum. Ma Fletcher didn't have that sort of money.'

'Believe me, she did, and I aim to share it with you. Just for once, Eliza, I have fallen upon my feet and I'm going to see that the ones I love the most are looked after. I've schemed and dreamt these last twelve or more years and at last, all is coming to fruition and I'm going to make the most of it.' Mary-Anne smiled across at Eliza. ' The world is ours, Eliza; now let's go and grab it.'

Chapter 3

The day of Priscilla's funeral dawned grey and overcast, as sombre as the family group that attended her grave. William stood looking proud and handsome as the vicar gave the body a blessing before the coffin was placed in the family vault. He was feeling guilty over the death of his wife but at the same time had a sense of relief that his life was now his own.

'I should have listened to her more when she was telling me of how you treated her,' Catherine Ellershaw whispered to her son. 'She'd still have been alive today if I'd have given her more care.' She looked at him, seeing not so much as a sign of emotion on his face. 'She was heartbroken when she told me of your lack of love for her, and now look how it has ended.'

'Oh, Mother, don't you start,' William said quietly. 'She was always complaining. She had everything a woman could ask for: security, a home, and all the dresses she could possibly wish for. But none of that made her happy.' However, he knew full well that what his mother said was true.

'She was shown no love by you, William,' Catherine retorted, 'and you know it. We women need the love of our husbands, else we are nothing.' She lifted her head to look around the churchyard, gasping at the sight of two figures in the distance. 'That had better not be who I think it is, standing under the branches of that yew tree. God, she has some cheek and she's brought her brat with her. Send her away, William; she's no right to be at this funeral!'

Catherine Ellershaw went to find comfort next to her daughter Grace as she watched William walk across the graveyard to where Mary-Anne and her daughter Victoria stood. She watched as William bent his head and kissed Mary-Anne on the cheek and put his arm around her waist while he talked to her. Her son had no shame; his wife was only just cold in her grave and he was romancing his lover in the very same churchyard.

'Don't watch, Mother,' Grace whispered, 'ignore them. We will walk to the carriages and make our way back to Levensthorpe for the funeral tea. He'll send her and Victoria on their way, of that I'm sure. George, take Mother's other arm and try to close your mouth and stop gawping at your brother.'

Grace linked her arm with her mother's and walked her down the churchyard path and to the waiting carriages with George linking his arm at the other side, not daring to say a word.

*

'Mary-Anne, what made you come here today? My mother is not at all pleased by your presence.' William looked across at Victoria, who blushed at the intimacy of him with her mother.

'We were intending to keep our distance, my love. But I came to pay my respects; after all, I did know her, and I even made her clothes at one time. I encouraged Victoria to join me as this is her true family and she has every right to be here.' Mary-Anne smiled at Victoria as William put his arm around her waist and just led her out of earshot.

'You shouldn't have come, nor should Victoria. Our time will come, but for now, this day is for mourning, not for revelling in a death that has set us both free. Now take Victoria home with you; there will be time enough for her to get to know me and my family. Though Lord knows why she'd want to do that, the mixed up bunch that we are. We are to return to Levensthorpe where I've had the staff prepare a funeral breakfast; although I must admit, it is a one-sided affair with only my family attending the funeral. I had thought her family might petition to have Priscilla buried alongside their own family but they have turned their back on her in death as they did in life. And they have washed their hands of me entirely.' William sighed and looked at the woman he loved; even in her sombre clothes she looked beautiful with a small, netted hat perched on her auburn hair.

'At least Priscilla's friend, Jessica Bentley, and her father are here; I saw them as they arrived, and Jessica looked terribly upset.' Mary-Anne glanced at her daughter. 'Will I see you later or will you not be able to escape your mother's clutches?'

'For pity's sake, go home. Get yourself gone. I have duties to perform here.' William smiled. 'But I may just see you later tonight.' He then walked away to his carriage, leaving Mary-Anne grinning as she took Victoria's arm.

'It seems we are not wanted, my dear. Never mind, we will go and visit your Aunt Eliza and tell her all about the funeral and perhaps treat ourselves to a cream tea.' Mary-Anne then sauntered off in the opposite direction to the mourners, arm in arm with her bewildered daughter, who was silently questioning her mother's decision to attend a funeral at which they were clearly not wanted.

*

'I just can't believe your barefaced cheek, Mary-Anne. What on earth possessed you to go and attend the funeral and to take Victoria with you?' Eliza folded her arms and looked at mother and daughter as they sat across from her in the cutting room above the shop.

'I went because I wanted to see if Edmund Ellershaw was in attendance, but he wasn't; the old bastard must be too ill. Victoria accompanied me because I wanted him to see her, to remind him that she was his child as much as William or Grace or George. They're hypocrites, the lot of them. Do you know Priscilla's family didn't even attend? They washed their hands of her. No one had the time of day for the empty-headed Priscilla once William had secured Levensthorpe Hall. It was a marriage of convenience; nothing more, nothing less. When I marry him, it will be because of love and perhaps a little bit of revenge on my part.' Mary-Anne smiled at Victoria. 'And to secure my lovely daughter here the fortune and home that is rightly hers.' Mary-Anne squeezed Victoria's hand and watched as her sister sat down across from them both.

'Don't you be making Victoria into the schemer that you are. I don't want you turning her head with talk of fortune and fancy houses. I don't want her to become as devious and as cunning as you, after all my years of protecting her and making sure she was brought up with manners and grace.' Eliza looked across at Victoria who blushed from head to toe as she was discussed between her aunt and mother.

'I am here, you know, and I do have my own mind, my dear mother and aunt. And I don't scheme, as you both do enough of that for me. I went with my mother, Aunt Eliza, because I was curious, if anything; I've never been to a funeral before and this one, as you are all eager to point out, was attended by my family, whether they accept me or not.' Victoria held her head up high.

'Oh, she's my girl is this one, Eliza. See, she's defiant and full of spirit.' Mary-Anne smiled at Victoria. 'Now, are you going to come and live with me or are you staying with your Aunt Eliza, now there is no more Ma Fletcher? Although the bloody cat she left behind in my care is harder work than any child, I swear it is.'

Eliza bit her tongue at the thought that Mary-Anne knew precious little about raising any child, given she had abandoned Victoria to her care at such a young age. Instead she said softly, 'You know you can stay with me for good if that's what you want, Victoria? But whatever you decide I will abide with.' Eliza looked across at her niece, hoping that she would stay with her as she knew, for all Mary-Anne's fine words, a home where her mother was openly courting so recent a widower as William Ellershaw would not be ideal for either of them.

'I think I'd still like to stay with you, Aunt, just for now. If you are to wed William Ellershaw, I would then, of course, come to live with you, Mother. That is if he would have me under the same roof. I can't help but feel that he's a bit ashamed of me when he looks at me the way he does. I think he would rather I was not there to remind him of his father's behaviour.' Victoria hung her head.

'I'm sure he doesn't; he still finds it hard to recognise that you're his half-sister. William accepts the wrong his father did and knows that I love you dearly and that I will not put him before you, no matter how wealthy he is or how much he loves me. However, perhaps it is better that you do stay with Eliza until we are wed; there is a sense in your words even at your young age. Besides, without you to play gooseberry—' Mary-Anne winked '—at least he can come and go as he likes until I have a ring on my finger and his name is mine.'

'You mean *you* can come and go as you like, sister. I know you better, don't forget. But I'm glad, Victoria, that you have chosen to stay with me; it's where you still belong and my Tom is not as hot-headed and as wild as William Ellershaw. He doesn't drink, gamble and stay out until all hours of the night. And he certainly will not be coming and going with me.' Eliza shook her head thinking of the scandalous behaviour that her sister and lover would get up to under the roof at Speakers' Corner now they were both free to do as they pleased.

'Anyone would think we were a right pair of rakes,' Mary-Anne scoffed.

'You are! You are both scandalous, and well you know it. Poor Victoria and I have to put up with hearing all the gossip. Neither of you have any shame: that's the top and bottom of it.' Eliza stared at her sister who just smiled back, unrepentant.

'Folk should have something better to talk about,' Mary-Anne said with a cheeky smile. 'Anyway, talking about gossip, has Grace said anything about the shop yet and her leaving? You must tell me as soon as you know and then we'll buy this place if it's what you want.'

'She's not said a word. It will all be nonsense; she loves this place and our clientele, and she'd never leave it all behind.' Eliza looked around her and hoped that she was right. Though truth be told, of late Grace had not shown a great deal of interest in the running of the shop, but she'd put that down to Grace's father being ill.

'Miss Grace isn't leaving, is she?' Victoria looked at both her mother and her aunt. Out of all the Ellershaws, Grace and

George had shown her the most kindness but even George had kept out of her way of late.

'We don't know, darling; it's just something your mother has heard. I personally hope not, else I don't quite know what I'll do.' Eliza came and put her arm around her worried-looking niece.

'You'll be right whatever, Eliza; I'll see to that,' Mary-Anne told her. 'I have the money now and, as I say, it's time to repay you for looking after this one here. She's dear to us both. Thick as thieves we three are and nobody can defeat us if we stick together. Three strong women that won't be ruled by any man.'

*

Catherine Ellershaw looked at her son as he poured her a glass of sherry in the drawing room of Levensthorpe Hall.

'William,' she whispered, as the rest of the family including the Bentleys came and seated themselves on the grand furniture of the room, 'what was that dreadful woman doing at Priscilla's funeral? Has she no shame? It was a private funeral and the last people we wanted there were her and her daughter.'

'Later, Mother, you can chastise me later. We have guests …' William smiled courteously at his fuming mother and then made a beeline for Jessica Bentley.

'Are you trying to escape your mother, William, or am I next in line for your charms?' Jessica said snippily, looking at William over the edge of her sherry glass, noting he looked concerned.

'You know me too well, Jessica. You're safe from my charms – I just needed to escape her clutches.' William sighed. 'Today has been hard enough without having a maternal lecture.'

'Well, if you will be such a libertine, what do you expect? Poor Priscilla was not even cold in her grave and your mistress was waiting in the wings. Lurking like a spectre at a feast with that child of hers. You do know people are talking about you? I even heard the other somebody say you had shot poor Priscilla, which I, of course, put right immediately.' Jessica put her head down and sighed. 'For all your faults, I know she didn't die by your hand. Poor Priscilla, why didn't she ask for help? I'd have been there for her; we all knew that she wasn't strong in spirit.' Jessica wiped a tear away from her cheek and looked at William. 'You were a bastard to her,' she chided him. 'You should never have married her; she needed someone to cherish her and treat her gently. But she loved every inch of you.'

'Please save your words. Everyone has cast me as an ogre that cursed and beat her every day when in truth I never laid a hand on her. The sad truth is that I never loved her. She and her money were convenient, an easy conquest that gave me the life that I craved. But she wanted something from me that I could never give her. It's really my grandfather to blame; he set us up as a match, regardless of whether we loved one another or not.' William looked down at his feet.

'And what of this Mrs Vasey? Mary-Anne Wild that was? Do you love her? Or is she just another convenient woman for you to use and amuse yourself with until you get bored?' Jessica looked at the man she had no respect for and waited for an answer.

'No, this time, I think it's a true match. We are both like-minded and need nothing from one another. In fact, Jessica, I love her and as soon as I can I will wed her if she will have me, no matter what folk say.'

'Oh, William, she comes from nothing. She has no class; she's a miner's daughter. Even your sister, Grace, who took Eliza out of their Pit Lane hovel, doesn't ever forget that. She might trust Eliza with the day-to-day running of her emporium but for all she's good with clients she will never be their equal. She doesn't have Grace's style or breeding, no matter how she tries – and no matter how she tries to raise that brat of theirs with fancy lessons. It's Grace's name above the door that gives them the calibre of customers that they have.'

'Like you, Grace is a snob. Besides, I'm sure she's told you that she is longing to leave and see a bit more of the world. I'm surprised she hasn't asked you to go with her.' William took a large sip of his sherry.

'She has, and I would have joined her, except my father needs me. I love him too much to desert him in his dotage.' Jessica looked across at her father as he spoke to Williams's mother and smiled at the grey-haired, aging man.

'Not like mine then; I haven't seen him for weeks now. I've been told to keep away. He's not so ill he wouldn't recognise me, the old hypocrite.' William took another swig of sherry and shook his head.

'He's still your father and you must be worried about him. Gossip is rife amongst my father's friends; they say that his finances are not strong. Can you not bring yourself to help him, William? I know from Grace he has disinherited you.' Jessica put her hand on her friend's sleeve.

William gave a snort. 'There's precious little to disinherit me from ... Besides, I've already helped him and any help I gave him he threw back in my face when he threw me out of my family home. As he has said to me, "the devil can look after his own", because I have washed my hands of him. However, I will be there for my mother if needs be.' William gulped back his last dregs of sherry and stood up. 'Now, if you'll excuse me, I need to see to an urgent matter awaiting me in my study.' Grace watched as William, without glancing at anybody else, walked out of the dining room and into his study.

Once there, he shut the doors behind him and lent back upon them, closing his eyes for a brief second, thankful to find peace away from the prying eyes of his family. He poured himself another drink from the decanter on the sideboard before sitting down at his desk, which was situated in the bay window that overlooked the estate of Levensthorpe Hall.

There he sat back and mused over the last few weeks. His life had been in turmoil, made worse by the death of Priscilla. It was not a case of him having not cared for her; he had, in a strange way, and nothing could have shocked him more than finding her dead after taking her own life. But both of them had been so unhappy in their marriage of convenience. As for his father ... well, he'd brought everything upon himself and William didn't feel bad about his situation. He'd never faced up to his responsibilities all his life and now he was paying for them.

He sat back in his chair and looked down the driveway down to the entrance to Levensthorpe. The gatehouse was empty at the moment but it was in need of some repair. Perhaps he should see about getting the builders in and then at least his mother would have somewhere to live if the worst came to the worst. But she'd have to know her place once Mary-Anne and he were married. As for Mary-Anne's daughter, Victoria, he didn't know how to feel. She was his father's, a bastard born out of his lust for vulnerable young girls that he could take advantage of. Plus she was the spit of them all with her dark hair and dark eyes; she and Grace looked like sisters and it would be plain to anyone who had an inkling of the scandals in their family who her father must be. Perhaps he should not welcome Victoria Wild into his family home after all, but for now he'd say nothing to Mary-Anne – not until after he'd wed her.

*

Fourteen-year-old Victoria lay on her bed in her bedroom at Aireville Mansions; she'd been crying but now decided to just lie there and compose herself before joining her aunt for dinner that evening. She'd never witnessed a funeral before and although they had not been mourners in the strictest sense of the word, she had found it moving.

Of course she had never met Priscilla Ellershaw but she had overheard her mother and aunt talk about her often enough. It seemed so sad to a young girl such as she – a woman driven to such depths of despair to take her own life. However, that was not the reason for her tears. It was the look that William Ellershaw had given her when he'd dismissed them. She felt ashamed: the Ellershaws' dirty secret that no one wanted. But it wasn't just the family; it was everybody. She neither fitted in with the ordinary working-class girls of her age nor the young women from well-to-do households. She was a misfit with no friends and no one to talk to. Even George, the bungling dandy, had given her a wide berth since the Guild Ball and now she was beginning to feel lonely with only her daily tutor and her aunt and mother as company.

She sighed and sat herself up on the edge of her bed, gazing at herself in the mirror. Why did she have to have such dark surly looks? Everyone could tell whose daughter she was. Her Aunt Eliza and mother told her often that she was beautiful and should be proud of her long black hair but she hated it. She knew it was an Ellershaw trait and it reminded her that she was of the same parentage as William and Grace, as well as the weak George, but without any standing in society and no money. She was worth nothing and even though her mother promised her everything, she knew that it was just a pipe dream, promises that would be unfulfilled like all the other promises she had made in the letters she used to send from America.

That's why she had opted to stay with her Aunt Eliza, although if she married Tom Thackeray they would not want her either. Not if they had a family of their own. Victoria looked at herself in the mirror once again and started to brush her long hair, securing it back with a couple of combs as she heard the maid coming up the stairs to tell her dinner was ready. She wiped her eyes and put on a smile as she answered the knock on her bedroom door.

'Dinner's served, Miss Victoria,' the maid said before she closed the door behind her.

'Thank you, Lizzie; I'll be down directly,' Victoria answered, and glanced at herself once more to check for any sign of the tears that she had been crying.

Even the maid, who was only a year or so older than her at most, hardly ever spoke to her, she thought, as she made her way down the stairs to the dining room. Though if her mother were to make good on her promises some day, when she married William Ellershaw, then Victoria would have a more certain place in society – she would have the wealth and connections to belong somewhere.

Chapter 4

Tom Thackeray stood in his office at the Rose Pit and looked around him, worried and concerned for his staff. It had been months now since he had been put in charge and although the pit was making money he was hardly benefiting in any way, neither in his own pocket nor with bills being paid and supplies being delivered more regularly. Having George Ellershaw in charge of the accounts was as good as useless; the youngest Ellershaw was happy to take the money that was coming in but he wasn't willing to part with any of it to keep the pit going. Thank heavens that they had come to an arrangement that Tom paid the men their wages before handing over any surplus to George, else there would have been a walkout a long time ago.

'Here, Tom.' Fred Parker, the man in charge of the yard, appeared at the office door, cap in hand and with a hangdog expression. 'This fellow says that he won't be leaving any of his coal sacks for us today because their firm hasn't been paid for the last two deliveries.'

Tom sighed. 'It's bloody George; he'll not have got around to paying him yet. Do we need them badly? I can pay him for this delivery and promise to chase up payment for the others if he's happy to do that.' Tom went to the petty cash tin, which he knew to hold hardly anything, with it being a Monday. Hopefully by Friday, when payday came around again, there would be enough cash in it to pay everyone.

Fred walked into the office. 'It would be a help if you could pay for these, else we won't be delivering to many homes this week ... I'm down to my last half dozen. That is if he'll just take payment for this delivery. He's a new man and he's a bit snotty, not to mention the size of him.' Fred shook his head. He knew Tom was doing his best; it was the buggers that owned the mine that was letting him down.

'Let me talk to him and then I'll go and walk down to Highfield House, see if I can prize any money out of George.' Tom patted Fred on the back and stepped out of his office and into the yard. The sack delivery man was over six foot tall and as broad-shouldered as Tom had ever seen, with muscles to match. 'Now then mate, I hear it's cash in hand else no sacks, is that right?'

'Aye, it is. My boss says I've at least to get something out of you, else I've to bring them back. He's heard that the Rose is in a bad way and that old Ellershaw hasn't a penny to his name. He's given you enough tick, so it's time to pay up or he'll stop supplying you.'

'Well, look, I can only do what I can. I'm in a bad spot. I need to keep my men working; they've families to feed but at the same time the bloody Ellershaws don't give a damn about anybody but themselves. I can pay you for this delivery and I promise to sort out what else is owed to you.' Tom looked at the hard-faced man and counted out what cash he had managed to pull together from the petty-cash tin and held it out for him to take.

'I don't know, my boss told me to insist on full payment. But then again, if the bank steps in he knows he won't get a penny.' The delivery man looked around the pit yard. He knew the Rose employed most of Woodlesford and even he had a heart when it came to keeping hard-working men in employment. 'Bugger it; give me what you've got and I'll leave the sacks this time on the understanding that you clear the account in the next month, else I'll not be coming back.' He reached out and took what money was on offer to him and summoned his lad on the back of the delivery cart to unload the sacks with the help of Fred.

'Good man, I'm grateful to you.' Tom patted the big man on his back. 'I'll see to getting the money to your boss. Working for old Ellershaw when he's on his deathbed is bloody hard work as his lad George is more than bloody useless.'

'Aye, I can understand that. But I'd be looking for a fresh pit to work at because this one is knackered from what I hear. But I'm not going to be the one that puts the nail in your coffin.' The delivery man walked over to his cart and turned before he pulled himself up on to the driving seat. 'A month ... my boss will need his money in a month, else I'll not be back.'

*

Tom stood, cap in hand, at the back door of Highfield House. He'd contemplated knocking on the front door but then thought better of it. The Ellershaws liked to think that their workers were way below them in status, no matter what position they held, so he'd made his way to the back of the house. He could hear raised female voices as he stood patiently waiting for the kitchen door to be opened to his knock, but he couldn't make out what the argument was about.

The old cook opened the door to him.

'Yes, what do you want?'

He knew her to be a gossip and she looked annoyed at being dragged to answer his call when she clearly would rather try and listen in to what the voices within were arguing over.

'I need to speak to Mr George Ellershaw,' Tom explained, 'it's a matter of some urgency.'

'He's not in. I'll tell him you've called if you can give me your name and what business you have here.' Madge Bailey had no time for her visitor when there was gossip to be had within the family.

'But it's urgent! Could I see Mrs Ellershaw? I must speak to someone now, right away. It's about the Rose Pit; I'm Tom Thackeray, the manager there.' Tom put his foot in the doorway and urged the cook to announce him as he heard a door slam from deep within the house and the arguing cease.

'I'll see if the mistress is free if you think it that urgent. She might not be willing, though; she's not having the best of mornings.' Madge shuffled off, leaving Tom feeling awkward upon the step as he awaited her return.

After a couple of minutes Madge returned, opening the kitchen door for him. 'The mistress says she'll see you now, but that she can't give you long.' She showed him through the kitchen and up into the hallway before knocking on the parlour door to announce Tom's arrival.

'Ah, Mr Thackeray, I believe you wish to see my son. I'm afraid he's not available and my husband is far too ill to discuss pit business, so you will have to make do with me.' Catherine Ellershaw stood proud and tall as she tried to hide the tears that were never too far from falling these days. 'Now, what can I do for you?'

'It's a rather delicate matter, ma'am. I know your son, George, is doing his best but I'm afraid he is not keeping his part of the bargain when it comes to the running of the Rose Pit. He's not paying any of the bills and consequently we are having problems gaining the supplies we need to do our jobs.' Tom looked down at his feet and felt embarrassed by his admission but it was no good beating around the bush. George was not paying the bills and that was the top and bottom of it. 'I've brought a list of what I know to be outstanding, but I know there will be more that I don't know about. The list is quite substantial, I'm afraid, ma'am.' Tom handed her the list and noticed her hand shake as she took it off him.

'Thank you, Mr Thackeray. Please leave it with me and I'll see that it is sorted. We are most grateful that you are running the pit so efficiently while my husband is indisposed. He really is a most ill man and I try not to burden him with the problems of running the house and business.' Catherine Ellershaw turned her back to Tom and looked out of the drawing-room window. It was yet another blow to her that morning and she felt that she could no longer cope with her lot in life.

'Thank you for your time, ma'am, I'm most grateful to you ... I'll leave it with you to sort then and I'll get back to the pit and men.' Tom stood and looked around him, taking in the furnishings of the grand room. One day he would like to live in a room like this, he thought, as Catherine Ellershaw rang the bell for someone to escort him out of the house.

'Ah, Mrs Bailey,' she said, when the red-faced cook appeared, standing in the doorway with flour down her apron, 'could you see Mr Thackeray to the door please, and when Master George returns can you tell him to join me in the study?'

'Yes, ma'am.' Madge stood with the parlour door open and waited for Tom to join her, before stomping off back down the hallway with him in close step behind her.

'Do this, do that ... I don't know how they think I have the bloody time. The butler's left,' Madge moaned to Tom indiscreetly, 'and half the servants too. I can't stand it any more and the groom says if he doesn't get paid this month he's off. And the old bastard upstairs still lives on and needs looking after all the time. It's him that's to blame for all this mess. No wonder Miss Grace is talking about leaving us all; I'd bugger off as well if I'd somewhere to go,' Madge growled as she opened the kitchen door for Tom to leave. 'I hope you haven't come for money because they haven't any, although that pompous George acts as if he's worth a mint, which he will be when he inherits his grandfather's money. And as for the mistress, she is in denial of everything. There's only one with any sense in the all lot of them and she sounds as if she's had enough.'

'So, it's true: Miss Grace is thinking of leaving. Are things that bad?' Tom put his cap back on his head.

'Bad! It's bloody hell here at the moment. If you knew what I know about this family … Let's just say the farther away you are from the Ellershaw family the better off you are. Old Edmund came from nowt and he's going back to nowt and he'll rot in hell when his time's up, of that I'm sure.'

Madge stood on the step and watched as Tom walked away with his head down, yet another casualty of the Ellershaw way of life.

Tom looked around him once back in his office at the pithead. He couldn't let the pit close; it could make good money and the workers were all good men bar one or two troublemakers. They were, on the whole, loyal to the Rose, dependable and the salt of the earth, with everyone reliant on the wage that they received every week to bring their families up upon.

Damn, Edmund Ellershaw, he whispered under his breath; he'd pissed, gambled and shagged all the money away that the Rose had made over the years, and now he was lying in his bed, unrepentant and uncaring about anything. Tom shook his head and cursed again; he didn't know how but he was not going to let the Rose close, not while he had breath in his body.

*

Catherine Ellershaw sat at the desk in her husband's study at Highfield House. She'd unlocked the roll-topped desk and gasped at the number of unpaid bills and final demands that she had come across, seemingly cast to one side by either her husband or George or both. Perhaps they had both thought that they would somehow miraculously disappear.

She sighed and sat back in her chair and looked around her. What was happening to her family? She'd tried so hard to bring up her children correctly and now they were all letting her down in their own individual ways, just when she needed them most. Now, after leafing through the account books of the pit, she had realised that they were almost entirely without funds. The bank had written to Edmund long before his stroke to say that they were going to have to meet with him to discuss his state of affairs. She knew that they must be showing clemency at the moment with him being near death's door, but it would only be a matter of time before their sympathies would run out, judging by the wording of the many letters.

Regardless of this, George had gone his own sweet way, still running up bills for clothes that he could not afford, and now Grace had told her of her plans to leave home and abandon her. She couldn't even rely on her eldest, William, to help them, given his estrangement from his father and his own selfish obsessions.

And as for Edmund ... her husband had let her down most of all. She almost wished he was dead. It was he that all her children took after: wilful, selfish and always needing more. She should never have married him. She'd put up with his womanising, drinking and cavorting but now, looking around her, the loyalty that she had given him had counted for nothing, and she was going to be lucky after his death to walk away with the clothes on her back.

Why had she not listened to her parents? She had the pick of suitors when she was younger; but, no, it had been Edmund Ellershaw that had taken her eye with his grand ideas for the future and his way with words that had made her feel special. She had been like putty in his hands, just like the succession of other young vulnerable women that he had bedded over the years. Only her fortune at the time had made her worthy of a ring, so he had wedded her. Now her dowry was long gone. What a fool she had been.

'Mama, you wanted to see me?' George was dressed as usual in his flamboyant style and with an abundance of youth. Standing in the doorway of the study, the expression on his face soon changed as he quickly realised that his mother had for once in her life looked into the family's finances. 'Oh, it's not as bad as it looks, Mama; I've been trying to keep on top of it, honest I have.' George stood in front of his mother like a petulant schoolchild and awaited his fate.

'You bear some of the blame for this state of affairs, young man, but even my cursory look into our finances has shown me that the damage was done long before you took over your father's concerns. However, at least your father had the sense to put what money we did have back into making the pit work so that we did have a bit of security. Now I don't know how that Tom Thackeray is managing to keep it all working with the amount that you have been squandering.' Catherine watched George's face turn nearly the same shade as his crimson waistcoat.

'Tom Thackeray needs to know his place!' George spouted as he sat down in a chair opposite his mother. 'He insists on telling me how to run the pit. He's an insolent beggar, and we would be better off without him.'

Catherine gave George a warning glance. 'He's an insolent beggar with brains and you have a lot to thank him for, else you would not have had the lifestyle you have been living these last few weeks by the looks of the bills in your name.'

'Well, Mother, if you can do any better, I'll leave you to it. I've just been having lunch with Bertie Baxter and he's invited me to lodge with him in his apartments in Leeds. He's such a jolly fine fellow and we are the best of friends so I agreed. After all, once I have received my inheritance in a month's time, I will be able to lead my own life. So you will not have me to worry about by the end of the week.' George crossed his legs and leaned back in his chair, oblivious to the pain and hurt on his mother's face.

'So, you have decided to leave me and your father too? What with Grace going and William washing his hands of your father, life is going to be lonely.' Catherine sighed. 'I'm to be left nursing your father and balancing a household that is bankrupt. Everyone did warn me that your children had a habit of breaking your heart but I never wanted to believe them.' Catherine started to sob.

'Oh, Mama, don't take on so,' George scoffed. 'We are not deserting you; we are just making our own way in the world. And surely things are not that bad when it comes to money.'

'You know nothing of the real world, George; you have been cossetted and mollycoddled all your life. You can go; just go now and find solace in your fine fellow's arms but don't for a moment think I don't know you're more than friends ...'

Catherine rushed out of the room with tears running down her cheeks. She raced up the sweeping stairs to the bedside of her sleeping husband. She reached for his hand but he didn't stir as she openly wept and sobbed to a man too gravely ill to help her in the troubles that were all of his making.

Chapter 5

'What's it like to be a single man again? Are the ladies already looking at my lover and thinking about what they could get up to with such a good-looking, handsome man?' Mary-Anne lay in the bed next to William, her skirts up around her thighs as they lay, legs entwined, exhausted after an afternoon romp.

'If they do, they don't let me know it. All I see is a load of gossiping ninnies that giggle, look slyly at me and then wander on their way. I've no time of day for them.' William put his arm around Mary-Anne, squeezing her tightly and pushing his body next to her while rubbing his hands over her breasts.

'I think you've had enough excitement for one afternoon, Mr Ellershaw. After all, remember that you are in mourning and that you are supposed to be hard at work running those mills of yours.' Mary-Anne grinned as she kissed him and snuggled deeper into his arms.

'Bugger the mills, they run themselves. A good overseer makes sure of it. And as for being in mourning, you know what I think of that. Why work myself into an early grave when I can spend time in a woman's arms satisfying the needs that I have been denied for so long.' William traced the outline of Mary-Anne's lips with his finger and kissed them again.

'I hope not just any woman. I hope that it will always be me; I don't aim to share you ever again. When are we to marry, William? I know what I said before about wanting to wait a little while but I want the world to know that you are mine and that we love one another.' Mary-Anne turned her head and looked at her lover; she needed him to wed her before his head was turned by other more suitable women, now that he was free of Priscilla.

'Have patience, my love; it's only right and decent that we wait a little while longer. Besides, I have other things on my mind at the moment. I fear my mother will be in need of my help shortly. My darling sister has plans to travel, and I heard yesterday that George has moved out of home and is living in Headingley with that idiot of a Bertie Baxter. Two of a kind they are: both brainless dandies who prefer male company to that of a full-bodied woman. How that has happened in my family I do not know.'

'And your father?' Mary-Anne enquired. 'How is he?'

At the mention of his father, William left Mary-Anne's arms and sat on the edge of the bed, putting his head in his hands. 'He's not long for this world, the old bastard. The sooner he's dead, the better. All he's given the world is grief.' He hated his father; he had always brought shame on his family, and with his death would come more, for once he died William was sure the banks would foreclose on his father's loans and mortgages.

'I'm sorry; I shouldn't have mentioned him.'

'No, don't apologise. He should be the one that's begging for forgiveness, given what he did to you and others. His death will leave my mother destitute, but I refuse to help her until he's dead and buried. I've decided that I'll offer to move her into the gatehouse at Levensthorpe. Because Highfield House will have to be sold to the highest bidder, and even then she will not be left with much money, if indeed any at all.'

'Oh, William, are things that bad?' Mary-Anne sat up and pulled her underskirts down and started to fasten her bodice before pulling her dress back on over her head. She smiled to herself; Ma Fletcher had been right all along when she told Mary-Anne to set her cap at William rather than avenging herself against his father. It was William who had amassed his own fortune but that was irrelevant, she was to marry William more for love than money now.

'Rumour has it that he has squandered everything, with the help of my feckless brother, George. His pit at Wakefield is worth nothing, and while the Rose is productive, it needs money spending on it. Grace was beside herself when she was telling me the state of father's business; I think that's partly why she seeks to get away from the whole sorry affair.'

'I'm sorry to hear that, especially when it comes to the Rose Pit. There are some good men who work there; they will need their jobs. As for your mother coming to live at the gatehouse, could you not set her up somewhere else? She will never approve of me, William; I will always be a common whore in her eyes.'

'I wouldn't let that worry you. Nobody is ever good enough for my mother when it comes to any of her family, even if you are bred into the aristocracy. She didn't even have the time of day for Priscilla, and yet she was related to the landed gentry.' William stood up and looked out of the bedroom window. 'What made you buy this house here? It's in a curious location – you've always got some big-mouthed lout just outside your doorstep that must give you cause for concern when they preach to the dissatisfied and work-shy that seem to amass at Speakers' Corner.'

'I like it here; it's a step up from Pit Lane and a solid house, which, once you're inside, opens up into my real world. I like to keep with my own people and although I dress and eat well, I'm still a working-class girl and will never forget where I come from. I like to listen to the speakers. They fight for the common cause, especially when you uncaring mill and pit owners don't do right by them.' Mary-Anne put her arms around Williams's waist and kissed his neck to soften the blow of her teasing words. 'We all know just how uncaring cads like you can be, William Ellershaw, and it's up to us commoners to keep you straight.' Mary-Anne smiled and ran her hand down his leg as he bent down and kissed her again.

'Leave me be, you wicked woman. I'm away to my work, else I'll end up in the same position as my father, with scarce a penny to my name, and that would never do.' But before leaving the bedroom, William grasped both of Mary-Anne's hands and pulled her tight against him. 'You drive me to distraction and well you know it, but sometimes I have to remember to keep my senses, else you and your wicked ways will get the better of me.' He smiled and then kissed her with passion before bounding down the stairs and out of the front door, looking up at the bedroom window where Mary-Anne stood, before weaving his way through the crowded busy street.

Mary-Anne watched as he went, and smiled; he was hers and he knew it. Her scheming had paid off and now she was going to enjoy life as much as she possibly could.

*

Eliza sat across from Grace and supped her tea while listening to what Grace told her, believing it to be fresh news.

'I know it will come as shock to you. But I feel I must make a move from my home, and I'm dying to see more of the world. There is nothing in the Leeds area for me and, to be quite honest, I'm a little tired of running a business. I want to do so much more with my life.' Grace looked across at Eliza and held her breath as Eliza placed her cup and saucer down upon the table and looked across at her. 'I aim to put my half of the shop up for sale, which puts you, I know, in a delicate situation. I will, however, be careful who I sell to and you, of course, will be able to meet them and have your say, unless of course you also wish to be free of your commitment to the shop. That would be the ideal solution as it would be more attractive to buyers, although I know your heart and soul has gone into the business.' Grace looked anxiously at Eliza; she hadn't expected her to take the news so calmly.

'To be honest, Grace, I'd already heard that you were thinking of withdrawing from the business, so your news does not come as a shock to me. Your brother William had told my sister, so don't fret that I'm going to take the news badly. I've just been waiting for you to tell me.' Eliza smiled at her business partner and watched the relief on her face as she realised that her news had spread.

'Our William never can keep his mouth closed. I've been building up for weeks to tell you and then he does it for me.' Grace sighed and looked hard at Eliza. 'Well, what do you think? Am I going to ruin your plans? Whoever does go into business with you will have to realise that you are the senior partner and that what you say goes. That is unless you are in a position to buy my share of the shop? I know that it would mean you perhaps borrowing money to finance it ... but you wouldn't be able to manage that, would you? You are still a single woman with your half of the shop and your little house as your only means of finance. Of course it wouldn't be enough,' Grace said dismissively. 'And you couldn't run the business by yourself, even if you could afford to buy me out.' Even though she thought herself friends with Eliza, she could never forget that they were of different classes. She had been generous in allowing Eliza a half share of the business, given it had been all her money that had funded it. If it hadn't been for her, Eliza would still be living in Pit Lane.

Eliza stared at Grace; she'd never had a cross word with her in the past, but she'd always known that Grace thought herself better than her and now she was saying as much. 'I'd like to know how much you would like for your half of the business; I don't want to go into a partnership with anyone else. But I can probably raise the money to buy you out. After all, while you may have funded it, the business runs on my designs and fashion; I don't want anyone taking advantage of my lowly beginnings in life as I'm sure some would. I aim to be independent of anyone, so think how much would be acceptable to you and I'll raise it.'

'Are you sure, Eliza? It will be a considerable sum!'

'I'm sure; the business will finally be mine and I can put my name alone over the doorway. I do have a lot to thank you for, Grace, but we both know if it had not been for my designs, neither of us would have the money and status that we now have. Yes, I know, my house is not so grand and that I'll never be the same as the ladies that come and purchase our wares, but I have more brains than all of them put together and I am not going to lose the business I love.' Eliza stood up and looked out of the window down onto Boar Lane and knew she was going to have to ask Mary-Anne for the money she had offered her. She only hoped that she had enough, because knowing Mary-Anne she might not have been left as much as she was bragging about. She turned and looked at her partner. 'Don't worry, Grace, you look after yourself; go and do what you want to do. I don't hold it again you for wanting to get out of Leeds and the business. You have nothing to hold you here, go and see the world. I wish I could, but my roots are here.'

'Oh, Eliza, I was dreading telling you. I'll not ask for the full asking price for the business if you think you can afford it. I'll get my accountant to put a fair price on it all and then I'll let you know. I do hope that you can buy it; you deserve it.' Grace moved over to Eliza and put her arms around her. 'I wish you well, you and Victoria; you deserve all the happiness that life can offer you.'

'We already have much more than I ever expected, so don't worry about us, and I have you to thank for enabling me to raise Victoria as a young lady,' Eliza sighed, eager to make peace between them.

'When will your sister take up the role of mother to Victoria, do you think? She seems to be too busy with my headstrong brother to bother with anything else. Although he is as bad; my mother is worried to death. Thank heavens my father is too ill to realise the romance that they are so publicly displaying.' Grace sat back down and waited for Eliza to reply.

'She does what she can, but motherhood has never come naturally to her. She does love Victoria and one day she insists she will take her to live with her, but for now, I'll keep Victoria level-headed and give her the love I can. As you say, William and Mary-Anne are the centre of gossip and she's better off staying with me at this moment in time.'

'But you have your own life. Have you and your sweet-heart still not set a date?' Grace smiled. 'Marriage and children of your own would suit you. It's not too late for you to look towards motherhood; after all, you are only in your mid-thirties.'

'And then who would look after this shop? No, I'm quite content with my lot at the moment, especially if I can buy your half of the business. It's more than I ever dreamt of.' Eliza gazed across at the mannequins that lined the office, dressed in her latest designs, and thought about what she might lose if she were to marry Tom.

'Be true to your heart, Eliza, don't let him slip away again. Your Tom loves you and that's precious. I have never felt the need to love or care for somebody in that way. I like my independence too much. Perhaps, my feeling might change when I leave here for my new life.'

'You will if you want to. Or perhaps you are not the marrying kind. Sometimes I do believe that life holds more for you if you remain single; after all, men always want to seem to control us women. I'll marry Tom when the time is right, but not just yet, even though I love him dearly.'

Grace laughed. 'Then we are both strong, wilful women, and, unlike your sister, we can live without a man.'

Eliza grinned. 'Oh, don't feel sorry for her; she can live without a man if she's a mind to. It's your brother I feel sorry for; he hasn't got a clue what he's taking on.'

'Nor her him. So they make a good pair. They should be happy together.' Grace laughed. 'Now, I'll go and speak to my accountant, and I'll let you know as soon as possible what I could willingly take for my half of our establishment. I'm glad that you are not too upset about my decision. I'd hate for us to part on bad terms.'

'That we would never do. Once you tell me how much you are expecting for the business I'll try and buy it as quick as I can if that is what you want to start you on your travels. Or will you be staying at Woodlesford for a while, seeing your father is so ill?'

'My mother will look after my father. We've never been close; the sooner I'm away the better. I don't want to still be here after his death, else my mother will expect me to stay with her for good and that would drive me quite mad, having to live with her all my life.' Grace rose from her chair. 'I'll let you know my price shortly; I do hope that you will be able to make it your own, Eliza; I know it should be yours, in all honesty.'

Eliza smiled at Grace and watched as she left the shop, stepping out along Boar Lane with her blue parasol shading her from the midday sun. 'Please let Mary-Anne have enough money,' she whispered to herself, her heart beating fast as she thought about being the complete owner of the business. She had worked hard all her life and now it was time for her to perhaps get what she deserved.

*

'How much does she want? Are you sure that figure is correct?' Mary-Anne looked again at the figure quoted on the accountant's document that a messenger had dropped off at Eliza's home. 'Is the bloody place clad in gold? Or does she think you are made of money?'

'It's what it is worth, according to the accounts. Though I hadn't realise just how much money she had been taking out of the business. I left her to take charge of the books – I don't think she expected the accountant to share them with me as part of the sale process. She's been taking advantage of me and I don't think I like how I feel about her now.' Eliza slumped down in the chair next to her sister and sighed. 'If you can't manage it, don't worry; I'll understand.'

'She's just like her bloody father, a two-faced thieving bastard.' Mary-Anne looked at the figures again and then looked at her sister's disappointed face. 'But it's a small price for me to pay to see my sister happy and to thank her for the years of love given to my daughter. Try to knock her down a little bit and then the money's yours. Let's buy this bloody posh shop and then I'll know you are happy; and, besides, with Grace out of the way she can't persuade William not to marry me, so that will be one less fly in the ointment.'

'Can you really afford it, our Mary-Anne? It's more money than I ever heard tell of in my life! At least that means I'm worth that much as well, or half of it, at least; not bad for a lass that started off with nothing. But honestly, Ma Fletcher didn't look to have enough money to feed herself, let alone have any savings.'

'Well, she did and there's much more besides, else I wouldn't be offering you this, so go and tell snooty Miss Grace that the shop's yours and you'll be handling the books from now on in. You no longer have to look up to her; you will soon own it, lock, stock and barrel.' Mary-Anne sat back and laughed at her sister's beaming face. 'That'll give bloody Edmund Ellershaw something to think about on his deathbed! That and the marriage of his son to me. What goes around comes around, and we are about to bite him on his bloody old scrawny arse, our Eliza. Our time has come, whether he likes it or not!'

Chapter 6

Eliza had a spring in her step and a determination in her heart as she walked along the drive to Highfield House, ready to tell Grace Ellershaw that she could agree to buy her half of their business and that the money was already in place once her solicitor had drawn up the agreement.

She smiled as she passed the flowerbeds filled with roses and couldn't help but think that hopefully one day, once she was in full control of her business, she too could have a home half as grand as Highfield. She stood in front of the large house and looked at the pillared front entrance, her old instincts telling her to go to the back door, the tradesman's entrance, but then she lifted her chin up and went to make herself known at the main door; after all, she was just as wealthy as them now, if not more so, if Tom's words were to be believed. She stepped into the entrance way and found the large oak door already open, with no sign of any servants as she shouted across the elegantly decorated hallway to make someone aware of her presence.

'Hello, is there anybody here?' Eliza yanked on the pull bell set inside the doorway to gain somebody's attention. Not a sound came from the great house as she walked into the hallway and made her way past many doors that led to the numerous rooms of the pit owner's home. Eliza couldn't help but gaze around her at the rich furnishings and remember just where she had come from. The two-up two-down miner's cottage where she and Mary-Anne has been raised had been tiny, with hardly any furniture. Their family had endured abject poverty over the years while Edmund Ellershaw and his family had been living in the decadence that surrounded her. She looked at the paintings and statues that adorned every wall and looked through to the plush furnishings of the drawing room as she turned the door handle into yet another empty room.

'Hello!' she yelled again around the empty house, hoping that somebody would hear her. She was so wanting to give Grace her news and set the process of buying her business outright into action. She walked back to the front door and was about to leave, when Madge Bailey, the cook at Highfield, came walking down the stairs, her face wet with tears as she stopped, surprised to see somebody standing in the hallway.

'I'm sorry ... I rang the bell but nobody heard me.' Eliza looked at the old cook, and realised immediately that something was wrong.

Madge Bailey pulled a handkerchief out from her apron pocket and blew her nose. 'I'm sorry. Most of the servants have gone. I'm the only one left and I'll not be here much longer now the master's died.' Madge started to cry again and looked across at Eliza as she shook her head. 'I've been told to go for the doctor, to confirm it, but he's dead is the old devil. The mistress and Miss Grace are at his bedside – the mistress is heartbroken. Now, if you'll excuse me, I'll have to walk down into Woodlesford and bring the doctor back with me.'

'Edmund Ellershaw is dead? Are you sure?' Eliza couldn't believe her ears.

'Yes, he drew his last breath about half hour ago. He just went while the mistress was talking to him; he took every-one by surprise. Now, I'll have to go, I'll tell Miss Grace that you called, but she won't be up to seeing callers for a while I don't expect. They'll be in mourning …' Madge Bailey rushed off into the kitchen and then out of the back door, running out of the back entrance of Highfield House.

Eliza walked across the hallway and glanced around her as she closed the front door of the grand house behind her. Edmund Ellershaw was at last dead, the man that both she and Mary-Anne had hated for so much of their lives.

But what would happen now? He still had a grip over them, even in death. Victoria had lost her father. And what would happen to Rose Pit? Tom would probably be out of work, and Eliza hung her head as she wondered if Grace would go back on the deal they had struck regarding the shop. Surely she would not leave her mother alone in the world; she would feel beholden to her and want to stay.

She made her way through Woodlesford to her home in Aireville Mansions and found Victoria at her lessons. The joy she had been feeling a mere hour ago dissipated like the early morning mist as she realised that her first duty was to tell Victoria and then Mary-Anne of Ellershaw's death. Her sister, she knew, would not shed any tears for the man that they both hated.

'Well, Aunt Eliza, I can't cry for a man I never really knew; he means nothing to me.' Victoria sat down next to her aunt and didn't quite know how to feel.

'He's still your father, Victoria,' Eliza whispered.

'He's no father of mine; a father shows you love and kindness and makes sure that you are looked after. I'm almost glad that he's dead; from what I've heard he's only brought sadness and sorrow to people all his life.'

'That's true; your mother will certainly not be upset over his death. I'm about to make my way to her; are you going to join me in telling her? I thought that we would get a cab and go and tell her the news, and I also need to talk to her about my business.' Eliza didn't know what to do with the money that Mary-Anne had deposited in her bank account for the purchase of Grace's part of the business; she hoped that the deal would still go through but at the moment it looked like Grace's plans could well be postponed.

'Yes, I'll come; I've finished my lessons and now that Mother lives on her own, I should visit her more. I really didn't like going when she was living with Mrs Fletcher; she reminded me of a witch. Especially when she had that cat on her knee.' Victoria pulled a face, thinking about the old woman who had been the one to shatter her dreams in the past by revealing to her who her father was.

'Your poor mother has to show that cat that it's loved; she owes everything to the animal. Part of the deal between her and Ma Fletcher is that she looks after it. Trouble is your mother has never liked cats, so it might just about get fed if it's lucky.' Eliza chuckled as she waited for Victoria to get ready to come with her to Speakers' Corner.

'It's the most scraggy, ugly feline I have ever seen; in fact, it looked like Ma Fletcher as you call her, and they were both ugly.' Victoria grinned as she opened the door for her aunt.

'Now, Victoria,' Eliza chastised, 'we can't be all blessed with your good looks. Ma Fletcher had a good heart and that's all that matters in this life.'

'No, Aunt, money also matters. You can't buy anything without money.' Victoria took her aunt's arm as they walked down the street.

'Except love, Victoria. You can't buy love and there's nothing more precious than love, as both your mother and I know. So never forget that.' Eliza smiled as she picked up her skirts to climb into the horse-driven cab; Victoria was truly her mother's daughter, especially now that she was beginning to realise just how much money and position in society counted.

Eliza knocked on the door of Mary-Anne's home and was just about to walk in when a pretty looking young woman dressed in a maid's uniform answered the door.

'Good morning, ma'am; whom may I say is calling?' she asked politely.

'It's all right, Nellie; don't stand on ceremony. You can let them both in. This is my sister, Eliza, and my daughter, Victoria.' Mary-Anne stood behind her latest hire and smiled as the servant girl bobbed a curtsy and went about the business of cleaning for her new mistress.

'You've got a maid!' Eliza grinned.

'Yes, what's wrong with that? I've done my fair share of cleaning and scrubbing, so I thought I'd indulge myself.' Mary-Anne looked at her sister and daughter and decided to give Victoria a hug as she entered into her home. 'Come through to the parlour; I'll get Nellie to make us some tea.' Mary-Anne called out to Nellie: 'Put the kettle on, lass, and bring it through to the posh end.'

Victoria smirked; her mother might have come up in the world in terms of her fortune but was so crude sometimes. She had no airs or graces, unlike herself and her aunt.

'Now, what brings you two to my door, not that it's not lovely to see you, and you both know you are welcome at any time.' Mary-Anne sat down in her favourite chair next to the marble fireplace and watched the faces of Eliza and Victoria as they looked around at the changes in her home. 'Oh, yes, I've been a bit busy; the place needed some time and money spending on it and now I've got both, I've done both. What do you think of my new chaise longue and curtains? I've got my eye on a nice whatnot in Smiths' window down in town; it'll go in that corner and display all my small ornaments nicely.'

'You've made it lovely, Mary-Anne. Hasn't she, Victoria?' Eliza turned to her niece, prompting her to say something while knowing that she was thinking the same as her: that everything was just a little too bright and vulgar.

'Yes, it's lovely. I bet Mr Tibbs doesn't know quite which house he is living in,' Victoria commented as tactfully as she could, realising that she had not seen the old tabby cat anywhere.

'He's not allowed in here; I caught him sharpening his claws on the chairs, so he's banned to the kitchen, the old fleabag. Now, what's new? There must be something, else you wouldn't both be here? Eliza, have you bought your shop yet and got rid of Grace Ellershaw at long last? She sounds as if she's been bleeding you dry, from what you've told me.' Mary-Anne went quiet as Nellie came in with the tea tray, placing it down in front of the group before leaving them to their secrets.

'I haven't seen Grace yet; I went this morning but I never got to see her because I chose a bad day to visit Highfield. The place was in chaos.' Eliza paused. 'Edmund Ellershaw died this morning. He'd just passed away when I got there. I didn't even get to see Grace.'

Mary-Anne gave a sigh. 'So, the old bugger's finally dead. I hope that he's gone to hell because that's where he belongs. I didn't think that this day would ever come; I've wished it on him for so long.' To her surprise Mary-Anne found a tear come to her eye but it was more in relief than because of a sense of any loss.

Eliza went and sat on the chair next to Mary-Anne and put her hand out for her to hold. 'Yes, he's gone and now we are free of him. Victoria never knew him, thank God, but we both know how evil he was. And that the world is a better place without him.'

Victoria came and knelt down by her mother's knee. 'Don't cry, Mama. He's gone, and now we can get on with our lives. I have never thought of him as my father, because I never knew him, so I'm shedding no tears.'

'I'm glad that you didn't know him, my love. You are the one good thing that he did have a hand in making, and I will never ever regret your birth. But when it comes to Edmund Ellershaw, then I do hope that he's dancing with the devil this day. I doubt that his legacy will be a good one; his wife will have been left with no money and the Rose will now close. If only you could have made your deal with Grace before the old bastard died, our Eliza. She'll not be able to leave her mother now; she'll need her income.'

'I'll give you your money back if she won't sell. It's only right that I do.' Eliza sighed.

'No, you keep it; you've earned it, bringing my lovely daughter up to be such a lady. It makes up for all the times when I was in America, promising you money which never came. I know you needed it then and that I really let you down but I aim to make it up to you now, now that I've come up in the world.' Mary-Anne ran her fingers through Victoria's long dark hair and smiled. 'She's the most precious thing in my life, regardless of what people are saying about me and William. I can't think of how upset he'll be at the death of his father. I hope his mother has had the decency to have told him, because even though he says he hates him, he's still his father. They are a lot alike, whether he likes it or not, except William is a lot more caring.'

'It's a complicated life you lead, Mary-Anne,' Eliza told her. 'You'd think if you had any sense that you would try and forget the Ellershaws, but instead you aim to marry into them. Even though you now have no need to.'

'I love him, Eliza; and besides, if we marry, Victoria will have the recognition of being an Ellershaw and have the position in life that she deserves. Money will only take us so far.' Mary-Anne smiled at her daughter.

'You don't have to marry just because of me, Mama. I'm proud of being known as Victoria Wild; I don't need Ellershaw as my surname.'

'It's not the Ellershaw name you need, Victoria, but you do need the connections in society that they have. You need to marry well and not live from day to day, hoping that you have enough money to pay the bills and keep a roof over your head. That is not what both your Aunt Eliza and I wish for you. We hope to ensure a better life for you and that is what we will endeavour to deliver. As for now, let us just celebrate that the man who has caused all three of us so much sorrow is dead and gone, and now is the time for us to grow stronger. These are tears of joy that are running down my cheeks, not of sadness. And as for Edmund Ellershaw, I curse you to hell, where the hottest fires will be stoked by you.'

*

Catherine Ellershaw sat by the bedside of her dead husband. Tears fell down her cheeks as Grace tried to console her.

'Father wouldn't want you to cry over him. He had a good life and proved that, even though you are working class, you can rise above it and become a self-made man.' Grace put her arm around her mother and looked across at George for support.

'Yes, he was a man of few words,' George added, 'but what he did say was always valid and strong, and even though he made his thoughts of my life and how I live it quite obvious, he never disowned me.' He bowed his head; he'd never been close to his father and, to be quite honest, he was glad that the old man had passed and was no longer able to lecture him.

All three turned their heads as the bedroom door opened and William walked in. Grace smiled sadly at her brother, and Catherine stood up and made for the arms of her eldest.

'So, he's gone? Leaving us all trying to think of good things to say about him, else he will probably come back and haunt us all.' William embraced his mother. 'There, there, Mother; we all knew he would not survive the stroke and that it was a matter of time. Now we must all be strong and be there for one another.' William kissed his mother on her cheek. 'Is the funeral arranged? Does his solicitor know he's died or would you like me to see to all? I am, after all, the eldest.'

'See to it, William.' Catherine sighed. 'I don't have the strength, and it isn't up to Grace; I wouldn't want her to have the further heartache that I know is going to unfold, and George has no idea of his father's affairs.'

'Mother, I'm not a simpleton; I can look to his affairs and see that we all get our dues.' George puffed up his chest.

'Dues, George … we will be lucky if we can afford to bury your father once the bank realises that he's dead. He's left us all with nothing, not a penny. Everything is in hock to the bank. You will be all right – you've got your grandfather's money, and Grace has got her business – but I will be left homeless for the whole of society to look upon and pity.' Catherine wiped the tears away from her eyes and looked at the dumbstruck members of her family.

'I'll see to everything, Mother,' William told her. 'I'll play for time and you will not be homeless. I've been spending money on the empty gatehouse at Levensthorpe Hall. I knew this day would arrive soon and I also knew that he had wasted every penny that he had earned. Let that be a warning to you, George, that a fool and his money are soon parted, so don't squander it on entertainment and clothes. I hear that you are keeping bad company now that you no longer live at home.'

'You, sir, are a hypocrite! How can you judge me when you are seen around town with that Pit Lane girl?' George blustered.

'A Pit Lane girl, who my father took advantage of and who, along with her sister, brings up our own half-sister.' William bit back.

'George, William … now is not the time,' Grace told her squabbling brothers. 'You are upsetting Mother and you shouldn't talk ill of the dead. William, go and see the vicar and we will leave you to sort his affairs. I will be needed here, and, George, you would do well to move back home for the time being.'

'I will not!' George snorted. 'If things are as bad as Mother says, I am not coming home, neither am I parting with my inheritance from Grandfather for the good of the family. Surely things will not be that bad.'

Grace shook her head as William held his mother close to him.

'Leave him now, Mother. Come downstairs and get Mrs Bailey to make you a pot of tea, and I'll see to Father, arrange the funeral and in the morning see the solicitor.' William guided his mother to the door.

'The doctor is sending someone to lay Father out,' Grace said. 'Don't bother with that, William. George, go down with William and Mother, and then you can open the door to the visitors that we will no doubt be having. Poor Mrs Bailey looks absolutely worn down to the bone; she's the only servant that has stayed loyal of late and I doubt that she will benefit from doing so.' Grace sat down next to her dead father and held her tears back. Though, in truth, she realised her tears were less for him and more for herself. She couldn't leave her mother now; all her plans would have to be put on hold. Even in death, her father was proving to be the stubborn, awkward old bastard that the family knew him to be.

'Me, be the butler?' George sniffed.

'Just go, George; for once in your life do something for your family and stop being so proud.' Grace bowed her head. God only knew what the future held for them all but William was the only one that had seen the truth behind his family and now he was needed by every one of them.

Chapter 7

William walked out of the vicarage in Woodlesford. His father's funeral was arranged for Saturday at three, to enable any of his workers that felt that they needed to show their respects to attend, but leaving them to have no need to disturb their working lives too much. Work should come first at the pit, and he knew it to be most unlikely that there would be many of his workers ready to lose an hour or two's pay to see their old boss laid to rest. He hadn't been the best-liked man and a large group of mourners was not to be expected – unlike the debtors, who seemed to be more numerous than the flies that circled around his horse in the muggy autumn afternoon's heat.

Since his father's death, Highfield House had many a frantic caller, not with notes of condolence, but with unpaid bills, demanding payment. George, Grace and the cook had begged for patience and time for payment once the funeral had taken place. It was this that William was now going to discuss with his father's banker, and then his last port of call was to his father's solicitor's, to see if anything at all was salvageable from his father's estate. He doubted it very much as he eased himself up into his horse's saddle and made off for the centre of Leeds, with its busy streets and temptations that had drained his father's pockets completely dry.

Harold Snodgrass looked full of commiseration as he sat down in his chair across from William and offered him a pinch of snuff.

'Ah, William, my lad, please sit down, make yourself comfortable, and before we talk business may I offer my condolences on the death of your father. He will be sadly missed here at Beckett's Bank.'

He sat back and studied the face of William, the son of one the bank's biggest debtors. He knew William to be of better character and fortune than his hapless father, and so he was hoping that he was here to settle his debts, which, until his illness the bank had thought repayable, but now on Edmund's death, things would have to be finally resolved.

'I'm here on behalf of my father. As you know he died on Monday and the family wishes for me to sort his affairs.' William crossed his legs and looked at the bank manager who he had been visiting with his father since he was barely knee high.

'I appreciate you attending to them so quickly; indeed it was only this morning that I looked at his account, knowing that it would be needed to be settled in the next few days.' Harold Snodgrass reached over to the side of his large oak dresser and picked up a bound red leather accounts book. 'I'm afraid that he left us with quite a debt for you to settle. I'm aware there is little left in his estate but I know that you have more than sufficient funds yourself to cover it on his behalf.' The old banker smiled as he pointed at the amount left owing by Edmund. Every pound and penny diligently written in red with interest added on and totalled page by page, leaving the grand sum of five thousand pounds owed.

William folded his arms. 'In case you are unaware, Mr Snodgrass, my father disowned me before his death and I have no legal requirement to settle his affairs. I'm not legally responsible because I was not in joint business with him. This is not my debt and I am not going to burden myself with it for the future. I helped him out in life only to be thrown out of the family home by him. I have only paid you a visit today to see just how much he owed you and to tell you to foreclose on his business and property after his funeral. My mother and family will not stand in your way; they realise how bad things are. It's the only way you'll get any of your loan back.'

'But you've got to stand by them; think of the scandal! Why yes, you may not be legally responsible for your father's debts but it's not only us that he owes money to. He will have accounts with most of the mining businesses in Leeds and none will be paid! Not to mention his private bills; they will be in the hundreds of pounds, the way he lived his life. This attitude is truly not good enough, William. A gentleman would do right by his father and save his family's name from being dragged through the mire. And this debt will bring some firms to their knees, not to mention the hurt that it will do to my bank.'

'Then I suggest you act quickly and recoup what you can. The pits are of no use to the family and my mother will be moving in with me. I ask for a little respect to be given until after the funeral but then, as I've said, I should think you will want to foreclose on my father's debts and sell what property he has.' William uncrossed his long legs and stood up ready to leave the shocked banker. 'I'm sure somebody will be interested in two worthless pits and a house that needs quite a bit of attention. Perhaps if my father had not been busy with other pursuits he would have been a man of worth by now.'

'William, whatever he may have done, he was your father; take care of what you say about the dead.' Harold Snodgrass shook his head in disbelief.

'Aye, he was my father and father to how many other children that he did not claim or brag about? I have no intention of honouring his name nor his bank account, so do your worst.' William walked out of the bank and onto the streets of Park Row, looking up at the spire of St Anne's Cathedral and the thunderclouds that were gathering around it. There was a storm coming, a storm that would bring change, but after its passing things would be calmer and settled, he thought. The coming weeks would be hard, especially for his mother, but at least she would not have to endure the pain of an unfaithful husband any longer, and she would have security in the gatehouse at Levensthorpe along with whatever selected items of family furniture he would move for her there, before the bailiffs seized it all to be sold.

William felt lower in spirits than he had done for some time as he stepped out of his father's solicitor's offices. It was as he had feared: there was nothing to be left to any of his father's family. Even though the most recent will had stated that his estate to go to his wife rather than any of his children, there was no estate to be had. He'd secretly hoped that his father had somehow hidden some of his wealth and that perhaps things were not as bad as they seemed but his solicitor had just told him the same tale: a story of a reckless, selfish man that had thought of only himself all his life. He hung his head and walked his horse through the streets to Briggate, tethering it outside the alleyway to Whitelocks, the alehouse where he meant to drown his worries, at least until the following morning.

'A gill of your best bitter.' William stood at the highly decorated tiled bar and reached into his pocket for money to pay the barman.

'I'll serve Mr Ellershaw; I have a bit of business to do with him.' The landlord moved the barman out of the way and poured William a gill of beer and passed it to him, taking his change straight away. 'I'll need a bit more than that if you are here to settle your father's tab. I sent my lad up to your home but he was sent away with a flea in his ear when he demanded payment. I hope the old bugger's debts are going to be honoured, else you can bugger off and the next caller on my behalf will not be as friendly.' The landlord leaned over the bar and looked threatening at William.

'It's nothing to do with me; my father and me never spoke to one another.' William swigged back the last few drops of his drink and stared at the big man. 'Now pull us another.'

'No, I don't think so. You can bugger off and get your arse out of my pub. You lot are all the same, all gob and shite and you think you can keep us workers in their place. Well, not in my place. Harold!' The landlord yelled at the barman at the other end of the bar who was as broad as he was tall with a face that looked like it had taken many a punch. 'Show this gentleman the door; his sort is not welcome here unless they honour their bills.'

'Be a reasonable man; my father's debts are not mine.' William stood his ground as he argued his case.

'Out, you toffee-nosed bastard,' the landlord yelled, as his barman grabbed William by the scruff of the neck. 'If I can't have your father's money, I'll at least have some satisfaction in not seeing your face at my bar again. You and your family are not welcome here ever again.' The landlord looked around him at the hardworking men of Leeds and heard a muttering of agreement as William was nearly lifted off his feet and propelled outside the doorway of the Whitelocks, leaving him looking somewhat dishevelled and frustrated with being held responsible for his father's misdemeanors.

*

'How could he do this to us all? I am so ashamed.' Catherine Ellershaw sat in her funeral finery, with her family all around her as she despaired of the situation her husband had left them in. Her head in her hands, she breathed in deeply and lifted her head. 'My mother told me not to marry him. The only good things that came out of this marriage are my children, who I am so thankful for; I know I can rely on you this day.' Catherine smiled wanly at her family and then wiped away a tear.

'Let us help you more, Mother. I'm sure all three of us would be willing to help clear father's debts ...?' Grace held her mother's hand tightly while William grimaced at his younger sister and George went red in the face, worried that she was just about to give his inheritance away.

'No, No definitely not. It is your father's doing. He's not going to ruin your lives like he has mine. You keep your money, all of you, and you enjoy your lives. William has secured me a home in his lodge and has moved some of my most precious items, which I don't want the bank to get their hands on. As for the pits, the one at Wakefield is not worth anything, and the Rose I will be glad to see the back of. It's just this house. Although I have always wanted better, it has served well as a family home and I would have liked to have seen out my days living in it. But it is the gossips I fear more. I'm sure everybody is talking about us and I keep hearing whispers about our situation, even from close friends.

'You get used to putting up with the gossips, Mama. We will be old news by next month and they will have found somebody else to pull apart and scrutinise.' William swigged his whisky back and looked out of the window at the funeral cortege awaiting them. 'Come on, let's get the old bugger buried and let's hope that it's the last time we will have a family reunion in a graveyard for a while. I think it's time for a bit of good luck just for a change.'

'So do I; two in a year is enough, although they always say death comes in threes.' Grace took her mother's arm and thanked George as he opened the front door for them to leave Highfield House for the very last time. She held back the tears as she raised her head high, not looking at the empty hall-way and the bare walls as she concentrated on being strong for her mother and keeping her dignity as she followed her father's coffin to the churchyard in Woodlesford.

Catherine was in tears by the time Mrs Bailey had served them tea in the parlour and made herself scarce. 'Oh Grace, what am I to do?' Her mother sighed. 'William says I've to move into the gatehouse fast before the bailiffs come and that I can't even afford to keep Mrs Bailey on!'

'Now, Mother, William says he is getting you a maid and I'm still here. I've no intentions of leaving you on your own. I've decided to change my plans and will stay with you for as long as you need me.'

'No, you do what you want to do with your life. You don't waste your days looking after me; I'll survive. I only hope that William doesn't do what he says he is going to do next spring by marrying that trollop! I loathe that family. The sooner you are out of business with her sister, the better; they are trouble, through and through. God rest his soul, they even got their claws into your father – making out that girl of theirs was his.' Catherine looked at her daughter, knowing that she herself had been friends with the Wild family, but she personally hated them.

'Poor Eliza; I've not had a chance to talk to her about our business of late; and, besides, I haven't really wanted to show my face in Leeds. Both William and George have had worrying experiences with people demanding they settle Father's debts now that it is common knowledge that his estate is as good as bankrupt!'

'Poor Eliza! Think of what you are saying, child. She's not poor; you've made her a fortune. And I bet she never thanks you. It should be that family that is in the gutter, not us. The gutter is where they came from and where they belong; I still feel faint when I think about Mary-Anne Wild, or Vasey as she calls herself, carrying on with William at the Guild Ball. That, I'm sure, added another nail to your father's coffin, not to mention the death of poor Priscilla! Oh, my Edmund, what am I going to do without him, I know he was not the man he should have been but he was always there and he was my husband.' Catherine gasped and fell into a cascade of tears.

'You'll survive, Mother. You will have a roof over your head, food on the table, a maid of all work and a family that cares. You may have lost your husband, but you'll have a lot more than most people have.'

Chapter 8

Tom Thackeray stood with the letter of authority in his hand from Beckett's Bank; it had arrived yesterday telling him of their intent to close the pit and to expect the bailiffs the following day. He stood looking out of his office window at the empty yard. The mighty pithead wheel was no longer turning, and the yards were silent without the usual banter of his men. His heart was heavy; he'd spent almost every day since the age of ten at the Rose, and he had a love of the pit and his fellow miners. A love that was all too obviously missing in the Ellershaw family, else they would have fought against its closure, no matter what their financial circumstances.

He sighed and thought about Edmund Ellershaw, the times he had cursed him, and the times that Ellershaw had used the office he was standing in for his illicit affairs. But at the end of the day, Edmund Ellershaw was at least a true miner; despite his shenanigans he knew where the coal seams ran and how to run a pit. Which was more than could be said for his family; they hadn't even had the decency to break the news to him and their workers in person. Edmund had died without a penny to his name and public notices had been posted in all the local papers and billboards telling of his demise, and for creditors to him to make themselves known to Beckett's Bank.

Tom himself had tried to make sure that he did right by the workforce at the pit, dividing what money he held in the office between the men, after telling them that the pit would close the following morning. He'd felt bad as he had shaken each man's hand and wished them all the best for the future, promising them that if he could give them employment he would, but knowing that it would be impossible to do once the bank locked the pit yard gates and reclaimed what was actually theirs. It had been hard watching grown men nearly cry as they said goodbye to the place they were dependant on for their families welfare all because Edmund Ellershaw and his family had spent money like water and had not thought once of the consequences. Damn the man. All he'd thought about was himself; he'd never once bothered about the lives that he was responsible for.

Tom turned to look as he saw four men from the bailiff's walk in through the yards gates and knock on the office's door.

'You've come to do your worst then.'

The man in the suit stepped forward.

'Now, we've not come to argue. You just behave and pass us over the keys to the yard and tell us what's left to sell and then go on your way.'

'You can have the keys, you can have the lot, but I'll not be showing you around nor telling you what's what. You've made seventy men out of work here; they could have proved to you that the pit was paying its way and you could have sold it as a going concern – but, no, you've just closed the Rose down.' Tom was angry; work was hard to come by and he felt helpless knowing that, with the man of the house jobless, some families would have to live on barely anything.

'Just give us the keys then, lad, and then get on your way. We are only doing our job like you yours.' The one in charge held his hand out for the keys, while the other three thick-set men set off to walk around the pit to assess the remaining assets.

'The third level is flooded but it's got a good seam running through it, and make sure the ponies get a good home. Don't be sending them to the knacker's yard.' Tom handed the keys over and found it hard to turn his back on his job.

'It's none of your concern any longer, lad. Now get on your way.'

Tom dragged his feet as he left the colliery behind. Not only had the lads at the pit lost their job, but so had he. He turned around just in time to see the bill of sale being posted to the mighty pit gates. If only he had the money, he'd soon make it pay its way.

The Rose was a good pit; it just needed proper investment and good management, which even Edmund Ellershaw had not seen fit to do in his last years. However, he couldn't change things. Tonight he would go and see Eliza and share his worries; she'd not want to marry him now with no money coming in. Even though he did at least own his mother's cottage, it was no way as near grand as Eliza's house on Aireville Mansions. Eliza had worked hard for all she had, that was the trouble; he didn't want to marry her without being able to pay his way, and she wasn't about to hand all her possessions and assets to him for the sake of a ring on her finger. He didn't blame her; he'd just have to court her for now and hopefully one day she would eventually marry him.

Eliza sat next to the love of her life and looked at the sadness in his eyes. 'Oh, Tom, what are you going to do?'

'There's not a lot I can do. The pit's closed. All the men that worked there will have to find fresh jobs, along with myself. The trouble is, would-be buyers will think it's worthless because it's not been being worked right. The books will show little or no profit, especially in the last month or two when George has been in charge of them. I doubt the Rose will ever work again; if they can't sell the land, it'll be like other pitheads that are left to rot and decay.

'Shall we walk down to the pit and look what the notice on the gate says? Do you think that the bank has also had to take Highfield House in repayment? It sounds as if Edmund Ellershaw had nothing … I just can't believe it. He used to strut around the town like a prize cock and all the time he owed the bank everything.' Eliza shook her head in disbelief at the situation.

'Aye, we can have a walk down if you want. But I'll find it hard; that pit and I go back a long way. I'm going to be lost without it. I suppose I can always go back and see if Master Bentley will take me back on at Eshald Mansion, but I fear he won't. I left him in a hurry and he'll be thinking that I'd do the same to him again. I might have to look for work over Wakefield way, but I don't want to move away from my home, or from you.' Tom rubbed his head and stood up as he waited for Eliza to get her shawl. 'I could do with buying the Rose, but it will be too much money, so I shouldn't even dream about it.' He smiled as Eliza linked her arm through his and they walked down the street together.

'That's buying work, and work that would not last forever. The coal seams will not be that strong.'

'Aye, but they are, Eliza; I've looked down and explored them more times than I've had hot dinners. There's enough coal down that pit to keep it open for many a year, but most folks don't know that.' Tom sighed.

'There's nothing you can do, Tom, and I can't help you. I have money from our Mary-Anne but I mean to use it to buy Grace Ellershaw's half of the shop ... that is if she is still set on selling it to me. Her father dying might have changed her mind and she might have decided to stay with her mother at Highfield House.'

'The bloody Ellershaw is still controlling our lives. Why your sister Mary-Anne bothers with that William, I don't know. He'll only break her heart and deceive her; that's all the men of that family do.' Tom sighed as they came to the top of

Pit Lane. 'Remember when we used to walk out together down this lane when we were so much younger, and here we are still doing it now. Marry me, Eliza, and stop keeping me hanging on. I know I've not got the best prospects at the moment but I'll find work.' Tom held her hand tightly and looked into her eyes and hoped that she would finally set a date.

'The time's not right, Tom. Let's see what happens in the next few months and perhaps next spring I'll be ready to set a date. Now, what does this notice say? ' Eliza looked up at the posting on the pithead gates and stood back and read it.

THE BANKRUPTCY ACT 1869

IN THE COUNTY COURT OF YORKSHIRE, HOLDEN AT LEEDS. IN THE MATTER OF PROCEEDINGS FOR LIQUIDATION BY ARRANGEMENT OR COMPOSITION OF THE AFFAIRS OF EDMUND ELLERSHAW (DECEASED) OF HIGHFIELD HOUSE, WOODLESFORD, LEEDS, CARRYING ON THE BUSINESS OF COLLIERY OWNER AT THE ROSE PIT, WOODLESFORD, AND AT THE NELLY JANE PIT AT WAKEFIELD.

WILLIAM SAUNDERS, OF NUMBER 2 PARK LANE, LEEDS, ACCOUNTANT, HAS BEEN APPOINTED A TRUSTEE OF THE DEBTOR. ALL PERSONS HAVING IN THEIR POSSESSION ANY OF THE EFFECTS OR PROPERTY OF THE DEBTOR MUST DELIVER THEM TO THE TRUSTEE, AND ALL DEBTS DUE TO THE DEBTOR MUST BE PAID TO THE TRUSTEE. CREDITORS WHO HAVE NOT YET PROVED

THEIR DEBTS MUST FORWARD THEIR PROOF OF THEM TO
THE TRUSTEE. – 26th OCTOBER 1878

Eliza stopped for a second and then carried on to read the
bill of sale.

BY ORDER OF THE COUNTY COURT OF YORKSHIRE
THE ROSE PIT
TO BE SOLD ON THE 1st DAY OF DECEMBER 1878,
BY AUCTION AT 2 PM.
THE PROPERTY TO BE PAID FOR ON THE DAY.

'Oh, my Lord, he must have left some debt!' Tom looked
at the notice, not quite believing, even though he had witnessed the bailiffs' arrival that morning.

'Who's going to have money to pay for the pit outright,
and with it being so near Christmas? No bank in their right
mind is going to lend money for a closed, bankrupt pit; I
doubt I've seen the last working days of the Rose and there's
nothing I can do about it.'

'It sounds as if he's been in real trouble. Now let's walk
down to Highfield House and see if they have included that in
his debts.' Eliza pulled on his arm urging him to walk the half
mile to Edmund Ellershaw's home. On arrival there they met
with the same notice as on the pit gates. Highfield House was
to be auctioned off along with all the furniture and belongings
inside on the same day as the Rose. Edmund Ellershaw and
his wife had lost everything that they had ever worked for.

'Poor Grace, she'll be beside herself. No wonder she hasn't got back to me about the sale of the business. She'll be frightened that she too could lose her money if the bank decides to look to her to settle her father's debts even though she had nothing to do with her father's business. Her assets are her own but us women are easy targets, and the law can easily be bent. Although I do believe that parliament is looking into changing things of late and I hope that they will shortly give women their own rights in the world when it comes to their affairs.' Eliza bowed her head and knew that perhaps her owning the shop outright on Briggate was not going to happen any time soon in view of the Ellershaws' circumstances.

'She might need the money yet, Eliza. I wouldn't give up hope of your dream. However, I've no sympathy with the Ellershaws; it's the men and their families' lives that they have ruined by Edmund squandering his money and in doing so closing down a perfectly good pit I have sympathy with. If I had the brass, I'd buy the Rose; it would soon pay for itself if run properly.'

'I too feel sympathy for the families but as you say there's not a lot we can do. I know Mary-Anne has given me this money in payment for looking after Victoria, but if I cannot buy Grace's half of the shop, then I will feel obliged to return it to Mary-Anne, no matter what she said.' Eliza put her arm through Tom's as they turned to walk home.

'It's time the hard-working men had their way. I'm sick and tired of being governed by those who don't give the working classes a second glance. Let alone worry how they make a living and keep their children fed while they gamble and drink their lives away. Grace Ellershaw is just the same – she has had you working with her all these years, and yet she's taken more than she was owed from the business. And were you ever asked to her home or for tea with her friends? No, she still thinks of you as below her and she always will. How I loathe the lot of them,' Tom growled as he walked homeward to Aireville Mansions.

Later that evening as Eliza lay in her bed, Tom's words echoed in her head. He was right; she had never been included in Grace's close circle of friends, and while Eliza's name was also above the door, most of their clientele deferred to Grace if she was in the shop. Perhaps Grace was no different from her father, and she had been used just as much as Mary-Anne had been used in her time.

Mary-Anne, meanwhile, was still playing them at their own game and had succeeded in her goals, especially if she was to marry William. Tomorrow she would visit her; no doubt her sister would be full of the news of Edmund's estate being bankrupt and how the land lay at Levensthorpe Hall.

*

'Couldn't have happened to a nicer family.' Mary-Anne sat back and laughed as she listened to her sister's news. 'At least William has had the sense not to waste his money on bailing out his father's estate just to keep his good name, although he is feeling guilty. But the old bastard did him no favours so why should he, and anyway Edmund's dead and gone now.'

'You are callous, our Mary-Anne. I can't help but think of all those miners' families that are now going without. Tom is worried about them too; he's actually partly blaming himself for it going rack and ruin. However, there was no way he could have saved the pit from closing. He was even saying that if he had money that he would buy it. I told him straight that he was talking nonsense.' Eliza sipped her tea and looked around her.

'He'd be a fool if he did; that mine must be nearly worked-out, surely?' Mary-Anne lifted an eyebrow and waited for an answer.

'Quite the contrary; Tom says he knows of a good rich seam, but that's of no consequence now. Anyway, I've come to talk about Grace Ellershaw and to offer you your money back if she does not want to sell me her half of the shop. Though quite how we can work together, now that I know how I've been abused by her, I'm not sure.' Eliza sighed.

'Well, she is an Ellershaw and if my views count, I've always thought she was a real snob. As for the money, I told you, it's yours; I owe you it, and, in fact, I owe you a great deal more for the care you have given Victoria over the years. I can never truly repay you for all you've done for her. Why don't you buy Tom his blasted pit? That would make me laugh good and proper. Us Wilds in charge of the pit that

Edmund Ellershaw worked for all his life; now that would be sweet revenge!'

'Don't be daft, Mary-Anne; I couldn't afford that. It isn't even worth giving the thought the time of day. Besides, if she's not for selling the shop, I will give you the money back.'

'How many times? The money is yours! Now, changing the subject, when will you have time to make me a new dress for my wedding this coming spring? I want to look like a million dollars and be the envy of the whole of Leeds.' Mary-Anne giggled.

'You're getting married in spring! You've set the date?' Eliza grinned.

'Yes, I've set the date, April the first; although I've yet to inform William. I'm not prepared to wait forever to get that ring on my finger, unlike you.'

'You'll be taking William to be an April Fool if you marry on the first of April,' Eliza exclaimed, 'and so he is with you tricking him all the time with your plans and schemes.'

'Well, sometime in April, then, a beautiful spring day is just right for me and William because there will be some merriment that day, I can tell you.' Mary-Anne sat back and sighed. 'I feel a lot more content knowing that Edmund Ellershaw is six feet under. I have hated him most of my life and it is just satisfying to put him behind me and look to the future. We have both come a long way in our lives, Eliza, and I have a feeling there is yet more to happen, but perhaps this time it will only be the good things in life.'

'I hope so, Mary-Anne, but at the moment all I see is uncertainty in mine. Victoria is growing up; she should have no problems when she is older to find a proper suitor. Her tutor is ever so pleased with her progress in all her studies but I do sometimes think she gets lonely, not quite fitting in anywhere. I know George was not to be encouraged but at least he was someone for her to talk to.' Eliza sighed.

'George is hardly fitting company for our Victoria, even more so now he's not answerable to his father and is sharing accommodation with his so-called "friend". William has washed his hands of him. Don't you worry about Victoria; she will soon find friends when she starts attending balls and functions. I expect her to be invited to a lot more once William and I are married. In time I hope he'll make her heir to his fortune and Levensthorpe Hall. You've taken care of her needs while she was young, shortly it will be my turn to ensure her a secure future. A future where she will want for nothing and will be loved and cosseted.' Mary-Anne smiled.

'That's all any mother wants for her child; that's why our poor dead mother married Bill and look how that ended.'

'Well, she won't be marrying anyone like that; I can assure you! I'll make sure she mixes with earls and viscounts and some of the wealthiest landowners in Yorkshire.'

'As long as they are kind and true, that will satisfy me, my dear sister. Money – as well you know – is not everything.'

Chapter 9

Eliza sat back in her chair in the small room that Grace and she used as an office in the upper part of the shop. She looked through the account book that she had been given the privilege of having more time to peruse and scrutinise, after being left alone by Grace since her father's death.

Eliza was no accountant but she had soon realised that things were not as equal when it came to the shop's affairs as she first had thought, particularly with their profits – that Grace was taking more of her fair share and had been for some time. Yes, she had paid the set-up costs of the shop but she had recouped her expenditure several times over. They should now be equal partners in their venture but the more Eliza looked at the figures the more annoyed she became. Yes, she owed Grace some loyalty but not to the extent of her working as an ordinary paid employee; that is not how things had been sorted when they first went into business together. They were supposed to be partners, neither of them being able to survive without the other one's knowledge or connections. However, the supposedly hidden figures of the pages told a different story, and Eliza now realised that she had been taken for an idiot.

As it was, she was now in two minds whether to go through with buying the shop even if it was still on offer to her. Also, knowing what she did now, it would not be at the original asking price, to make up for the years of deceit that lay within the accounts' pages. Along with her new-found knowledge, there were also Mary-Anne's words playing over and over again in her mind. 'Why don't you buy the Rose Pit, for Tom?' She'd not even dared to think about it, but now she couldn't stop herself from toying with the idea. In fact, if she didn't buy the shop from Grace, and the pit went for next to nothing, she could probably afford to buy it, but the money to run it along with the wages would be the problem. The door opened and Grace entering the room made her stop her dreaming as she glanced up at her so-called partner and noticed the worried look on her face.

'Good morning, Eliza. I got your message that you wanted to see me.' Grace sat down next to her and knew immediately that something was wrong.

'Are you still in a position to sell me the shop or have things changed with the death of your father?' Eliza got straight to the point, her hand resting deliberately on the accounts book as she tried to keep her feelings hidden.

'No, I still wish to sell it, Eliza. In fact, my need to sell it is even greater now, as I'm sure that you have been made aware of the situation that my father has left his affairs in. It seems the whole of Leeds is talking about us at this moment in time.' Grace sighed and smiled, hoping to find some sympathy from Eliza.

'Well, I'm no longer sure that I wish to buy the property or not. The accounts tell me that you have been taking liberties with the profits and that over the years we have been anything but equal partners. In fact, I have only been receiving slightly more than what our senior seamstress receives, while you have been seeing to it that you receive large regular payments out of our funds. I thought we were friends, Grace, I thought that I could trust you to balance our books and all the time you have not played fair with me. A fact I would never have known if your father hadn't have died and you hadn't given me time to look deeper into the shop's affairs.' Eliza glared across at Grace, whose face suddenly looked like thunder.

'How could we ever be equal partners? You put nothing into the business; it all came from my own funds. You have no qualifications, no breeding, no connections; you are just good with a needle and thread, and you've me to thank for being where you are in life. I helped you buy your house and now I'm giving you the chance to own this property and business outright, something that you could never have aspired to do if I had left you and that child that you pamper so much back in Pit Lane.' Grace hadn't expected this of Eliza and her words in retaliation were harsh.

'That child is your half-sister! She should have had as many rights to a decent life as you all did. If your father had had an ounce of decency in him.' Eliza glared.

'We have only ever had your sister's word on that. A woman who is throwing herself at my brother and is responsible for poor Priscilla's death. Maybe she did the same with my father all those years ago. My father is proving to be right; I should never have got involved with the Wild sisters. Wild by name and Wild by nature, that's what he used to say.'

'Well, let's face it, he was no angel. He'd know all about being a wild one. And Mary-Anne was scarce older than Victoria when he took her virtue! However, this slandering is not getting us to settle the sale of this property. After looking through the figures, I've decided to withdraw my original offer and offer you half that. That seems fair to me and makes up for all the years that you have not paid me in full.' Eliza sat back and waited for a reaction. Her feelings were torn as she had always seen Grace as a friend but now she realised that she had just been a convenience for her, a lass from the working classes who she could make money out of as long as she kept her sweet.

'Eliza, that's not fair; we had an agreement. The money was there and ready to be handed over to me if it had not been for my father dying. Now it is you that is taking advantage of the situation that I'm in. I was already selling the business to you at a reasonable price. I've had plenty of offers, so don't tempt your luck; else I will sell my half to someone else!' Grace looked at Eliza, realising that there would be no compromising with her now she had digested the years of unfair payments to herself.

'I tell you what, Grace: I don't think I want to be part of this business any more. I'm bored with pampering old women and waiting on young women who will always think themselves better than me. If you won't take my reduced offer, let us put both halves of the business up for sale and share the profits. I could never feel the same about this place now anyway, not with all the hateful words said today and the fact that I've been conned all these years. I know I've still had a good life but it could have been so much better. I was never included in your little soirees with your intimate friends and I always wondered why. Now I know: I was just not good enough. You were still ashamed of me and my upbringing. Well, I'm ashamed of you now; your father was a lecherous drunk and you're not to be trusted. I no longer want to be associated with you in business.' Eliza couldn't help herself as the tears started to build up in her eyes.

'Eliza, you don't understand. You'll never be the same as me; you would have been uncomfortable with the friends I keep. Please don't do this; I know you love this place. I'll take a smaller offer but not as low as the one you are offering; that would be ludicrous. But we can reach an agreement, I'm sure of it …' Grace reached over to take Eliza's hand but she pulled it away.

'No, I've made up my mind; the shop is for sale. I'm making other plans for my money and every penny will help me in achieving my goal. I aim to be an independent woman and have no help from anyone. So, the sooner this shop goes up for sale the better, although I will of course honour any orders that need finishing. I'm not having people badmouthing me around Leeds; instead they can believe that we are selling because of your family problems.'

'Eliza, you are saying things you don't mean. Don't be so hasty. We will pay you the same as me, and I'll not sell the place, and things can go on just as they were. You love this shop!' Grace stood up and looked out of the window high up in the rafters of the main building, down onto Briggate where the people looked as small as ants as they went about their business.

'No, Grace, my mind is made up. Ellershaw and Wild is no more. You can get the full asking price and do as you wish with your half and I can fulfil my plans. Things will never be the same between us, although,' Eliza added as a parting shot, raising her head and looking up at Grace determinedly, 'we will have to be civil if Mary-Anne is to marry your brother William.'

'Over my dead body! Your sister has already hastened my father's demise; she can just remove her claws from my brother and go back where she belongs, and you with her if that's how you feel.' Grace made for the door and then turned back to grab the accounts book from under Eliza's nose. 'I'll see to the sale details; after all, I'm the one with the connections and I'll leave you to run this place until it's sold. You'll only hear from my solicitor when a price is agreed upon by both of us, but it will be considerably more than what you were willing to offer me. After all, we will both need as much as we can possibly raise.'

Grace opened the door and slammed it behind her, catching her breath at the top of the stairs before lifting her skirts and running down them. She hadn't expected what the afternoon had brought at all. She had thought that Eliza would have told her that she had the money and was willing for the deal to go ahead. There was more to the stubborn hard-headed woman than she had given her credit for. She thought that she had hidden the differences in pay well, but obviously not well enough. Now both their lives were to change because of their stubbornness. However, Grace needed every penny possible if she was to escape the clutches of her family and make a new life for herself in London away from the scandal that her father had brought about and that her brother's wedding to a lowly pit lass would cause. She looked around her as she stepped onto the shop floor. This had been her empire, the place that she was proud of, and now she was walking away from it. Her father had been right: Eliza Wild had shown her true colours and had kicked her when she was at her most vulnerable, not even thanking her for all her investment and years of support. Had she really expected to take as much dividend out of the firm as herself? After all, she was only a glorified seamstress, a common lass with no formal education. No, she'd been right in what she had done; after all, Eliza would never have the refinements that she possessed, no matter how much money she had made for the firm. Good luck to her in her new venture because she would surely fail without Grace's good name to support her.

Grace held her head up high and walked out of the rotating brass doors, looking up at the sign above the door that glistened in the autumn sunshine. So, this was to be the end of Ellershaw and Wild. Well, let it be resolved quickly … she wanted to be away by the time winter arrived and the farcical marriage of William, which she knew that she could never stop, even if she set her heart on it.

*

Eliza sat with her head in her hands and tears running down her face. She'd always trusted Grace; she thought she was the decent one out of the Ellershaw family, and now she had found out that she'd been wrong. She was also beginning to realise the consequences of her words said in anger and the fact that she had just told Grace to sell her much-loved shop from under her feet.

She fought back the tears and blew her nose on her handkerchief as she looked around the room. She'd have to watch Grace Ellershaw when it came to the sale of the shop; she was not going to get away with swindling her out of money again. With the money made from the sale of the shop and Mary-Anne's gift, she would have no financial worries. In fact, she just might take Mary-Anne's advice to heart and attend the auction sale of the Rose. Tom said it could be profitable in the right hands; well, in his hands it would be made so, of that she was sure, and she would be giving employment to the miners and their families instead of pandering to the upper classes. She might look the part of a lady, but in her heart she was still a miner's daughter and her class of folk wouldn't steal and cheat from one another, unlike the toffee-nosed lot that she had been courteous to for the last number of years. She'd go back and try to do good for her own community, and not line the pockets of the upper classes.

Grace had better get a good deal for the shop because she had plenty of ideas about how to spend the money raised, and this time she would be her own boss. This evening she would tell Tom of her plans and hope that he saw her point of view. As for telling Victoria, she knew that she would be upset as she enjoyed the fact that her aunt was in haute couture and dressed the most fashionable ladies in Leeds. But pretty dresses were not everything and the sooner she learned that the better. Eliza hung her head and swore under her breath. Bloody Mary-Anne … she'd been led by her suggestions again. There was everything at stake because of her and her fancies. However, her eyes had been opened to Grace's antics and perhaps she was right. Perhaps she should look into buying the pit.

'Go on, what have you done? I know that look on your face.' Tom put his cap on his knee and sat down next to Eliza, while Victoria sat looking out of the window doing her cross-stitch and sulking.

'She's ruined my life,' Victoria said sharply, 'that's what she's done. We will end up with no money, no friends and

I'll never get to attend a ball again. And it's all because of you and that bloody pit.' She slammed her needlework down and stormed out of the room.

'Victoria, you come back into this room at once and apologise. I will not have language coming out of your mouth like that.' Eliza got up from her chair and walked into the hallway, stopping Victoria from running up the stairs.

'Why should I? My mother uses those words every day and after everything I'm going to be a Pit Lane girl, just like I used to be. Because of your selfishness.' Victoria pulled her arm out of the reach of Eliza, and stood defiantly on the stairs.

'Is that what you really think? We will own the pit, Victoria, and we will still have a roof over our heads and be living here; nothing will change for you. In fact, I thought you were prepared to go and live with your mother when she weds, so what I do does not even concern you.' Eliza looked at the young girl standing in front of her; she had blown her news out of all proportion.

'I liked Miss Grace; she was always kind. And she's my sister – she even looks like me … And now you have fallen out with her she'll no longer talk to me or treat me like her equal. I'll have nobody! And I don't want to live with my mother,' Victoria blurted. 'She's selfish too.' She ran up to the safety of her bedroom, throwing herself onto her bed and sobbing into her pillow.

Downstairs Tom walked into the hallway and put his arm around Eliza's waist as she tried not to cry over the outburst from Victoria.

'Now, what have you two fallen out over, and what's this about a pit?'

'Oh, Tom, I don't know if I've been a fool today or not. I've told Grace that I'm no longer interested in buying her half of the shop and that she should put it all up for sale. Since I found out that she had been fiddling the books and that she wasn't being fair with me when it came to my share of the profits, it's made me angry. That, along with Mary-Anne putting stupid ideas into my head, I just got my dander up, and I found myself saying what I thought of the whole situation. Me and my big mouth.' Eliza sighed.

'And where exactly does the pit come into it?' Tom held her tight.

Eliza held her breath and said the words she had wished to say to Tom all day. 'If it sells cheaply enough, I'm going to buy the Rose with the money I get from the sale of the shop; along with Mary-Anne's money there should be ample.'

'Oh, Eliza, you would leave well-paid employment to run the Rose. Are you mad?' Tom shook his head and couldn't believe his ears.

'But I wouldn't be running it: you would. And I'd be spending money and keeping my own people in work instead of amusing the rich. I've never fitted into the so-called upper circles of Leeds. At least this way I know who I am and I give back to my own. You know why I'm doing it? For us. You think like me; that's why we make such a strong couple. Just think, Tom, you could run that pit with one hand tied behind your back if you had my support. You could open that new seam and give the miners of this area employment, decent employment, with good wages paid if they were prepared to work for them. That would give me so much satisfaction, more than pandering to the rich's demands. I thought you'd be happy with my news.' Eliza's face was a picture of disappointment as she looked at Tom taking in her news.

'Eliza Wild, you impulsive woman. I thought the Rose would be the last place you wanted to stay open, with all the links that it has to Edmund Ellershaw and what happened to your mother and sister. And now you are telling me that you are going to buy it.' Tom sighed. 'But, aye.' He nodded his head and grinned. 'The idea sounds a good one to me; there's brass to be made in the old mine yet and I know just the men to work there. We need to extend level three, put pumps in so that it doesn't flood as bad; there's a seam down there that will nearly run to Wakefield if I've got it right.' Tom was thinking fast and his eyes lit up with hope for the future. 'Bloody hell, Eliza, I'm glad, just for once, that you listened to your Mary-Anne. But you are sure it's what you want to do, that you'll not regret it?'

She took Tom's hand. 'No, I'll not regret it. You might when you are working all the hours God sends and having to account for every penny we spend.'

'Well, then maybe I will. Happen now you will marry me and become a true partnership.' Tom looked at Eliza; he so wanted her to put his ring on her finger and walk down the aisle with her.

'Perhaps, once we have dealt with the purchase. I'll go and see the solicitor who is dealing with the auction tomorrow and ask him if we can look around the premises.' Eliza smiled, trying to change the subject.

'Nay, you needn't do that; I know it like the back of my hand. I've worked there both man and boy; it's not going to change overnight. I just hope that you can afford it, Eliza; even at rock bottom prices it might be too much for you. I hope that you haven't thrown everything in your life away.'

'If I have, I have. I couldn't work with Grace ever again; she's shown her true colours to me today. I only hope William doesn't hurt our Mary-Anne because I know she loves him deeply now, even though she knows that he can be the devil himself when he wants to be.' Eliza sat down and thought about both her future and that of Mary-Anne's.

'Your Mary-Anne is as tough as old boots; she'll keep him in his place once they are wed and Victoria will get to attend more balls and have more young men lusting after her than she will know what to do with when she's old enough. So, don't you fret about them, think of yourself for once and make sure you are happy with what you are about to do. Whatever you decide I will be there for you and will be until the day I die.' Tom kissed Eliza's hand and held it tight, thinking everything would be perfect if only she would marry him and be rightly his.

Chapter 10

'Well, Grace,' Catherine Ellershaw exclaimed, as she listened to Grace and her woes, 'you only have yourself to blame. When you summoned the courage up to tell us that you had made that terrible Wild woman a partner, I told you that it would all end in tears. They have both brought nothing but shame to this family. And they are not done yet. That terrible woman, her sister, who has got her claws into William … I wish she was dead! She's causing our family so much shame.'

'I know, Mother; perhaps it is my fault when it comes to Eliza. I should have kept her in her place and never offered her a partnership. She isn't our class nor ever will be. I had to teach her so much and yet she still reverts back to the class that she came from with that socialist sweetheart of hers that she will never marry if she has any sense at all. Do you know that she often attends rallies and talks with him? Certainly no place for a lady to be seen; she could do so much better for herself. However, I have always respected her in a way; she and her sister, at least they have lives of their own and minds of their own, instead of being dominated by men.' Grace breathed in deeply.

'That's where they have gone wrong and it is where you are going wrong too, Grace. You need to settle down and start your own family.' Catherine looked across at her scowling daughter. 'Graham Todd always asks after you. You should take an interest in him; he's got his own steel business and a lovely home. Your father always hoped that he could marry you off to him.'

'He's at least fifty, Mother, and his breath smells. Besides, I'm not interested in finding myself a man. I still aim to travel. Once I have sold the shop, I will have no commitments so I will be free to do as I wish.' Grace had no intention of staying with her mother; the last few weeks living with her in the confines of the small gatehouse had nearly driven her to her limits.

'And what about me? Does anyone care that I will be living in this wretched hole with no one to look after me apart from that gormless maid that William has sent me? No wonder he has got rid of her from his employment,' Catherine moaned. 'She really is the most feckless creature I have ever had serve me.'

'You'll survive, Mother, and Jenny is not that bad; she's just not used to your ways. You had better get used to her because I don't aim to be here forever. Indeed, I would like to be gone before winter sets in and hopefully will be if the shop sells quickly.' Grace rose from her seat.

'You can't leave me, Grace,' Catherine wailed, 'not now. I will have nobody.'

'You have, William – he is but a hundred yards away – and George, for what he is worth, in Leeds. I need to live my life, Mother, before I find myself becoming a bitter and twisted old woman, looking back on a life that I have not lived, because of others.'

'You are selfish, Grace,' Catherine yelled at her daughter. 'Your role is to be here for me in my dotage.'

'Mother, you are still capable of looking after yourself as of yet; and, who knows, I may return. Now, if you'll excuse me, I have to inform Gerald Evans that my shop is on the market. He said he would have bought it off me before but didn't fancy taking on Eliza as a partner. He made me a good offer, but I felt beholden to give Eliza the first chance.' Grace walked away from her mother, not feeling any empathy at all towards her situation. She had to get away from her family, the family she no longer wanted to be part of.

'Your father would have something to say about this,' Catherine yelled at her self-centered daughter, and then looked around her at the home she now regarded as her prison. Perhaps it would look better once William had replaced the furniture that was being concealed from the bank in one of his outbuildings. But she knew it would take more than having her own things around her to make her feel content in the gatehouse. As for William, at the moment she could make no sense of him. He had even asked her to have tea with him and his hussy, and was expecting her to be civil to her! Well, he could think again.

*

'Bloody hell, Eliza, when you do something, you really do something. I didn't mean for you to risk everything for sake of Tom and his dreams.' Mary-Anne sat back in a chair in the parlour of Aireville Mansions and looked at her sister. 'I find it amusing that you are going to actually hurt the Ellershaw family's pride more than me. Just fancy, you the owner of the Rose; all you need is their house at Highfield, and then between us we will have everything that bastard Edmund worked for.'

'Don't even tempt me; when I looked through the gates, I wanted to go in and look around it. The only time I was in it, I thought it so grand. I would love to live there.' Eliza sipped her tea.

'Have you been in touch with his solicitor yet? Perhaps when you view the pit you could also view the house; from what William has told me the bank will be desperate to sell both, they'll want what money they can get and they will not be bothered where it comes from.'

'Don't you do this to me again! Look at the mess I'm already in because of you putting ideas into my head. I've not contacted the solicitor; Tom and I are just going to go and bid at the auction. He knows the pit back to front, so there's no need. He's also putting the word out that the pit is near to being worked out so that it discourages any would-be bidders. The less we have to pay for it the better.'

'You mean the less you have to pay for it the more money you have left to buy Highfield House. Just go to the solicitors ... tell them that you are interested in the house alone, and we will both go and have a nosy. I've always wanted to see how the Ellershaws lived; I bet they wanted for nothing when we were living like dogs. Go on, Eliza, we will both go. Victoria could join us. It would cheer her up with the thought of it being a new home.' Mary-Anne egged her younger sister on, knowing that it would not take a lot of encouragement to change her mind.

'Victoria will soon be moving in with you and William; she will have the grand home that you have always promised her once you are both wed. And what would I need a large house like Highfield for? Even if I do wed Tom, I doubt that we will ever have children.' Eliza gazed out of the window and held back the tears.

'How do you know? Have you and Tom been at it and trying? You sly devils!' Mary-Anne teased. 'You better get him wed then and bid for the house; what have you to lose?'

'I'm not loose like you, Mary-Anne, and I'm in no rush to be married, no matter how much I love Tom. I want to be my own woman just for a little longer. You of all people should understand that.'

'But Tom isn't like that, and well you know it. Go on, Eliza; let's have a look around Highfield. You never know,

I might fancy it. But I'll not tell William that I've viewed it with you. Did I tell you that I'm invited to Levensthorpe Hall on Friday? He wants me to meet his mother and charm her; I'm not looking forward to that! She's a right old bitch!'

'She's going to be your mother-in-law! You've made this complicated life for yourself, by courting William; you will have to grin and bear it.' Eliza looked at her sister coyly. 'I suppose it wouldn't hurt to have a look around Highfield. Should we go and see if that's possible tomorrow afternoon? I'll not tell Tom; he wouldn't be so agreeable to my ideas of grandeur, and of course I can only dream of it until the business is sold. And I doubt I'll be able to afford both pit and house, no matter what a tempting picture you paint with your words.'

Mary-Anne chuckled. 'Yes, we will and we'll take Victoria. It will do her good and we can all have tea in the tea shop that we could never afford in the middle of Woodlesford. That can be my treat. Us women of leisure should make the most of our time and be seen; especially as both of us are going to become higher up in society, whether they like it or not.'

'Mary-Anne, I sometimes wonder how we have already got this far. We've come from nothing and sometimes I worry about where this will all end. When Edmund Ellershaw died, I thought that we would both be satisfied but now with Grace not being true I feel hurt all over again.'

'Then let's make the best of things tomorrow. We will both go to the solicitor, ask for the key to Highfield, and you should aspire to purchase it along with the pit if you have the money from the shop sale by then. And don't you feel guilty; it's our turn to be cock of the midden so don't be afraid to crow about it and show off.'

Eliza stood outside the solicitors in the centre of Leeds with the keys to Highfield House in her hand. Her stomach was churning as she crossed the street to where Mary-Anne and Victoria waited for her.

'You've got them then?' Mary-Anne looked at her sister and smiled.

'Yes, he's also registered my interest. He mentioned the Rose too, and said that he had little or no interest in either of them.' Eliza smiled.

'No wonder; nobody would want a pit. Especially one that is not worth anything. I still can't forgive you, Aunt Eliza, for putting the shop up for sale to try and buy it,' Victoria quietly said as the three of them walked elegantly down the street stopping at a Hackney Cab stand to take them back into Woodlesford.

'Now, Victoria, it's your aunt's life. She knows what she is doing. Besides, it will have no reflection upon you. In fact, if anything, your life is about to improve. Just you wait until you have looked around Highfield House and once I have been introduced officially to William's mother, then you will be able to visit him at Levensthorpe Hall. Two great houses that you may well soon call home. I'd say your future looks rosy.' Mary-Anne winked at her daughter, as they all climbed into the cab and sat back as the horse made its way out of the hustle and bustle of Leeds to the mining village that all three had once regarded as their home.

Pulling up outside the locked gates of Highfield House, Eliza thanked the cab driver and paid him before unlocking the padlock and opening the gate onto the driveway. She looked around at Victoria and Mary-Anne and felt a strange feeling as they both smiled and set foot onto the gravel and walked the few yards to the pillared doorway, which Mary-Anne and Eliza had only dared to glance at when they were children.

'Well, at least it's still standing. I always envied these gardens when I was a child; we only had a backyard and the Ellershaws had all these immaculate gardens with lawns and flowerbeds. Do you remember the gardener, Eliza? He always swore at us if he saw us at the gates. We used to stick our tongues out at him and then run like hell down the road.' Mary-Anne looked around her and the memories came flooding back.

'Yes, and Mother sometimes passed the time of day with the cook; she was still there when Edmund died. She was a right old gossip.' Eliza smiled at Victoria

'Go on then, girl. Open the door; let's have a proper look into the world of the Ellershaws.' Mary-Anne waited with baited breath as Eliza put the key into the keyhole and pushed the oak door open, letting light into the hallway that was empty and bare.

'You see, Victoria, it is more than thrice the size of our home. Look at the stairs and there's a parlour and a drawing room, and a study, not to mention the kitchen and the various other rooms. There's still furniture and furnishings in some; they must have had to leave them all behind. I suppose they belong to the bank now.' Eliza went and opened each individual door and gazed into each room, hardly able to contain the excitement she was feeling within her.

'You forget that I've been here once before as guest to George. I know what the house is like, but I don't understand why you are even here and looking around it. Surely we can never afford a place like this, and why would you want it if the family within has caused us so much heartache over the years?' Victoria watched as both her mother and aunt nearly ran from room to room admiring certain aspects and disagreeing over other features.

'I would love to live here; I've always wanted to live here. Your mother knows that.' Eliza twirled around in the hallway, her skirts flowing out around her. 'It's just a dream, Victoria; everyone has to follow their dreams, but sometimes dreams do come true, and I do wish this one would.

'You always were the fanciful one, Eliza. Just look at you; you'd swear you were Victoria's age.' Mary-Anne laughed. 'I knew once you had seen inside properly you'd set your head on having it. Perhaps I shouldn't have been so cruel as to make you come and see it. The shop might not sell, you might get outbid for the Rose Pit and then you'll not have money for either.' Mary-Anne followed Eliza and Victoria up the curving staircase and entered each room with them, looking around and wondering to herself which room

Edmund had slept in with his wife. It was a strange feeling to have and she hoped that the ghost of the old bastard did not haunt the house of Eliza's dreams.

'If I can, I will buy this place, Mary-Anne. Perhaps my fall out with Grace was meant to be, else I would never have dreamt of this.' Eliza sighed as she waltzed back down the stairs.

'I will help you all that I can, dear sister, if your heart is set upon it. But for now it is a waiting game; it depends on who is interested in the pit and who wants the house, and if your shop sells beforehand. But for now, lock the door and let's go and have tea; I'm really looking forward to having a fancy or two and sticking my nose up in the air like the Ellershaws and Bentleys used to do. We are just as fine as them nowadays and our Victoria here is going to marry such a young man as never we could have imagined back then, when she is old enough, one of such high status that she will want for nothing.' Mary-Anne linked her arm through Victoria's as they all made their way down the drive from Highfield and onto the road into Woodlesford. The three of them, dressed in their finest, all looked like perfect ladies of society as they entered the small tea room, choosing the table next to the window.

The other diners' heads turned and whispers and knowing looks were given between the other women that were taking tea there.

'Well, Eliza, they are either talking about you or they are talking about me.' Mary-Anne grinned as she whispered from behind the ornate menu that she was reading. 'Whichever it is, they have plenty to gossip about.'

'Mary-Anne, behave. Be a lady for once and let us enjoy our tea in peace.' Eliza gave her sister a warning glance as she heard one of the better-to-do ladies voice her opinion on the clientele that the small select tea room was attracting nowadays.

'I think I'd quite like a hot buttered crumpet, rather than a cake.' Victoria tried to keep the peace between sisters. 'With a drink of coffee for a change.' She smiled at both her aunt and mother, and hoped that they would give their attention to the menu that both of them were half-heartedly looking at.

'Well, I too will have coffee along with a slice of lemon cake, which just leaves you, Mary-Anne.' Eliza glanced at her sister and could see that she was eavesdropping on the next table's conversation.

'Well, I think I will have a tart of some kind,' Mary-Anne said loudly. 'It must be good as I keep hearing it talked about by these fine ladies next to us. Yes, here it is: Manchester tart. It takes one to know one, except I'm a common Leeds tart, according to some.' She laughed as the three women who had been seated on the adjoining table picked up their skirts and gave disagreeing looks and sounds as they left the table and walked out of the tea room in disgust.

'Mary-Anne, you cannot keep your mouth closed, can you?' Eliza whispered and smiled sweetly at the young girl who came for their order.

'Could we have the following, please?' Eliza gave her and Victoria's order to the serving girl and then looked across at Mary-Anne. 'And what are you really having now that you have made your point?'

'I'll have the same as my sister, a piece of lemon cake and a coffee, please. Thank you, dear.' Mary-Anne grinned. 'I had to say something; they were after me like a terrier after a rabbit, and I wasn't going to put up with that. Anyway, it was quite tame for me.'

Victoria blushed and then raised her head and looked around her. 'I've never been in here before; I used to pass it on my way home from school and see all the well-to-do ladies sipping their tea but I never thought that I'd be in here myself.'

'We were just the same when we were young; we used to press our noses up at the window and gaze in at everybody in their finery. That was until the owner came and shoed us away.' Eliza smiled, remembering her childhood. 'Of course your mother has been in here once before with Grace and William and their friends – that was back when we were living in Pit Lane. She came back and told me all about it, and I was so jealous because all that I'd had to eat was bread and dripping, and she had been given sandwiches and cake and had been made a real fuss of.'

'That was only because you couldn't be bothered to deliver the dress to poor Priscilla Eavesham, else it would have been you that got the treat.' Mary-Anne smiled.

'No, it wouldn't; William was sweet on you even back then. He used to call into our little shop to catch a glimpse of you and you know it. He only paid for that dress for her so that he could be with you, I'm sure. And now look, we've gone full circle; you are to marry him and we both have enough money to buy our own fancy tea.' Eliza looked up and thanked the waitress as she placed what they had ordered in front of them.

'It seems a lifetime ago, and yet it is not so long since. So many things have happened, some good, some bad but at least we are all here for one another now.'

'Better things are around the corner; I just know it. All three of us can look to the future with certainty, of that I'm sure.' Eliza reached for Victoria's hand and squeezed it. 'As long as we are strong and here for one another.'

Chapter 11

'Do I look all right? Will your mother approve? Mary-Anne asked nervously of William, sitting next to him in the carriage as they drove up the roadway to Levensthorpe Hall. 'Although I don't know why I'm even asking that as I know your mother will approve of nothing I do.'

'You look as beautiful as ever. Stop worrying; I won't let her eat you alive. She can be very tart with her words, but I'm sure by the time we leave, you will have her eating out of your hand. And if not, then it is her loss.' William smiled at the love of his life, and just hoped that his mother would behave and not be as outspoken as she had threatened. 'I've never known you worry about what people think of you before, so why worry about my mother?'

'Because I need her to realise that I do love you. That I'm not the scarlet woman that everyone portrays me as and that I do genuinely care for you. I need to win her over despite our differences else she could make life difficult for us both. Besides, we have a lot in common; your father was unfaithful to her and abused her just as much as he abused the other women in his life.' Mary-Anne sighed as they entered the gates of Levensthorpe, past the gatehouse, which she knew to be Catherine's new home. Even though she had become hard over the years, the fact of having afternoon tea with Catherine Ellershaw was making her feel quite ill. Butterflies were churning in her stomach, which she knew was quite ridiculous at her age, even though she had tried her best to quell her nerves.

'Here we are then, time to meet the old dragon and to step into your future home, no matter what my mother has to say upon the matter.' William opened the carriage door before his servant even had time to do so, leaping out of the coach and offering Mary-Anne his hand as it came to a standstill at the bottom of the steps leading up to Levensthorpe Hall. 'Come along, don't worry. Look, everyone is waiting for us; they all know to make you welcome.'

Mary-Anne looked at the pompous butler and the house-keeper who were awaiting them at the top of the steps and breathed in deeply, trying to calm herself. She smiled at all the servants as she passed them and acknowledged their greeting to William and her as she walked into the large hall-way of Levensthorpe.

'Is my mother here, Briggs?' William passed his butler his top hat and cane.

'She is indeed, sir; she's in the drawing room awaiting your arrival.' Briggs gave a small smile, his long face giving nothing away as he took his master's belongings.

'Mrs Appleby, I take it tea will be served to us shortly? I hope that there is some shortbread; Mother loves Cook's shortbread and I need to keep her sweet this afternoon.' William grinned at Mary-Anne as she waited on him while he addressed the housekeeper.

'There is, sir, and some maids-of-honour; we know how she likes them.' Mrs Appleby curtsied.

'This is Mrs Vasey, Mrs Appleby. This is her very first visit here, but it will not be her last. If she is in need of anything please see to her requirements and treat her like you would myself.'

The housekeeper looked up and down at Mary-Anne.

'Yes, sir, of course, sir.' Mrs Appleby curtsied for Mary-Anne and then started to walk away to her duties. She'd heard all the gossip about the guest and now she had seen her for herself; she could see why William's head had been turned by the common beauty.

'Mrs Appleby and Briggs will see to your needs while you are here; if there is anything you need just let myself or them know. Now, let's face the dragon; it would seem that she is already ensconced in the drawing room and awaiting the pleasure of meeting you.' William took Mary-Anne's hand and walked across the beautiful ornate hallway. 'I see that you are admiring the sculptures? Priscilla's father had them imported from Italy after he did the Grand Tour with some of his friends. They are beautifully carved and must have cost him a great deal and that is a portrait of his father, Priscilla's grandfather, painted I believe by Joshua

Reynolds.' William looked up to a portrait hanging halfway up the stairs and looked at the reaction of Mary-Anne's face.

'It's a beautiful home, William; I'd no idea that it was so lavish. My small dwelling is nothing compared to yours.' Mary-Anne stood and gazed around her. Everything was on such a grand scale and was truly beautiful.

'Nonsense, yours at least is paid for. The Eaveshams were good at spending money and have plenty to show for it in their home, but alas did not have the means to back it up. Not too dissimilar to my own father, much to my disdain. I hope that I am never in that situation, but you can never be sure what life throws at you. Now, let us face Mama.' William opened the drawing-room door and walked in with Mary-Anne on his arm. 'Now, then, Mama, we are here. Let me introduce you to Mrs Mary-Anne Vasey, though you might remember her as Mary-Anne Wild. She is the sister of Eliza, Grace's business partner. I don't believe you have met before, certainly not on an equal footing as now.'

'Equal? Now can she ever be equal to us?' Catherine turned and looked at Mary-Anne as she entered the drawing room.

'Now, Mama, be civil. You really don't know Mary-Anne at all; today will give you the chance to do just that.' William smiled at Mary-Anne and offered her a chair next to his mother.

'Good afternoon, Mrs Ellershaw. It's a pleasure to be having tea with you and William this afternoon.' Mary-Anne bit her tongue and acted graciously as she accepted her seat.

'I suppose if you weren't having tea with us, you'd be bedding my son, so at least I can thank myself for that. Mind, I can see why he's attracted to you. I remember you and your sister. You always were the good-looking one but I think age has blessed you with better looks than before. No wonder he can't take his eyes off you,' Catherine growled as she leaned forward and stared at Mary-Anne.

'I'm sorry to hear of the loss of your husband and your bad fortune. Hopefully things will improve now you are in William's care.' Mary-Anne tried to ignore the slight against her and to sound genuinely sorry when it came to the death of Edmund; she knew she had to rub along with her mother-in-law if she was to wed William.

'You, sorry at Edmund dying?' Catherine sneered. 'Now tell the truth, lass. He hurt you just as much as he hurt me, if what I've heard and been told is true. Had you not had enough of the Ellershaws, and did you not think twice when galli-vanting with my William? Or is it his money you are after?'

'So, you know about your husband and me? You must also know that I have a daughter, Victoria, of whom he's the father, although he'd never admit it. She was not born out of love, but out of sheer lust on your husband's part. I did not want his attention, believe me. I wasn't much more than a girl at the time. But you don't have to worry when it comes to William; my love for him is genuine and I don't need his money.' Mary-Anne could feel tears welling up in her eyes, remembering Edmund's actions and having to tell his widow of his wicked ways.

'You probably tempted my late husband at some point. His eye was always taken by a young bit of a thing; don't you think I was ignorant about his doings. Now he's gone, I've realised that there was no love left in his life for me. He's left me penniless and homeless, aye and heartbroken, at the mercy of the banks. All because of his whoring with the likes of you. And now you have your claws in my William.' Catherine cursed under her breath.

'Mother! She needs no claws; I love her, and I've always loved her, when I now think back. Father took advantage of his position as he did with many. You know how I feel about that.' William stood up and looked down at his mother and tried to reassure Mary-Anne.

'I'll go. Your mother hates me and I am adding insult to injury by being here. All I can say is that I did not willingly bed your husband, Mrs Ellershaw, just as I didn't mean to fall in love with your son. However, I have, and he means everything to me, along with my daughter.' Mary-Anne stood up and was about to go when the maid came in with a tray laden with tea and cakes.

'You'll stay,' William said firmly to the pair of them. 'You will stay and have tea. Mama, you will be civil; none of us can help our pasts. None of us are blameless for what has been done, and I need the women I love the most to get along. After all, I aim to marry Mary-Anne and if you are to live in the gatehouse,' William threatened as Mary-Anne sat back down in her chair, 'I will not have any ill feeling towards her.'

'Marry her?' Catherine muttered. 'Now you are talking stupid.'

'Yes, Mama, we are to marry this coming spring, and she is to live with me here as my wife.' William glared at his mother.

'Lord help us! First, you marry a lunatic and now you are to marry a whore!' Catherine said in front of the maid who blushed and left quickly.

'I'm sorry, William; I've tried my best but your mother is never going to accept me.' Mary-Anne stood up once again.

'Yes, she will, or else she can find somewhere else to live,' William warned his mother. 'Perhaps her precious George will take her because I don't want her anywhere near us once we are married if she keeps acting like this.'

'You wouldn't dare. I'm your mother; I deserve some respect,' Catherine exclaimed.

'And so to does my wife-to-be. Now, Mary-Anne sit down and let us start again and act like civilised human beings while we have our tea. The past is behind us all and we have to move forward and make the best of our lives together.' William looked at both women who shared a hatred of his father and thought how different they were; perhaps they would never be friends but at least they could learn to accept one another for his sake.

'Very well, I'll try, but you must understand that this conversation is hard for me. That you, Mary-Anne, have intimate knowledge of my husband and now you mean to marry my son ... Now that I know just how unfaithful my husband was, I can perhaps see your side of things when it comes to him, but my William is dear to my heart and I wanted better for him, especially after such a dreadful marriage to Priscilla. She may have come with a fortune but it was a high price to pay by William, having a wife who really should have been placed inside a lunatic asylum.'

'I can understand you thinking you need to protect William, especially as you know me for who I originally was: a working-class lass from Pit Lane with not a penny to her name. However, I have come up in the world, Mrs Ellershaw; I now have money of my own, and my own house. I will not be marrying William for his money or to bring him shame; it is for love alone.' Mary-Anne looked across at William and smiled. She loved him with all her heart and every word she said now was true.

'And your daughter? What do you aim to do about your daughter? I have problems accepting her as Edmund's; she could, after all, be anybody's.' Catherine could hardly say the words that she had been thinking of since the day William had told her the truth about Mary-Anne's child.

'Yes, I'm sorry; she is your husband's child. I was very young when your husband … I had never been with a man until that night and I didn't think I would ever again once he had his way with me. But Victoria is blameless in this. She has your family traits, dark hair and blue eyes and can be so stubborn when she wants to be. However, my sister, Eliza, has raised her like a lady and I hope for her to join both William and myself once we are married, here at the hall.'

'I have seen her briefly; George was once friends with her and has brought her to our home. I didn't realise then that they were of the same parentage; however, I'm not that petty that I would take it out upon the girl. Perhaps I should meet her; after all, she is my husband's daughter.'

'We can soon arrange that, Mama; I'll bring Victoria to visit next weekend and we can all have dinner together, including Grace if she wishes. I know Grace and Victoria enjoy one another's company and when you see them they are very much alike.' William smiled as he sensed a chink of weakness in his mother's armour.

'I believe Grace has a buyer for her shop and aims to leave me high and dry. Victoria might just fill the void that she is about to leave in my life. Sons are a blessing but daughters are more needed to be there for you in your old age, and perhaps if I get to know Victoria, she may be company for me; she seemed amicable, the little that I saw of her.' Catherine looked at Mary-Anne as she offered an olive branch of peace out to her.

'Grace has sold the shop!' Mary-Anne was taken by surprise.

'Yes, so your sister will be pleased if that is what she wanted. I believe Grace was going to see the solicitor today so the deal must be going through. I'll be honest and say that I've never encouraged the partnership between them. I thought that it would fail in the first few months. However, it has been a success overall and I do believe that Grace has secured a good deal for both herself and your sister in its sale. So she, too, will be thankful for having some dealings with my family. It seems that despite Edmund's unforgivable ways you are both now benefitting from our connection. Perhaps it was meant to be and is just reward for what he must have put you both through.' Catherine hung her head and tried not to show the hurt that knowing and facing the truth about her late husband gave her.

'Mama, don't be upset. I'm sure Victoria will be happy with an offer of companionship; you can teach her much. What do you think, Mary-Anne; would she be willing?'

'I don't know; we will see. I would like her to come and live with us here, William, once we are married. I know I've only just broached the subject in the past but I'm hoping that would be possible. If she is to be partly your mother's companion it would make sense.' Mary-Anne was beginning to have some respect for Catherine Ellershaw; after all she had been used and abused by Edmund just as much as Mary-Anne had. Over the years he had robbed Catherine of her fortune and any self-respect that she had, and now he had torn her family apart with his death and bankruptcy.

'I must admit, I wanted us to start our married life alone. I wasn't planning on having Victoria as part of our lives. It is strange for me to think that she is my half-sister and I was rather hoping that Eliza would continue to be her guardian, rather than her live with us.' William looked at Mary-Anne and saw that she was not happy with what he said.

'I need her to be with us, William; she has every right to live with me once we are married. Besides, Eliza has her own life. She has done enough for my family, and it's time for her to live her own life.' Mary-Anne looked across at William and noticed his mother smiling as she sipped her tea.

'It seems to me that you two have been so busy flirting and cavorting that you've only thought of your own lives and what you want instead of looking at the life you will have to lead and the effect on folk around you. Perhaps you need to talk things through and, when you both know what the other wants and needs, see if you still feel marriage is the path you should go down. This time, William, it is your choice; make the right one.' Catherine put her teacup down and noticed William's face cloud over as he realised that Victoria would have to be part of his newly married life whether he liked it or not.

Catherine was glad that she had mentioned Mary-Anne's daughter; she might just prove to be the one thing that they did not agree upon and be the fly in the ointment. Perhaps there would be no marriage after all if they could not agree.

*

'I thought you understood that I wanted Victoria to live with us,' Mary-Anne said in an annoyed voice to William as they returned to her house on Speakers' Corner.

'I know you mentioned it, but you only just skirted around the idea. I didn't think that we had agreed to her living with us immediately after we are wed,' William growled.

Mary-Anne flung her shawl at her maid to put away and went through into the parlour. 'When I get married to you I expect her to come and live with us and for you to make her part of our family.'

'But she isn't my daughter, she's my sister,' William spat. 'Not even that, she's my half-sister. My father didn't even recognise her as his, so why should I?'

'Perhaps because you love me and want to do right by me?' Mary-Anne spat back. She couldn't believe that he was willing to dismiss Victoria from his life and expected her to do the same. 'Victoria is more precious to me than life itself; I need to be her true mother and she needs to know where she belongs and that she has a future as your rightful heir, just like she should have been to her father.'

'My heir now, is it? Perhaps that's all you see in me, after all: my money and position. Perhaps my mother is right!' William stood holding the chair back and glowered at Mary-Anne; this was not the first argument that they had had but this time he found himself fuming with Mary-Anne's assumption of Victoria becoming his heir.

'William, don't be so silly. I love you. I just naturally assumed that Victoria would be joining me once we were wed and that hopefully in time you would think her as your own and make her part of our family,' Mary-Anne said loudly. 'And as such she would be a rightful heir to your estates along with any other children that we may have between us.'

'Children? Who said anything about children?' William stormed. 'Is that what you want? For us to be surrounded by children whining and demanding attention. I haven't the time to be bothered with children, nor the inclination. Not yet anyway. All I want is time with you and to have a good life. Besides, you and I are not getting any younger; why should we bother with children? Why do you think I have been so careful when we have lain together; I don't want to be caught out like my father.'

'Caught out! Do you think I'd want to catch you out with being in child to you? Never again do I want to be in that position of bearing a child and not having the father stand up to his responsibilities.' Mary-Anne scowled at William. 'Once we are married, however, I thought that you would expect me to have children of our own, if it's not too late; as you say, we are not that young any more, but my Victoria will always be loved, no matter what family we have together.'

'Well, perhaps my mother is right. Perhaps, we have been led by our desires and have not talked about the things we should have. I think that it is best now that I leave; it will give us time to simmer down as both of us are of a volatile nature when roused.' William walked to the doorway and looked back at Mary-Anne who did not even move from her seat. 'Perhaps I'll see you on Friday if you wish?'

'We will see; I may be doing something else that demands my attention,' Mary-Anne said with a surly look on her face.

'Suit yourself. I'll let your new maid show me out. She's a pretty bit of a thing; you've got a good eye for a beauty, Mary-Anne.' William looked at the disdain on Mary-Anne's face as he added his parting words, knowing that it would make her think that he had no desire to be faithful to her.

*

Mary-Anne cursed under her breath as she heard William flirting with Nellie before leaving. She knew he was doing it on purpose but it still annoyed her. In fact, the whole afternoon had annoyed her; they had rowed over nothing, really, as she wasn't particularly bothered whether William and she had children in the future. Besides, she didn't even seem to be able to conceive any more, the amount of times she and John had lain together. And while William had indeed mostly careful, he wasn't always, but it was the same every month: no sign of being pregnant no matter how many times she had lain with her lover. But she had just thought it inevitable that when married William would want to try for children. However, he would have to concede when it came to Victoria. She would live with them and she would be his heir, whether he liked it or not.

Chapter 12

Grace sat across from Eliza and watched as Eliza scrutinised the agreement of sale between Gerald Evans and themselves. 'It's a good deal, Eliza; he even wants all the stock, which you will see he's made a separate offer for and he wants to buy it quickly, which suits me as I wish to be on my travels before winter sets in.'

'I didn't expect for the shop to sell so fast. However, it does look a particularly good deal. He does have the money, does he? It's easy for anybody to say they want something but that doesn't necessarily mean that they have the means to buy it.' Eliza couldn't quite believe the amount that was set out in writing in front of her. It was almost double what she had planned to offer to Grace and that was just for her share.

'Oh, Eliza, he's worth a small fortune. This amount is nothing to him. He owns shops in Wakefield, Bradford, and Sheffield, and has been after somewhere larger in Leeds for a while. He already has that pretty little hat shop in the Victoria Arcade; you know the one that I like and envy. He's itching to move in. He was really annoyed that I was selling to you originally so he couldn't believe when I got back to him.' Grace sat back and watched as Eliza looked through the offer again. 'Are you regretting your decision now? Because I'm not about to go back on my agreement to him, I gave him my word.'

'No, I just want to make sure that all is in place and that I'm not being duped.' Eliza looked across at Grace and let her know that she was still not forgiven her for underpaying her for years.

'You certainly aren't with this sale; in fact, you will be a very wealthy woman by the time this has gone through. You will never have to work again, and will be a most eligible woman with good marriage prospects if you wanted to be. So I hope that your pitman appreciates that.' Grace looked down her nose and waited for the papers to be returned to her.

'My pitman, as you call him, is the only man I need. Money does not turn his head, nor mine, come to that.' Eliza signed the papers and passed them back to Grace. 'Well, that's the end of our business together, I suppose. It's a pity it ended on such a sour note; we've had some good times together and I must admit I do owe you a lot for being where I am today. However, the money will be put to good use; I have plans for it already.' Eliza sat back and held her tears back; she was going to miss the shop and she was jumping into the unknown with her possible plans to buy the pit.

139

'Really? I thought you would just like to have some time to yourself and Victoria. It sounds as if you have a new business venture in mind already?' Grace folded the papers into her bag and looked at Eliza with surprise at her news.

Eliza smiled. 'I don't want to say yet, that would be tempting fate. But it involves looking after my own people and my own community.'

'Ah, a little tea shop or something on those lines, I expect. Woodlesford could do with a place for the working classes to pass the time of day and treat themselves. Well, I wish you well, Eliza, in whatever you do. You are made of stern stuff and you work hard; you deserve this money.' Grace stood up and held her hand to be shaken.

Eliza took it and shook it. 'I take it Mr Evans will be in touch shortly as he will want to look around and know what is what.'

'Oh, did I not say? He's planning to knock the shop down and rebuild it. He wants the land more than the building. None of the staff will be wanted, I'm afraid; he will be hiring new from scratch once he's rebuilt it. And as for the stock, he's placing it into his own shops elsewhere. I think he's doing quite right; after all, this building is so out of fashion with the rest of the shops. I was beginning to be embarrassed by its exterior. Ladies deserve better premises than these to be pampered in.' Grace stood silent as she watched the horror on Eliza's face, thinking of all the staff losing their jobs.

Eliza gasped. 'But, you can't do that to our loyal staff! They will be devastated when you tell them. What will they do? Where will they go?'

'I don't aim to be the one to tell them. After all, I've always left the staff to you. I just look after the finances, remember? I'm sure they will understand when you tell them how much money you have made out of your venture; after all, they will soon find other employment, don't you think?' Grace pulled on her gloves. 'Goodbye, Eliza; make sure when you have received your money that you hand the shop keys into the solicitor's, not that they'll be needed, unfortunately.' Grace said as she swept out of the office, closing the door behind her.

Eliza slumped in her chair. How could she? How could she be so heartless? She knew that the seven staff employed by them would struggle to find work once the store had closed. And how could Grace place all the blame on her? If she hadn't have been so underhanded and selfish, there would have been no problem. As it was, she was now hopefully going to save the mine and its workers at the cost of losing the store and its workers. Life was just not fair.

'The bitch!' Mary-Anne sat back and listened to Eliza's woes. 'Do you know, I never thought that Grace was like that. I always thought that she was nearly one of us, down to earth and not bothered about getting her hands dirty.'

'So did I. Just shows how wrong we both were. Anyway, my dear little shop will be gone by the end of the month.

Even the building will be just a pile of rubble and I'll be without income or purpose.' Eliza nearly sobbed as at that moment everything looked dark and gloomy in her life.

'Oh, don't be so dramatic, Eliza; you know you'll have money and that the next step is to buy the Rose Pit. You are neither without money nor a home, so things aren't that bad – unlike for me who has made a complete mess of her life by arguing with William over something that was of no real consequence, and not backing down when I should have just bided my time,' Mary-Anne growled. She had not slept for the last few nights for worrying over the fact that she had argued with William and, to make things worse, she had not heard from him since.

'He'll come around. He'll be sulking; that family is good at sulking. What is stopping you from going to see him? Why don't you take Victoria to visit his mother and then take her to Levensthorpe? It will do you both good to stand together – and if his old mother has expressed an interest in her perhaps that is a way to win William round. After all, he'll not want to pander to his mother's every need, so he will look at Victoria as a godsend if they both get on. Grace has been selfish with her own family too but perhaps Victoria will take her place. Catherine Ellershaw is more of a lady than the rest of the family and it would not hurt Victoria to be seen with her.'

'She was no lady when she was talking to me. But I do respect her for looking after her own and she did show an interest in Victoria, despite her knowing the circumstances of her birth. You might be right, our Eliza; perhaps I should visit Levensthorpe with Victoria. I'll call this coming Sunday and will take Victoria with me. It's time she saw her new home, if all is well between me and William. And it will be; I'll make sure of that. I can't afford to do any other.' Mary-Anne smiled. 'Anyway, they are going to be in for a shock once you have bought the Rose along with their old home. It'll give that Grace something to think about; she might learn that you stand by your family, no matter what. That's what we have always done and it's what we will continue to do.'

*

'I'm so nervous, Mother. She's going to hate me.' Victoria stood outside the gates leading up to Levensthorpe Hall and felt her stomach churn with the thought of meeting Catherine Ellershaw.

'Nonsense; she showed much interest in you. She practically begged to see you. Now, chin up, and remember your manners no matter what she says to you.' Mary-Anne linked her arm through her daughter's, stepped through the gates of the drive and turned towards the small garden path that led to the studded arched doorway of the gatehouse.

There, mother and daughter shot a glance at each other as Mary-Anne reached for the door pull, hearing it ring loudly within the square squat gatehouse and then the sound of footsteps as the heavy door was opened.

A small, fair-haired maid, with her frilly cap askew, answered the door and quickly asked them their names and business, without any grace or manners.

'Could you tell Mrs Ellershaw that it is Mary-Anne Vasey and her daughter, Victoria Wild, who would like to pay her a visit if it is convenient.' Mary-Anne and Victoria were left standing on the step as the maid scurried away to see if the mistress of the small gatehouse was taking guests. Mary-Anne smiled reassuringly at Victoria as she looked troubled at the thought of seeing Catherine Ellershaw.

The maid returned, her cap having been hastily straightened. Smiling, she invited them into the small hallway. 'Mrs Ellershaw said she can see you for a short time but she is expecting more visitors later this afternoon.' Mary-Anne and Victoria were ushered through a doorway that led to a small sitting room where Catherine Ellershaw sat waiting for them at the window. Mary-Anne quickly looked around her; although it was pleasantly furnished, the gatehouse was quite a comedown from Mrs Ellershaw's previous residence at Highfield House.

'Good afternoon, Mary-Anne. This must be Victoria, I presume?' Catherine didn't rise from her seat and didn't hold her hand out in greeting. Instead, she stared at Victoria, taking in each detail of the girl that stood in front of her. 'I suppose you had better take a seat; please make yourselves comfortable on the sofa.' Catherine couldn't help but notice that Victoria bore a startling resemblance to her daughter Grace. It seemed more than likely that they shared some of the same parentage.

'It is good of you to receive us, Mrs Ellershaw. I hope that we have not called at an inconvenient moment? It's just that you showed an interest in meeting Victoria so we took the opportunity to call upon you while out for our Sunday stroll. The weather is a little inclement today; autumn is upon us and it will not be long before winter winds keep us in our homes.' Mary-Anne, minding her manners for once, decided to make conversation about the good old English topic of the weather to break the awkward silence between the trio.

'Yes, indeed.' Catherine Ellershaw leaned forward and stared at Victoria, making her blush under the old woman's penetrating gaze. 'So, Victoria, you have a mixture of your mother's and your father's looks. I can see now why your mother is so certain about your parentage. My husband, it seems, was a manipulating old rogue and I am truly ashamed of his actions. However, sometimes some good comes out of bad and it seems that you are a young lady of manners, beauty and brains, if what I hear is correct.'

'Thank you. I try to do my best for both my mama and my Aunt Eliza.' Victoria bowed her head and felt uncomfortable being talked about so openly.

'Ah, yes, your Aunt Eliza brought you up. Indeed she seems a woman of many skills; Grace has spoken quite highly of her in the past. However, I understand that the business relationship has come to an end. Perhaps it is for the best; Grace needs her own life it seems and your aunt would miss her financial skills.' Catherine glanced across at Mary-Anne and noticed her scowl as she battled to not say her thoughts on the matter. 'It will give your aunt more time to enjoy her niece, unless your mother has other ideas for your future. It would seem that my son is as obsessed with your mother as my husband was. How do you feel about that, Victoria? I'm sure the idea of living at Levensthorpe would be more than your wildest dreams, given who you are and where you have come from …?' Catherine was sharp with her words and noticed how uncomfortable she had made her young guest feel.

'I may be working class, but I do have manners,' Victoria bit back and glanced angrily at her mother for putting her in the position in the first place. 'Mama can live her life as she sees fit, and I wish her and Mr Ellershaw happiness if they love one another. It may be a lovely house but money is not everything; I've learned that even in my short life.'

'And a girl of spirit! Mary-Anne, would you be willing to leave Victoria and I together for a while. I have a feeling that given time we would be able to become quite close. And after all, I would like to rectify part of the wrong my husband has done to you. I'm in need of a young companion to keep me company now that my daughter has set her mind on travelling.' Catherine smiled, noticing the worried glance between daughter and mother. 'Don't worry, child, I don't bite. In fact, we will start by ordering some tea and progress from there. If the maid that William has provided me with can manage that small demand. She is the most stupid person I have ever known; that's why I need someone on my own level to converse with and keep me entertained in this godforsaken hole. Even though I still find it hard to come to terms with what Edmund did behind my back, I am not that blinkered to take my wrath out on you.' Catherine reached for the bell and rang it loudly and sat back in her chair.

'You don't have to stay on your own, Victoria. We can both leave or I can stay.' Mary-Anne looked at her daughter protectively and then at Catherine.

'She'll be fine, I will look after her, and I thought she could read to me for a while. I've just purchased a copy of *Une page d'amour* by Émile Zola but my eyesight is getting so poor I'd appreciate someone to read it to me. Grace hasn't time to do so; and, besides, her pronunciation of French is appalling. I presume you can read and speak French, child?'

'Yes, I enjoy French; Aunt Eliza made me learn it from a young age. I've heard of Émile Zola but I've never read anything by him,' Victoria said and watched as Catherine reached for the book from beside her bell.

'Well, then, here you are. Let's enjoy it together. Now, where is that wretched maid? Mary-Anne, would you mind chasing her up while your daughter and I get better acquainted?' Catherine smiled at Victoria and passed her the book, watching approvingly as Victoria looked at the cover and lovingly opened it.

'You will be all right, won't you, Victoria, if I leave you for a while?' Mary-Anne looked at her daughter who was already reading the preface to herself.

'Of course, Mama.' Victoria smiled. 'I'll enjoy reading this.'

'Go, go, Mary-Anne, the child is fine. Let me get to know her.' Catherine looked up as the maid eventually entered the room. 'About time, tea for two and perhaps a slice of Bakewell tart each?' Catherine smiled at Victoria and acknowledged Victoria's agreement to the maid.

'Mr William is here, ma'am; he's just talking to his groom outside. Should I bring refreshments for him too?' the maid enquired.

'No, I'm sure that he and Miss Wild will have better things to do than take tea with Victoria and I. Are you in agreement?' Catherine looked across at Mary-Anne, expecting her to make herself scarce, enabling her to get to know Victoria in her own time.

'Yes, of course, if that's what you wish.' Mary-Anne rose from her seat and followed the maid out into the hallway. She held her head up as she walked out onto the driveway where she could hear William's voice as she talked to his groom. She'd not bothered seeing him on the previous Friday, hoping to make him think that she was not dependent upon him and that her absence may make the heart grow fonder after their petty argument.

'Mary-Anne, what are you doing here?' William patted his horse on the withers and dismissed his groom as he turned to talk to her. 'You did not meet me on Friday. I waited for you at the Rose and Crown for over an hour. I missed you, and I regret our spat.' William walked over to her and held her in his arms.

'Not as much as I missed you,' Mary-Anne whispered. 'It was all over nothing anyway; I am not bothered if we don't have any children. But I'm still adamant that Victoria is able to live with us if we are still to marry.' She looked up into his eyes.

'This is why you are here, isn't it? Is Victoria with my mother? You are introducing her to the family by the back door, hoping to win my mother over with her? Well, if she can accept her into the family, then I suppose I can. Who knows, we might even have a child of our own, a brother or sister for her. I'm sorry, Mary-Anne; I'm used to having my own way and I tend to tread like an ignorant fool over people's feelings.' William bent down and kissed Mary-Anne passionately before whispering in her ear, 'I'm a fool and I love you more than life itself. Will you forgive me?'

'Oh, William, I've been so upset. Victoria is everything to me; I need for her to have good prospects and not to struggle in life. It's all I've ever wanted for her, so I am just as stubborn as you. If you can only forget that Victoria is your father's child and accept her as your own.' Mary-Anne buried her head in his jacket and hugged him close to her; she loved him and had hated the way they had fallen out.

'I tell you what, Mary-Anne, this Christmas I will organise a ball. We can announce our wedding and we can use the event as the opportunity to introduce Victoria to polite society and acknowledge her as part of the family. There's been enough gloom and doom this year; let's put the past behind us and look to the future together, all three of us.'

William tilted Mary-Anne's chin up to him and kissed her passionately.

'That would be wonderful, William; she would love that and she would feel loved by that act alone.'

'Then consider it done, my darling. Now, let's see how things are going between my mother and Victoria. I bet she's got her reading to her; that is all she wants Grace to do all day. No wonder my sister is so keen on escaping her clutches.' William laughed.

'That won't worry Victoria; she loves her books. But I must admit the book they are reading would baffle me; it's all in French. When does Grace leave and where is she going?' Mary-Anne asked, eager to glean information to give to Eliza.

'She's due to leave at the end of next week; she's just heard that she's been accepted as a candidate to attend the Royal Free Hospital as a medical student. She is hoping to become a doctor, which is an absolutely ridiculous thing to want to achieve. A woman a doctor! She will be no good; she will be forever fainting and having fits of the vapours. We all thought that she just was going to travel and see the world and then she tells us that. Apparently it has been her dream all along but she wasn't sure if she would be accepted!' William scoffed.

'Good for her! Women are just as good as any man. But what a change it will be for her. She is not exactly popular with both Eliza and me; we both wish she had been more honest with Eliza over the shop's accounts. Poor Eliza is being made out to be the bad one in the partnership, having to tell the staff they are no longer wanted by the new purchaser of the building.' Mary-Anne sighed.

'That's just like Grace ... wants everyone to think the best of her when really she is more devious than any one of us. London is the right place for her; she'll meet her match and find out that life is sometimes hard if you are not being cossetted at home.' William laughed.

'Oh, William, I'm glad that we have forgiven one another; now let's go and tell Victoria our news of the ball.' Mary-Anne put her arm through William's; she had got her man back, and he had realised that Victoria was everything to her.

Chapter 13

'Hell, has it come to that, Tom Thackeray delivering coal to me?!' Fred Parker stood in his kitchen doorway, looking out at his small yard, as he watched his old boss empty sacks down his outside coal hole.

'Needs must, Fred. Have you not got a job yet?' Tom stood up straight after replacing the metal coal cover and grinned at his old right-hand man from the Rose.

'No, not a snifter; there's no work in the whole of Leeds. Anyway, you must know that, if you are the new delivery boy for the Rothwell Pit. You deserve better than that.' Tall, grey-haired Fred pulled his braces back on and looked hard at his old boss.

'Aye, well, it's only for the time being. Plans are afoot. I'll hopefully not be delivering for them for much longer; it's just a stopgap. In fact, if you are still out of work in another few months with a bit of luck I'll be able to offer you some work. But you say nowt to nobody.' Tom stood and saw a glint of excitement in his old friend's eyes.

'What are you up to, you bugger? I know that look. What bother are you giving folk now?' Fred grinned.

'Well, between you and me, my lass Eliza has set her head on buying the Rose, but you keep it quiet. Both you and I know that there's a good seam on level three, but nobody else knows that. Everybody thinks that it's worked-out and that's what I want them to think. That it's worth nowt to nobody.' Tom leaned next to his old mate as he watched Fred's young children gather around their father's legs. 'You'll need a job by the looks of this tribe; I didn't know you'd this many children, you old dog!' He smiled down at their dirty faces and shoeless feet and knew that if Eliza was successful with her purchase of the pit his first job would be to ensure Fred a good position at the Rose.

'Aye, I've five of them for my sins. The missis is out collecting washing; it's a good job, and she can make some money.' Fred tussled the hair of his oldest son and smiled at him. 'I think that you are mad buying the Rose. Level three floods at the least bit of rain; you'll need some new pumps and they will cost. Old Ellershaw never bothered with it because it would have cost him too much. But then again he was a tight old bastard. If you get it bought and your offer is still there, count me in; there's enough coal on other levels to last for a year or two without touching that lower level. I need the money, as you can see; in fact, we were keeping out of your way until I recognised you because we haven't a ha'penny to rub together, so don't expect payment for your delivery.' Fred looked shamefaced; he'd complained many a time when the Rose Pit's delivery man had returned empty-handed from some of the worse-off homes.

'Don't worry, mate; I'll tell them that it got pinched off the back of my cart in Harehills. It makes no difference to me; I'd rather yours were warm and fed.' Tom slapped his mate on the back and looked down again at the children that were staring at him in curiosity. 'I'll be in touch, with a bit of luck. I hope my lass buys the bloody place; it'd be the answer to many a prayer.'

'Too bloody true, mate. You'll keep in touch?' Fred watched as Tom closed the garden gate behind and climbed up onto the coal-black cart, whipping his horse into action.

'Aye, as soon as I know something, I'll be knocking on your door,' Tom shouted as he trundled off down the road.

*

Eliza stood in the empty main room of her beloved shop. Her eyes were filled with tears as she lovingly swept her hand along the shop's large counter and looked around the empty shelves and abandoned shop dummies that were usually so finely dressed. What had she done? And all for sake of pride and money that she really didn't need anyway, she thought to herself. Why had she been stupid enough to sell everything that she loved when she and Grace had fallen out? No amount of money could make up for the years of happiness that she had enjoyed being in charge of the shop that had once only been a dream.

The worst thing was it might have been sold for nothing if her plans for the pit did not bear fruit; she was gambling with her life and her security, and it was all because Mary-Anne had put ideas in her head and made her feel as if anything was possible with the money that she had given her. A worked-out coal pit, for this fine old shop; she must be mad in the head, she thought, as she looked out of the shop's window and saw the new owner walking towards it to pick up the key and take legal possession of his property. It had been a terrible morning already, saying farewell to staff that she had valued, and knowing that they would perhaps not be able to keep their families fed, all because of her stupid pride and even stupider decision to sell up and buy the Rose, and now she had to smile and be polite to Graham Todd, who was the most hard-nosed businessman she had ever met.

'Now then, lass, I see all the stock has been sent over to my shop in Wakefield. That's a good job done; I can get on with knocking this old spot down and putting up something with a bit of style about it.' Graham Todd looked around him and raised his stick to poke it into the skirting board that had a sign of rot in it. 'It's rotten, is this place. Mind, you had it bonny, but underneath all the trimmings the shop's worth nowt. Time to move with the times and have a fresh look, like the shopping arcades further up the street. So that folk can pass their time and enjoy the experience even on a wet day.' Graham Todd was brash and had no care for the feelings that were flitting around in Eliza's head.

'It's Miss Wild, if you have forgotten, Mr Todd; my name's above the door along with Grace Ellershaw's.' Eliza had not been called lass for as long as she could remember and she wasn't going to be called it now. 'I suppose you want the keys and then that's me done.' A lump came into Eliza's throat as she passed the bunch of keys to the new owner who didn't give a damn about her feelings.

'Aye, we'll soon have it pulled down; the keys will be not needed for long. You'll admire the new place; it's to be built in best Portland stone with plenty of windows to let some light in and show off our wares. Folk will flock for miles to see it when I open it,' Graham Todd boasted.

'I'm sure you will be successful, but now if you'll excuse me, I'll make my way home.'

Eliza could not hold back the tears any longer as she walked down Briggate. She hated the bloated Graham Todd; he never designed his own dresses, and he'd certainly never even sewn or stitched a thing in his life. What did he know about women's fashion? But he had the money and money talked. Unlike her when she had started out with Grace, he could buy anybody or anything he wanted. Well, when she bought the Rose Pit, she would have connections and money too and, if she was successful in buying Highfield House, she'd make sure she only invited who she wanted to entertain, not who she hoped to impress. She was going to be her own woman and, with that in mind, she stepped out down Briggate, head held high. She was more than just a lass; she was a lady who owned her own property, had money in the bank and a bright future ahead of her.

Chapter 14

'I forbid you to leave me, Grace,' Catherine Ellershaw shouted at her daughter as she watched her put on her dark-coloured hat which matched her skirt and boots and fasten the button of her smart tweed jacket over her frilled high-necked white blouse.

'Oh, Mother! Please don't do this again. You know that I'm going; my place is all arranged, and I have no intention of staying a minute longer.' Grace secured her hat with a pearl-edged hatpin, ready for her travels, and glared at her mother for making their parting so dramatic.

Catherine sighed. 'I really can't understand why you think you should become a doctor; it's not a fitting role for a lady's career and you don't know the first thing about medicine. Why won't you just be happy with your lot?'

'You know I've been reading biology and medical journals since Father was taken ill. It's something I feel that I could excel at rather than just waste my life making silly conversation with empty-headed women and, besides, seeing my father in so much pain made me realise what I wanted to do with my life. You should be proud that I have been accepted into the college; it's the first intake of female students.' Grace picked up her amply filled Gladstone bag and stood in the doorway looking back at her mother shedding tears. 'You know where I'm staying – twenty-two Cromwell Street, along with other professional ladies. I'm assured that it is of a good standard so you must not worry about my well-being.' A pang of guilt washed over her as she saw how genuinely upset her mother was at her leaving. 'I'll write regularly and, if you need me, I can soon catch the train from King's Cross back up to Yorkshire.'

'Grace, please don't go. I always thought that I had you if nobody else.' Catherine wiped her eyes and got up from her usual chair next to the window and walked over to embrace her daughter.

'You'll be fine, Mother, William is on your doorstep and you have your friends to have tea and gossip with. A week further down the line and you'll be grateful to have got rid of me,' she joked, as her mother held her tight and kissed her on the cheek. 'Now, I must go; my carriage is waiting and the train to London will not wait just for me.'

'You will write, won't you? And you will take care? London is a lot larger than Leeds.' Catherine stood back and looked at her daughter; she was going to miss her but she knew Grace needed more out of life to keep her satisfied.

'Yes, of course, I will. I mean to make you proud of me, Mother, when I qualify as a doctor.' Grace quickly looked around her and then rushed to the carriage waiting for her outside the gatehouse.

Once inside, she felt her heart beating fast as she was conveyed to Leeds Station. The station was busy with all classes of passengers, gentleman and ladies awaiting embarkation in the first-class areas, the less wealthy finding seating in the second- and third- class carriages, having to jostle for their seats once the steam train had pulled in and anxiously standing on the platform edge under the watchful eye of the station master and porters as they tried to be first to secure a seat.

Under the station's glass roof was a mixture of smoke and steam from the many engines coming and going. The huge wheels and the brass funnels of the coal-driven beasts shining in the glint of daylight that streamed down onto them. A paper seller yelled out the latest news as he made his way through the crowds, making easy money as he sold to people who bought one in hope that it would make their journeys go quicker. Grace smiled as she heard him shout the headlines out.

'Act of the Married Women's Property Act passed. Women to control their own money! Here, miss, do you want a copy?' the cheeky young lad said as he noticed her smiling.

'No, I've heard what I wanted to know,' Grace said to the lad as he shouted out the headlines again. Times were changing; women were getting more rights and soon they would be regarded in the same standing as any man.

'Grace, Grace!' Jessica Bentley pushed her way through the standing crowds just as her train arrived. 'Please, please let me through, I need to catch my friend.'

Grace turned just as she was about to board the first-class compartment of the train. 'Jessica, what are you doing here? I thought we said goodbye last week at your home.'

'I just needed to say goodbye again and give you this to remember me by. I'm hoping that it will be useful to you.' Jessica held up a small wooden box secured with a lock to guard the contents. 'It's a microscope; I thought that you'd appreciate it in your new vocation.' She reached into her pocket and fished out the key and placed it into Grace's palm. 'I'm going to miss you.' Jessica held back her tears.

'And I you, dear friend.' Grace smiled as she quickly gave Jessica a hug. 'Thank you, I will take great care of it and will always think of you when I use it.'

'Now, go, go else you will miss the train.' Jessica nearly shoved her closest friend into her carriage as the station master blew his whistle. 'Write to me,' Jessica yelled above the steam engine's noise as she watched Grace sit down between two other well-dressed ladies. Grace was doing something more daring than she had ever dreamt of and how she was going to miss her.

*

'Now then, Miss Wild. What is it like to be a lady of leisure?' Mary-Anne asked, as she, Eliza and Victoria sat in Eliza's parlour, embroidering.

'I'm absolutely bored to death, along with nattering myself silly with worry wondering if I've done the right thing. I was happy enough working with Grace; you don't realise what you've got until you have lost it. I think I must be slightly mad to have listened to you and Tom. What if I can't afford the pit? And I don't even dare think about buying Highfield House.' Eliza dropped her embroidery onto her knee and looked across at Victoria as she made a disapproving noise. 'I'm doing this for you too, young lady, so don't make that noise and give me that face.'

'No, you are doing it for yourself and Tom,' Victoria quickly replied. 'This time I don't enter into it.'

'And so she should; you are to be living with me at Levensthorpe Hall once William and I are married. Your aunt deserves a life of her own; she might even be brave enough to get married herself if she has heard the news.' Mary-Anne grinned and took the newspaper that she had been carrying from her bag and offered it to her sister. 'There you go, no excuses now. As soon as the act is passed, any money that you have got will always be yours. You are not obliged to give it to your husband.'

Eliza read the news with growing triumph, knowing that the bill would make all the difference to women of all classes. 'I can't believe that it is going through Parliament; this is a really good thing for all women. You'll not be beholden to William and I can leave my money to Victoria after my day and know that no man can touch it.'

'You might have children of your own if you get a move on with getting wed. Not that Victoria would turn her nose up at an inheritance from you.' Mary-Anne laughed.

'Mother! Don't talk of such things. I hope Aunt Eliza will be with us for a long time yet.'

Eliza folded the newspaper and answered quickly. 'You just mind your own business, Mary-Anne. Marriage has not been mentioned for a while, so I'll keep it that way just for a while longer until I've seen where the next months are to lead me.'

'There's no excuse now, so don't hide behind buying the pit, else you'll lose him again,' Mary-Anne warned.

'I'm just not ready yet but I have no intention of losing him.' Eliza looked at her sister. 'Is it true what Victoria tells me, that William is to hold a Christmas Ball at Levensthorpe? Is it not too soon after his wife and father's death? What will people think? Does he have no respect for the dead?' Eliza quizzed her sister.

'He says life must go on and that it is no good mourning over people that didn't really love him. He thinks that it is a good way to introduce both Victoria and I officially to his family, friends and associates. I, myself, think that it is brilliant news and can't wait to see what he arranges, but Christmas is a good way off yet. Many things are to happen before then. Victoria, did you tell your aunt that Catherine Ellershaw requested you to call on her again? I really do think she's taken to you and enjoys your company. I suppose she thinks that you will be there to replace Grace now that she's gone.' Mary-Anne smiled at Victoria; she had done well in impressing Catherine, and she needed her help to win Catherine Ellershaw's approval.

'I did, Mama, but I don't know if I want to go again; she is quite strict, although she did make a fuss of me, especially when I played her the piano. She said Grace used to play and sing like a tormented cat, which made me laugh.' Victoria smiled and folded her sewing away; she hated needlecraft but her aunt said that she might one day need it and that it was best she learned.

'A cat that needs strangling!' Eliza spoke up, remembering how Grace had described her own singing voice to her in happier times. 'Have you walked down into Leeds and looked where my beautiful shop once stood? There is nothing more than a pile of rubble, it broke my heart to see it that way.'

'I have, Eliza. He means to rebuild, doesn't he? It will soon look beautiful again and will fit in with the new buildings that are going up in Leeds all around it. Now stop feeling so miserable; let's have a drink and perhaps a game of cards, Whist, I think, I'm not keen on playing gin rummy. Do you have a pack of cards or will you be tempting the devil?'

'I'll ring for Lizzie to make us some tea. It's a long time since I've played but, no, I used to enjoy a game of Whist. There's a packet of cards in the desk, right at the back of the drawer in the other room. Victoria, would you be good enough to go and get them?' Eliza was about to ring for her maid's attention when Mary-Anne stopped her. 'Don't bother with tea; I have a bit of something better.' Mary-Anne opened her bag and pulled out a bottle of gin. 'I thought we both have nothing to do and not so many worries, so let's have a drink together.'

'Oh, Mary-Anne, you really know how to lead me astray. I haven't had a drop of gin for years. One glass of that and I'll be giggling like an idiot,' Eliza said coyly, as she grinned at her sister. 'Go on then, glasses are on the dresser; I'll clear this table and we'll play an afternoon of Whist. It will have to be Knockout Whist; Victoria doesn't know any other and we haven't enough players to make two sets up.'

'I don't mind playing that; I remember sitting around the table with our mother and father and you getting so excited when you thought you were going to win. You or I always won because Mother and Father could see what cards we had in our hands and played their cards so that we won!' Mary-Anne set three glasses out on the table and filled two of them to the top with gin. 'Can Victoria try the gin? It's shop bought so isn't that potent if she only has a small drop, mixed with a drop of cordial.'

'Go on then, just half a glass; she'll have to get used to drink sometime and she's better drinking with us than with someone she couldn't trust.' Eliza looked across at Mary-Anne as she tipped the clear liquid into Victoria's glass. 'Whoa, that's enough; she'll be tiddly on that amount, don't give her any more.'

'What is this?' Victoria asked as she came back into the room. 'I've only known you drink the occasional sherry at Christmas and I've never been allowed to drink anything before.' Victoria put the pack of cards on the table and looked at both her aunt and mother sipping the drink.

'We've just given you half a glass to try; you may not like it. It's got a smell and taste all of its own.' Eliza felt the colour rising in her cheeks as the alcohol hit her.

Victoria looked at the small crystal-cut glasses and smelt the liqueur inside it before sipping the smallest of mouthfuls. 'I don't know if I like it or not; it's a bit odd but warming at the same time. Do people actually drink this for pleasure? I find myself wondering if I dare take another sip.' Victoria smacked her lips and tasted the juniper berry upon them.

'Two sips in and you'll enjoy it and will probably ask for more once you get that nice warm feeling that it gives you. But that will be enough for you today; it is only your first tasting and neither of us wants you the worse for wear. Now, let's deal these cards. Seven cards each; I'll shuffle them first and deal, and then will split the remaining cards to find the trump.' Mary-Anne smiled across at her daughter as she took another tentative drink of the gin while pulling a face as the liquid ran down her throat. 'Well, there is one thing: you are not a drinker!' She laughed as she dealt the three of them their cards. 'But are you a gambler?' she joked as she turned the top card left in the pack to reveal the Queen of Hearts. 'Now, that's our card, my dears; the Queen of Hearts, because we are the queens of many a heart and our lovely Victoria will be just the same as her aunt and mother when she comes of age.' Mary-Anne looked across at her daughter and felt a glow of pride at how beautiful her daughter looked.

'Now, I'll start with the first trick,' she told them. 'Just to remind you of how you play; Victoria, you have to place a card of the same suit on mine, hopefully higher in number then you can win that trick. If you have none of that suit you can trump my card by placing a heart upon it, but be warned – we can have higher cards than you. You can also throw a card of a different suit away, instead of using a trump; it's better to throw cards of small value like a two or three if you have to do that. The person who holds the most tricks at the end of the game is the winner. Now, I'll start with the King of Spades; he reminds me of William, with his superb beard and moustache.' Mary-Anne laughed at the picture of the king on the card, and waited for Eliza to play her hand as she fanned out the cards out in her hand.

'I've only got one spade. You'll have to take my queen,' Eliza grumbled as she placed her card on the table. Then both women looked at Victoria, watching her slowly smile as she placed her card upon the two already on the table.

'Well, you both lose because I've got an ace; I win the first trick!' She grinned at both her guardians and felt happy for the first time in a long time. This was the family she wanted and both her mother and aunt were enjoying themselves in their family home.

The afternoon soon passed and as nightfall came there was a great deal of giggling and playful squabbling within the drawing room of Aireville Mansions. Both sisters had drunk more than they had intended to do as Mary-Anne listened to the clock in the hallway chime. 'Oh, my Lord, it's seven o'clock. I've been here over six hours!' She looked across at her sister, who was sitting next to Victoria who had the biggest smile on her face as she watched her relatives. Both women realised that the day was nearly at an end and so was the bottle of gin.

'I feel quite tipsy, Mary-Anne; it's all your doing. You're a bad influence.' Eliza put her hand to her head and tried to get up from her seat. 'I'll ring Lizzie for some supper to revive us.' She pushed herself up and swayed unsteadily before sitting back down.

'It's all right, Aunt Eliza. She's made some ham sandwiches in the kitchen, and I'll go and get them. I told her to do so and to go home about an hour ago when I realised that you two were the worse for wear. If anything was going to put me off drinking it's you two; what a load of rubbish you both come out with when you are drunk!' Victoria grinned.

'Us drunk? We are not! We're just a bit merry, thank you very much!' Mary-Anne's indignation was betrayed by a slight slur in her words, which made them all laugh. 'You are such a beautiful child; you can't possibly be mine.'

'She is yours, and you know it. But I've looked after her all her life, so I'm more her mother,' Eliza answered honestly.

'Now, don't you start arguing over me. I'll bring the sandwiches in and make some tea and then you will both revive.' Victoria shook her head. What a pair, but she loved them both and that was all that mattered. She laughed as Eliza tried to stand up with her empty glass in her hand and propose a toast to 'Ladies of means and independence'. They were both certainly independent, as no man in his right mind would want them in the state they were currently in. They were definitely not the ladies that they tried so very hard to be every day to the rest of the outside world, but they were family and they loved her.

Chapter 15

The month of October had come in with wild and windy weather. The trees were quickly losing their leaves as the rain and wind battered them into submission. Now, with two days to go before the auction for the Rose Pit, Eliza was on edge, questioning the sense in even showing any interest in it as she sat with Tom in her sitting room at Aireville Mansions.

'I wish it would stop raining … I'd at least then be able to go for a walk, which might help quell my worries. I think I must be slightly mad in thinking that I can purchase the Rose. You should not have let me talk myself into it. I'm a dressmaker, not a pit owner. What do I want with the place anyway? Everyone is saying that it's worth nothing.' Eliza turned to Tom and wrung her hands in despair.

'That's what I've been telling them, Eliza,' Tom reassured her once again. 'You know that it's what we want them to believe. And you should be thankful for this weather. Level three will be flooded and nobody thinking of buying the pit

169

will be able to inspect that at length, making them think that it is worth nowt.' Tom put his arm around Eliza and held her to him. 'You are doing it for us and for the miners' families that have always been reliant on the Rose. They won't be able to thank you enough when they hear that it is not lost forever.' Tom kissed Eliza on her brow and smelt the perfume on her hair. He loved her so much and he knew how much she was fretting, but worry would not make the day of the auction come any sooner, nor effect its outcome.

'And my shop staff? They don't sing my praises; in fact, they walk on the other side of the street and blank me. They too should have every right to work.' Eliza looked up at Tom.

'They were mainly young lasses; they'll get work in other shops in Leeds. And, besides, that was not your fault – it was Grace Ellershaw's – so stop worrying about that. You'll be giving the men of the families employment if you buy the pit. That'll mean that you give that miner his pride back and money to feed his children and security for his wife. That should give you more pride in the long run.' Tom squeezed her tight. 'I wish you'd marry me, Eliza. I can't understand why you haven't named the date; we both love one another.'

Eliza withdrew from his arms. 'One thing at a time; let's get the Rose bought first. Also, as you may have gathered by now, I've been thinking I might attend the auction for Highfield House as well. Just out of curiosity more than anything and because since I was a young girl I have stood at the garden gates and looked in at it and wanted to live there. Now, that would make a good family home because I do love you Tom and we will be married, but not just yet. Besides, Mary-Anne is to marry come spring, I don't want to spoil her big day, and it will be the wedding of the season if she has anything to say about it. They are already planning a Christmas Ball to tell everyone of the date they are to wed. I, myself, think that they have no shame and that they should wait a year or two before marrying discreetly and keep it small. After all, it is not that long since poor Priscilla shot herself. Neither Mary-Anne nor William seems to care.' Eliza shook her head and looked out of the window. 'She was telling me of the dress that she would like me to make for her; she's got such big plans.'

'It wouldn't be Mary-Anne if she didn't make a big splash of her wedding day. She's got her man and her fortune – a lot has happened this year for her. Our time is yet to come, but we would be stronger if you would marry me. Please think about a date again, Eliza, and ease my aching heart. I am yours whenever you wish and it is not for money that I wish to marry you, it's for love.' Tom reached out for her hand and squeezed it tight.

'I know. Be patient with me; just give me a little more time and then we will wed. But for now, let us hope that the Rose will become ours on Thursday and who knows, perhaps Highfield House if it is sold cheaply.' Eliza turned and sat down.

'You are still determined to buy Highfield? The contents were sold last Thursday? Did you not go to that? They were on display in the Institute and Thompson the auctioneer sold them for what he could get. The lads at the Rothwell Pit were on about it, some of their wives thought that they could perhaps get real bargains. Nobody, however, had enough money on them and if they did they weren't about to line the pockets of the banks so nobody bid much for anything.'

'No, what is the use of more furniture? I have what I need for here and I suspect owning Highfield House is just a dream and that I am foolish to even think about it, let alone buy furniture to place within it. I'll never have Highfield, I should be happy with this home here. It is lovely and it is large enough for when we do get married.' Eliza smiled.

'So, you are looking to the future when we are man and wife? I thought perhaps that day would never come. That you keep me hanging on but never intend to marry me.'

'Of course I am, but not just yet; as I say, let Mary-Anne marry first and then it will be our turn. Victoria will be with her mother then, and I won't have the responsibility of her welfare. I'll be able to give you all my attention and to any family we may be blessed by having.' Eliza smiled.

'Some children of our own ... now that would be something that would be precious to us both. Victoria is a lovely girl, but she is not yours and, to be truthful, I would rather she did live with Mary-Anne once she is married.' Tom looked worried. 'You've spent all your life looking after her and now her mother should look after her. She'll soon be a woman and will have a mind of her own. She may not accept me.'

'I don't know why you think that. She always talks highly of you already; she knows that you are a good man. If she was here I'd ask her to tell you so, but she's gone to read to Catherine Ellershaw, while her mother visits William there at the hall. Mary-Anne is adamant that Victoria will join them when she is married, so stop worrying over nothing.' Eliza held out for Tom's hand and held it tight.

'You have brought her up so well and I'm only a colliery man. She knows much more than I'll ever will. I'm not surprised Catherine Ellershaw has taken her under her wing; she will replace Grace perfectly if Mrs Ellershaw can come to terms with her parentage. It must be strange looking at a child you know to be your husband's and for the mother of that child to be marrying your son. When she finds out that you are to buy the Rose and perhaps Highfield she will most definitely feel slighted. In fact, I can feel a bit of sympathy for her; she was used by Edmund Ellershaw perhaps more than anyone.'

'I know, but she must have known what he was like. But I feel sympathy for her. She's put everything into her children's lives, forfeiting things for herself, only for Edmund to leave her with nothing. She did deserve better than that.' Eliza looked at Tom and shook her head. 'Do you think we are doing the right thing or will we be cursed by Edmund's ghost? He must be turning in his grave if he knows what we are about.'

'The old bugger's not in his grave; he's stalking the fires of hell. Don't you worry about stuff like that ... you know as well as I do it's the buggers that are alive that hurt you most, not them that are dead.' Tom held her tight.

'Oh, Tom, I hope that you are right.' Eliza looked up into Tom's eyes and kissed him on the lips. 'I do love you. You do know that, don't you?'

'Aye, I know it. We've always been meant for one another, you and I. It's just taken us a while to realise it.' Tom hugged her close to him.

'Perhaps it's time to prove my love to you.' Eliza left his arms and pulled on his hand. 'Now, seeing Victoria is not here, how about we find other ways of pleasure on this wet and miserable day. It's taken me a while but I'm willing to be yours and yours alone.' Eliza smiled and blushed at being so forward with her suggestion.

'Bloody hell, lass! How fast can you run up those stairs, Eliza Wild? I'll give you a head start of two steps before I grab hold of you and show you my passion for you. Now, get running!' Tom laughed as he smacked her bottom through the many layers of her skirts. 'It isn't just William Ellershaw that has the upper hand in lovemaking; this colliery lad can do just as well.' He grinned as he watched Eliza beam widely at him as she made for the stairs for their first afternoon of desire and passion.

The day of the auction soon came around and, like the rest of the month's weather, it was showing no mercy as Eliza climbed into the hackney carriage to take her there. Even the horse and coachman that drove her there looked miserable;

both were soaked to the skin but knew that they had to earn a living if they were to eat that night.

The Rose yard looked grey and foreboding as Eliza stepped down from her carriage; the yard was filled with puddles and the pit wheel looked like a huge rusty skeleton against the backdrop of the grey skies. She paid the coachman and quickly ran across the yard to what she knew to be the offices of the pit and noticed a few people standing to look out of the window at the gloom outside. She could see that Tom was one of them and her heart started beating fast as now she knew there was no turning back, that she had to go through with the deal if she was able.

'Ah, Miss Wild, Tom here told me you were on your way, and that you still have an interest in its purchase. It's a terrible day to be doing business on but needs must, I'm afraid.' Bernard Thompson looked at the two bankers who were sitting at the desk that once was Edmund Ellershaw's and smiled. 'It seems we don't have much interest in the pit, but let's hope that the bids are high; we need to raise as much money as possible today.' The grey-haired auctioneer with mutton chop whiskers smiled as he looked up to see Mary-Anne enter into the office, thinking that there were going to be more spectators than buyers as surely the two women could not be seriously considering making a bid. Coal mining was a man's profession and it was better left to the likes of Elijah Shore from the Shore Pit and Reginald Sidebottom from the pits at Methley, who were sitting in a corner plotting together as they glanced at Tom

Thackeray, who they thought might be a threat to their purchasing the Rose at a price that they had come to an agreement between themselves.

'We will just wait another ten minutes and then I'll start the proceedings. I expected more interest than this, although I know perhaps the pit has been neglected of late.' Bernard Thompson looked at his silver pocket watch and went to sit down by the bankers and await any more interested parties as Mary-Anne, Eliza and Tom all stood together, hoping that no one else would be attending.

'Do you know those two men?' Eliza whispered as they finally took their seats.

'Aye, they are both pit owners,' Tom whispered, 'but they are both as tight as duck's arses. They'll not want to pay a lot for it. If anything, they'll just want it to close and no longer be opposition for their workings. It sounds as if they are going to be bidding as a team, so the bank will not be happy with that.'

'I feel sick; I should have left it for you to bid, Tom. They are all looking at both me and Mary-Anne, wondering what two women are doing here in the first place.'

'I'll give them something to bloody well think about if they don't stop looking at us,' Mary-Anne blustered. 'The dirty old sods. You take no notice of them and you get this pit bought; that'll stop them in their tracks.'

'Hold your noise, Mary-Anne; we've got to keep things sweet,' Tom whispered and glanced up at Bernard Thompson as he stood up in readiness to start the auction.

'Good day, gentleman and ladies,' Bernard Thompson said. 'I'm afraid the inclement weather has not been in our favour today and that there are not as many of you as my colleagues and I would have liked to have seen here.' Bernard acknowledged the two gentlemen by his side and looked at the small group of would-be bidders. 'Anyway, to business; I aim to sell the Rose this morning and then move on to Highfield House this afternoon. Perhaps the weather will be kinder to us then. Now, where do we start? Three hundred guineas, that's a fair amount for this fine place.' Bernard Thompson looked at the potential bidders and saw a look of disdain on the mine owners' faces. 'Two hundred guineas then; come on now, it's worth all of that.'

'It's a bloody hole filled with water, nothing more,' Elijah Shore answered. 'Half of these buildings need flattening. I'll give you one hundred and fifty, not a penny more.'

Tom looked at Eliza as she gasped at how little the pit was being auctioned for and knew that her time had come to make her bid. 'One hundred and sixty-five. I'll bid one sixty-five,' Eliza shouted, and watched as the two pit owners mumbled to one another.

'Gentleman, the lady is offering one hundred and sixty-five guineas. Are you to offer more?' Bernard Thompson looked at the two and waited.

'They don't like you outbidding them,' Tom whispered to Eliza, 'and to make it worse you're a woman. Just look at their faces; if looks could kill you'd be six foot under by now. They thought it was me who would be their opposition and they'd know I couldn't afford to go high.'

'One hundred and seventy; I'll make it one hundred and seventy, but it's not bloody worth that.' Elijah spat onto the floor and put his head down.

'Madam, the bid is with you; are you willing to counter offer?' The auctioneer paused and glanced at the two bankers who were not happy at such poor offers being made.

Eliza saw Mary-Anne wink at her as she shouted out, 'One hundred and seventy-five. One hundred and seventy-five guineas and I can give you a cheque here and now.' She couldn't stop herself from smiling as she saw the disappointment on the two pit owners' faces. She'd been prepared to pay over two hundred guineas to secure the property, but obviously they had not, as Elijah shook his head and cursed under his breath.

'Sir, are you willing to counter bid?' the auctioneer enquired.

'No, she can bloody well have the godforsaken place. It's worth nowt to nobody, so it's a hundred and seventy-five guineas wasted. Old Ellershaw's run it into the ground; it's not worth the clothes upon my back let alone seventy-five guineas. Let's away, Reg, I've seen it all now: a woman buying a pit! This must be your doing, Tom Thackeray, the way you are grinning at us.' The two men stood up and pushed their way past Tom and the auctioneer, slamming the door behind them as they left.

'Bloody hell, lass, you own the Rose. It's yours!' Mary-Anne cried and hugged her sister.

'Not quite yet, madam; there is the small matter of payment to be made to these two gentlemen.' Bernard Thompson looked across at Eliza and ushered her towards the two gentlemen who were awaiting payment, and who were disappointed that the pit had sold for so little.

'That was a good buy on your part, madam. I'm afraid it is not, however, good news for the bank. We are going to struggle to cover all the late Mr Ellershaw's debts.' The bank clerk quickly made a bill of sale out, while the other checked that he was about to hand over the correct deeds while Eliza with trembling hands wrote a cheque out to cover the payment.

'Yes, I didn't expect it to be sold for such a low sum, however, I'm quite happy that it has. I'll now be able to show interest in buying Highfield House this afternoon.' Eliza looked at the cheque she had just signed and written.

'You are interested in buying Highfield as well as the pit?' The older of the bank clerks looked at his partner and smiled.

'Yes, providing that the price is not too high.' Eliza felt a rush of excitement as she and the clerk exchanged deeds and cheque, and she turned to see Tom and Mary-Anne looking at her in anticipation, realising that part of their joint dreams had come true.

'It is possible, Miss Wild, for us to accept an offer for Highfield, here and now. There's been very little interest in either of the Ellershaws' properties and I'm sure that my partner and Mr Thompson would accept a reasonable sum now, without taking it to auction this afternoon. It would save time and money, both of which are precious to us all.' The clerk looked at the woman that seemed to have her head set on buying the Ellershaw estate.

Mary-Anne and Tom stepped forward and linked arms with Eliza as she hesitated, wondering what to do.

'What would be the asking price?' Mary-Anne interjected on her sister's behalf, as Eliza struggled to dare ask the question.

'I believe one hundred guineas would purchase it here and now. It's a decent building and worth every penny of that.' The clerk looked up at Bernard Thompson and waited for his confirmation of valuation.

'Nay, I've been thinking around the one fifty to two hundred guinea mark. But it might go higher if someone was to bid against you; you could save money if you bought it here and now.' Bernard looked at the two sisters and Tom, who he knew to be behind persuading Eliza Wild to buy the pit.

'It's a case of a bird in the hand, Miss Wild. You want the house and we want a buyer and it would seem that we can conclude our business here and now if you were to offer us somewhere within the region of one hundred and fifty guineas.' The clerk grinned and showed his well-worn teeth as he tried to convince her to buy the property that the bank wanted shot of.

'Go on, Eliza make him an offer.' Mary-Anne squeezed her sister's hand tight.

'Aye, go on lass; you know you want it. If you can afford it, buy it.' Tom looked at Eliza as she faltered in giving her answer.

'I don't know, it's a big house; what would I do with it? I never thought in my wildest dreams that I could afford both, although I had hoped on the quiet.' Eliza felt her heart pounding as she looked at both Mary-Anne and Tom. She breathed in deeply. 'I'd be able to offer one hundred and twenty-five guineas. Would that be enough?'

All three held their breath and watched as the clerk looked down at his paperwork and glanced at his colleague.

'Miss Wild, you are now the new owner of Highfield House, and I hope that you spend many pleasurable years there. Now let us settle the paperwork here and now and then perhaps you would like to go and view your new home, Bill here has the keys and the deeds; all we need now is payment once again.' The clerk looked at the blushing Eliza and smiled. 'You have made two good purchases today; you can be proud of yourself,' he said as she signed yet another cheque and passed it across with shaking hands.

'I've never ever spent so much money in such a short time. It is quite frightening.' Eliza passed over the cheque and then took hold of the title deeds to Highfield House and the large sturdy keys that rattled on an iron ring and had always done so since the house was first built. She turned to look at Mary-Anne and Tom. 'Well, I've done it now; I've bought work for myself and you Tom and I've also bought what should have partly been Victoria's inheritance.'

'You won't regret it for one moment; I'll soon have the pit up and working and I'll have most of the men back on the payroll and working as they've never worked before.

This time they'll know that they will be looked after by their boss.' Tom went and hugged her tight as she looked at Mary-Anne over his shoulder.

'You've done it, lass, you've got what you have always wanted. I'm proud of you; we've both got what we deserve from life. And more to the point, we have no Edmund Ellershaw to cause us any bother, seeing as he's six foot under.' Mary-Anne looked across at the bankers who were getting ready to leave along with Bernard Thompson.

'I'm loathe to speak ill of the dead,' one of the bankers began, 'but I'm afraid to say Mr Ellershaw had very few friends when it comes down to it. And even fewer now that his estate is not going to cover his debts, but that is not your concern.' The banker sighed. 'Now, I know you have bought both properties outright, but if you need any further advice, or indeed a loan in the future, please do call in to see us at the bank. I couldn't help but overhear that this gentleman here is going to be reopening the pit and managing it for you. I wish you every success with it. I'm glad that it didn't fall into the hands of the other interested parties, as they were after it for the wrong reasons. Good day to you all.' The two bankers walked out into the rain-soaked yard and Bernard Thompson smiled knowingly as he made his way through the doorway.

'It's all yours now, lass; you can do what you want with it. No doubt that fella of yours knows more than he's letting on, else he'd not be letting you throw good money away.' He winked at all three and then turned his coat collar up to the rain as he walked across the puddled yard and through the gates.

'I've got to sit down; my legs feel like jelly!' Eliza grabbed the side of the desk and sat in what used to be Edmund Ellershaw's chair. 'I can't believe what I've just done. All this is mine and the house too, and I've still some money left in the bank. Or will do once I've sold my house at Aireville Mansions. Oh, my Lord, I can't believe it: I own Rose Pit.'

'You can be a lady of leisure now if you ever actually get around to marrying me. Let me do all the work for you. I know there's coal down there; now it's up to me to find it and get it out. We'll need some pumps and some new ponies and everything needs stocking up and then you'll have the wages to pay. It might be hard going for the first year but then you'll start showing good returns. I bet them two buggers that were bidding against us won't be happy; they were looking at getting the Rose's contracts. Well, I'll soon have those back on our books.' Tom ran his fingers through his hair. 'It's absolutely pissing down; it's not fit for a dog to be out, else I'd be tempted to go and have a look down the pit now, just to see what state it is in.'

'Well, I don't know about you two but I think we should have a drink to celebrate. Do you think we should go into town and have lunch at Whitelocks along with a gin or two?' Mary-Anne looked at Tom and Eliza and saw that her suggestion was not going to be accepted by the looks on their faces. 'All right then, if you are not up for that, can I make the first move to redecorate this bloody office?' She went to the far wall and reached up for a painting that hung there. 'Take that, you old bastard. Your days have been and gone, and my sister is in charge now, so rot in hell.' She got hold of the paper knife that was on the desk and stabbed time and time again at the portrait of Edmund Ellershaw, shredding it in bits. 'That makes me feel good; pity it wasn't the man himself. While you are spending money, Eliza, get Tom here a new office. I can't abide standing in here; it brings back too many memories of the old letch.' Mary-Anne slung the painting on the floor and shuddered. 'How many times did our mother come in here, begging for his mercy and getting none? I remember when I stood in front of him, trembling and frightened because he ruled our lives and I had no powers. Well, it is different now; I know a good man is going to be in charge, that my sister will want for nothing and that Victoria and I have our lives ahead of us with William by my side. Your ghost will not haunt us, Edmund Ellershaw, but we may haunt you, albeit in hell.' Mary-Anne's eyes filled with tears as she looked at her sister with Tom standing behind her, his hand on her shoulder. 'I'm proud of you, our Eliza; we've all come a long way since Pit Lane. Now, for God's sake, put this poor bugger out of his misery and marry him.' Mary-Anne smiled at Tom but got no reply from Eliza who pretended to be engrossed in reading the deeds to both properties.

Chapter 16

'Well, what do you think, will you be happy here?' Mary-Anne asked as, a few days later, she stood with Victoria and Eliza in the dining room of Highfield House.

'How could I not be? Just look at it. All these rooms and I can decorate them just as I wish. I can't wait to choose wallpapers and curtains and transform this place to how I want it. It's a pity that I didn't have the foresight of going to the furniture auction and buy some of the original furniture back, but I never thought that I'd be able to afford this. I'm so lucky.'

'Luck doesn't enter into, my dear sister; you've worked hard for what you have got and achieved. Now enjoy it.' Mary-Anne smiled.

'You are going to need more than the one maid, Aunt Eliza; there are at least six fires to light in a morning and the kitchen is larger than our two main rooms at home. You need a cook and really a butler if you are going to live correctly here.' Victoria gazed around her.

'Don't be daft, me having a butler! I'm not that posh. But you are right; we will need more staff than just Betsy. I'll have to advertise. It's all right me buying this house but its upkeep is going to keep me on my toes. Then there's the garden and stable; I need a gardener and stable boy as I think I should have my own horse and carriage now I own the Rose; it makes more sense than walking everywhere.' Eliza still couldn't believe her luck and her mind was working overtime with what she was going to do with her new home.

'What you need to do is marry that man of yours first,' Mary-Anne said curtly. 'You've no excuses now. Poor Tom, you keep him hanging on and all he wants to do is put a ring on your finger. You completely ignored my prompting the other day and you should have seen the hurt on his face when you didn't even look up and say anything in reply. You'll lose him again if you are not careful.'

'I'll not lose him. Don't worry, I will marry him and I won't make him wait much longer; I just need the new act in Parliament to become law and then I'll feel more easier when I know my money is my own and always will be. I've seen too many women lose everything because of their husband's ways.' Eliza's face told of her worries and Mary-Anne put her arm around her.

'Our past still haunts us. Doesn't it, my dear sister? But you have to learn to trust else you will become a bitter old woman in a big house, all alone. I've moved on; I'm marrying William in trust and in love. No longer is it for revenge;

I truly love him and him me. Victoria is being welcomed into the family by his mother; in fact, they both enjoy one another's company, especially now Grace is no longer around to keep her mother amused.' Mary-Anne looked across at her daughter and smiled.

'Yes, I quite like my time with Mrs Ellershaw; she's an intelligent woman. At first, I was a little frightened of her because she was quite strict but she has warmed to me and we have good conversations covering a wide range of subjects. It's a pity that George and Grace do not give her the time she deserves since their father has died.' Victoria looked at her mother and wanted to tell her Aunt Eliza to go with her heart and not her head and marry Tom as she knew he made her happy.

'Well, I'm afraid to say that I now realise Grace only ever did look after herself. She will never marry; she's not that sort. And as for George, he's a lost soul from what I understand. He loses himself in his dens of iniquity; he's the one that takes after his father from what I hear, though not with the ladies.' Eliza looked at the two people she loved the most and realised that both of them only wanted the best for her, unlike the family of Catherine Ellershaw. 'I will marry Tom, I do love him and now I've got what I've always wanted in life, I should put him out of his misery.'

'Good! Where is he today? I suppose he's looking around his kingdom and doing the same as us, imagine how great he can make the pit now it's virtually his to run.' Mary-Anne grinned.

'He's offering work to his old work colleagues. He can't do anything without workers, so he's going from house to house offering his old crew work. Most of them have only been taken on as casual labour like he was and they will appreciate a permanent job, with a decent wage and a good boss.' Eliza looked around her. 'We are both going to be busy over the next few weeks.'

'You are. Also, don't forget, I need a wedding dress designed and sewn, not to mention the ballgowns that we all need for William's Christmas Ball. It's going to be such a grand affair. Both Victoria and I are to visit Levensthorpe next Saturday to hear of his plans and to tell him who we wish to invite. I'm glad for Victoria; it is what I wished and hoped for.' Mary-Anne smiled at her daughter. 'We have all achieved what we have wished for; let's hope that it continues.'

*

Tom walked through the back streets of Leeds, finding the men that used to work at the Rose and giving them hope in their desperate lives as he offered them a chance to earn money and put food in their children's bellies. He despaired at the poverty that he saw all around him, the filth of the open gutters and the overcrowding in the back-to-back slums, where people lived in worse conditions than the rats that scuttled along the open sewers.

He was met with thanks by all his old work colleagues and their wives openly fought back tears as they heard that their husbands had work once more. Most of the miners' children were shoeless and dressed in hand-me-downs. Times were hard for the ordinary working man, and well he knew it. There might be a change in the centre of the city of Leeds but in the backstreets of Harehills and Hunslet, there was much needed to be done to improve the ordinary man's lot in life. He walked back out of Leeds with a heavy heart before calling on his right-hand man Fred Parker and his family. He needed Fred to be his deputy manager and knew he could rely on him to keep the coal supply regular while he sorted the problems of level three and the water he knew flooded it. A regular income would be needed if he was to make the coal deposits at level three assessable and that would mean having someone he could trust as his deputy.

'I thought it was you. I said to Betty: here comes Tom Thackeray; let's pray that he brings good news with him.' Fred Parker had opened his front door before Tom had even walked up the path to his home. 'Well, my friend, have you got what you wished for? Is the Rose saved and do we have jobs?' Fred patted his old friend on the back and urged him inside his humble home. 'Here, sit down. Betty put the kettle on and leave that baby to its wailing.'

Tom walked into the small cottage that was home to his best friend and his family and looked around him. The house was spotless but sparsely furnished, every penny spent on keeping the roof above their heads and their children fed. The flagstone floor was polished to a shine and the pine kitchen table was scrubbed white as Betty tried to pacify the crying baby on her hip, while putting the kettle on to boil on the fire. Tom looked at Betty and noticed how haggard and tired she looked; it was always the women of the family that carried the brunt of the worries when their men were out of work.

'Thank you, my friend, but save your tea; it's late enough and I've not yet finished my business for the day so I can't stay. You'll be glad to know that my lass has bought the Rose. It's in safe hands now and that is why I'm here; I need you to start work for us both tomorrow morning if you can. I'm in need of a deputy manager, someone to help with the running of the colliery, while I see to getting a pump and pump house built to get rid of the water in level three.'

'Oh, thank the Lord!' Betty cried as she slumped down in a chair next to the barely lit fire. She then hugged the wailing baby to her and fell into tears as she realised that perhaps some of their worries would soon be over. The rest of her family huddled together on a makeshift bed in the corner of the room and stared at the man that had made their mother cry.

'You don't know what that means to me, Tom; I'd start work right now if I could. Things were beginning to be desperate; there's no work around here and I've all these mouths to feed. We were beginning to fear that the next step was the workhouse for the lot of us.' Fred hung his head and then raised it up. 'I can't thank you enough, mate; you can count on me, and I'll do whatever is needed to make that pit work. Have you got all the old gang back working for you or is just me?'

'Most of them. Jack Beatey is in Armey jail; he's been done for pinching a flitch of bacon from the butchers on Briggate. Arthur Mason is in the workhouse because he's got pneumonia but most of the lads are back with us and are grateful that I've called on them and offered them work. I can't say it's going to be a bed of roses. Nothing's been looked after since the gates were closed in early summer, so there's a lot to be done in the coming weeks. I have a fella coming to see me in the morning from Worsley Iron Company; I need them to give me some idea how much it will cost for a pump to be fitted and built. Level three has always needed one, but Ellershaw would never spend that much money on his pit, even though I believe that he'd easily have made the money back within a year. I suppose I'll soon find out if I'm right once I know the price and if it can be done.'

'Aye, that will make all the difference; there's a good seam under all that water. We all knew that but he couldn't be arsed to do anything about it, or happen couldn't, seeing he'd spent every penny he had on women and booze. Chance would be a nice thing.' Fred smiled across at his wife as she blew her nose and composed herself.

Tom rose from his chair. 'You want nowt with neither. You look after what you've got; they are worth ten times more than any drink or harlot. Here, fill your bellies tonight; have supper on me.' Tom put a florin onto the table. 'You'll earn this and more besides by the time that pit is how I want it to be run. Now, I'll see you at six in the morning at the yard along with the other lads. Stop your crying, Betty; you'll not be going hungry again if Eliza and me have our way.' Tom looked with pity at the broken woman. Edmund Ellershaw was better off dead and buried; at least Eliza and him would make sure some families of Leeds were looked after and fed.

Tom looked at the man in front of him and sighed. 'I didn't realise it was going to cost that much. I knew it would be expensive but hadn't bargained for that amount. Perhaps I've been hasty with my thoughts of a pump and perhaps Edmund Ellershaw was right not to fit one. I'll have to see if it's all right by Miss Wild; she has the say on major spending.'

'A woman in charge of a colliery; now that does make a change. Bloody hell, these women think they can take over the world. They'll be thinking they'll get the vote and stand for parliament if this government isn't careful.' Stanley Arkwright laughed and then looked at the worry on Tom's face. 'If you put a steam engine in to drive the pump you could also make it operate the winding gear for the cage and bring up the coal from the face. It's safer for your men and a lot less work. It would pay for itself within no time. We've just put the same into a pit at Pleasley, and it soon got rid of their flooding problems. In fact, it worked so well that people complained that the natural springs in the district were running dry as the natural water table lessened in that area. You've no problem getting rid of the excess water pumped out; we will just drain it down into the Aire. You'll need to build a pump room for this new machinery. Where would it go, do you think?'

Tom looked to where all his new employees were busy working, some above the ground clearing the pithead and making the pit yard more respectable, and some below on level one, where the miners knew there was little coal but the seam was safe. 'It could really do with being where the office is at. Could we perhaps knock it down and build an extension on the pump room to serve the same purpose as the one that is standing now?'

Stanley knew, with each question asked, his price to the new owner was rising, but in the long run the alterations would make it one of the best pits in the district, providing Tom Thackeray was right in knowing that there was a strong seam of coal on the level that nearly always flooded every year. 'I know it sounds a lot, but it will be the making of this pit.'

'Could we still mine in level one and two while you are fitting this pump and its workings? We can't afford to lose income and spend money as fast as the water we will be draining away.' Tom was worried; could Eliza afford all these extra costs and had he been wrong to push her into buying the Rose?

'Aye, you can do that. You might have to stop for perhaps a week or ten days until we actually go down the shaft and fit the bottom pumps, but the majority of the time will be spent in the actual building of the pump house and the machinery inside it. It's what Edmund Ellershaw should have done years ago; I told him so last time we met, but he'd have none of it. He knew there was coal down there and all, but he wasn't man enough to go and look for it. He was too busy being guided by his dick, the old sod.'

'So, you knew him then?' Tom looked at Stanley and tried to weigh up if he was telling him that just to secure the job.

'Aye, I knew him, although I don't brag about it. He was definitely not a gentleman. Now, we can do the job and we will do it well and we can start work before Christmas if Miss Wild agrees. So, I suggest you let me go and draw up your plans after I've given the main shaft a quick survey, and then I'll give you a quote on how much it's going to cost and then you should discuss if you want to go ahead with it. I know your money will be precious and that it's a big decision.' Stanley waited for Tom's reply.

'Let me talk to Eliza first before you inspect the main shaft. I know to level one is safe but any further and I'd be hesitant to let you down there before I inspect it myself. I've told my men to stay clear of it this morning; unlike Edmund, I like to preserve life not lose it. This is our first day open since the pit closed in spring and I have a lot to do to make sure things are in good order and safe for all my men.' Tom held his hand out to be shaken. 'I will want you back though; I'm determined to make something of this mine, so once I've confirmed that Eliza is happy with what you plan to do, come and do your survey and then start work.'

Stanley shook his hand and smiled. 'Eliza, is it? Are we on good terms with the woman that owns the pit? Good for you, lad, a woman with brass … get her wed if she isn't wed already. '

'I aim to as soon as she sets a date. But I loved her long before she had any money. Money's never had anything to do with our love for one another. She's everything to me.'

'Well, I hope all turns out well for you both. Just let me know when you want me back; you know where I'm at.' Stanley Arkwright tipped his hat and left Tom standing, looking around him, wondering if Eliza could afford the improvements and if she would agree to them going ahead.

*

'Oh, Tom, this sounds expensive. I'm beginning to wonder if I've not been a little hasty when buying the Rose. You are sure that level three will yield enough coal to make it worth our while to spend all this time and money on it?' Eliza looked worried; the pump was going to cut deep into her savings and she was afraid that she'd lose everything if there was no sign of the fabled seam of coal once it had been cleared of water.

'Believe me, there's coal down there. Stanley Arkwright knows there is as well, as it's not the first time a pump has been mentioned for the Rose. Seemingly Edmund Ellershaw knew there was coal down there but he wasn't prepared to do anything about it.' Tom put his hand through his hair and smiled at Eliza. 'Trust me, I'd not see you destitute. I crave a better life, too; I don't ever want to have to work for the Ellershaws of the world ever again.'

'If you are sure, then yes tell him to come back and do his survey. The money I raise from selling here at Airedale Mansions should go a long way to paying for the pump and I'll just have to wait for my ideas with decorating my new home at Highfield.' Eliza looked around her; she'd hoped at first to rent out her first home instead of selling it but now she had no choice if she wanted to make sure her bank balance was as full as she was content with. She sighed; she had really been looking forward to choosing furnishings for her new home but now they would have to wait. Long-term success was more important to her than any fancy trappings, and, if Tom was right, there'd be money in the future if the golden seam of coal was there.

Chapter 17

'I want you to know that I don't agree for one minute that you are having a Christmas Ball this year, nor that you are marrying Mary-Anne Wild come spring. We've lost your father, and poor Priscilla; this year is not a year for celebration. And that is not even mentioning the disgrace and scandal that your father has brought upon us by leaving me penniless.' Catherine Ellershaw sat in the drawing room of Levensthorpe Hall, sipping her tea and awaiting Mary-Anne and Victoria to join her and William to discuss the plans for Christmas. 'You really do like rubbing my nose in it, William. Not only are you to marry your father's mistress, but her sister, I hear, has bought both your father's pit and our old home for a song, and I'm supposed to smile and be pleasant with the family. It really is too much to ask of me.' Catherine Ellershaw sighed and looked into her teacup.

'Mother, life goes on. How am I expected to mourn two people who made my life a misery? The world is better off without them. I'm sorry, but my father never had time for either of us, and you know that.' William stood by the Adams fireplace and looked out of the arched window, and saw a carriage pulling up with Mary-Anne and Victoria inside it. 'Now, our guests are here; please remember to be pleasant to Mary-Anne and Victoria. Remember, Mary-Anne was as used as the rest of us by my father.'

'Phh ... she may have been used by your father, but she's got you just where she wants you. However, I must admit that I am growing to admire her daughter. Victoria is a very intelligent young woman and she shows great promise now that I have spent some time with her, despite her origins.' Catherine went quiet as the butler opened the drawing-room door and showed Victoria and Mary-Anne inside.

'Good afternoon, Mrs Ellershaw.' Mary-Anne and Victoria both acknowledged Catherine first and then MaryAnne went to the side of William, kissing him gently on the cheek as Victoria sat down beside Catherine on the elegant green plush sofa of the drawing room. 'It's cold out there today. Autumn is well and truly upon us now. The trees looks so bare now that the frost has made them shed their leaves.' Mary-Anne made polite conversation, noticing that Catherine Ellershaw did not greet them with much warmth.

'Yes, it soon will be Christmas,' William said. 'All the more reason for us to gather this afternoon and put paid to our plans for the Christmas Ball and Christmas itself. I was hoping, Mary-Anne, that you and Victoria would have Christmas here with me, at Levensthorpe, and perhaps stay until the New Year?' William looked at his mother as her face clouded over and then at Victoria as she beamed with delight at thinking of spending Christmas at the hall.

'William, think of what you are saying?' Catherine Ellershaw snapped. 'The gossip!'

'There will be no gossip,' William retorted, 'as I aim to make it known to everyone on the evening of the ball that Mary-Anne and I are to marry, and that once married I will recognise Victoria as my own daughter. Besides, there will be other guests staying so I am sure it will not be such a scandal.' William turned and smiled at Mary-Anne.

'That would be lovely, William. Do you not think so, Victoria? Christmas at Levensthorpe; that would be so special.' Mary-Anne looked at her daughter and felt a sense of pride as the young woman composed herself and held back the tears that were so near falling after William spoke of accepting her as his own.

'Yes, that would be very special. Plus I could spend some time with you, Mrs Ellershaw, which would be most agreeable.' Victoria looked at Catherine Ellershaw and hoped that her hand of peace would be accepted.

'Grace will be returning for Christmas, along with George, so my days will be busy,' Catherine said sharply. 'You will have to stay with your mother here at Levensthorpe. I have children of my own who naturally come first.'

'Of course, I understand.' Victoria bowed her head and knew that she had been put in her place because Catherine Ellershaw did not agree with her son's wishes.

'Never mind, Victoria. We will still have a good Christmas; William will see to that.' Mary-Anne smiled at both Victoria and William before sitting down in a chair opposite to Catherine and her daughter. She hated the fact that Catherine Ellershaw wanted Victoria to know her place within her family and would never accept either her or Victoria fully.

'Yes, of course, I will. There will be plenty to do and people for you to meet; I aim to celebrate this Christmas in style. Now, what I need you all here for today is to give me the names of guests for the ball, including you, Mama. I'm sure you have a list of friends that you would like to include; I don't want to miss anyone when I get the invitations printed and delivered.' William smiled at all three women as they looked up at him.

Catherine Ellershaw could stand it no more; she secretly hated Mary-Anne and, although she did have more time for Victoria, she still could not forget how she had come about. 'This is a farce, William. I am going to have nothing to do with it. I wouldn't invite my friends if you paid me. You are going to be the talk of the district yet again! Announcing your marriage to your father's whore, who is only after your money and status for her daughter. For God's sake open your eyes and realise what you are doing. No good will come of it; your father and Priscilla will be turning in their graves. I will stay in my own home along with Grace and George as my guests.' Catherine Ellershaw could take it no more as she stood up and said exactly what she thought yet again upon what she felt was an unholy alliance. She'd bitten her tongue for too long but now, looking at Mary-Anne and her daughter sitting as if they were already part of her family, she had to say something.

'Mother, stop it! You have only just told me how much you enjoy Victoria's company and think that she is blossoming into a young lady.' William glanced across at Victoria as she sobbed. 'I love Mary-Anne and she me. Money has nothing to do with it.' William looked at Mary-Anne who sat with her head down and silent as she placed her arm around her sobbing daughter.

'I'm sorry, William; I am walking home. If you carry on with this sham, on your own head be it,' Catherine snarled at her son. 'And I will not be attending your wedding either. It is a shame for Victoria. I did not mind encouraging her in learning her etiquette and education, despite her being my husband's bastard, but for you to make her yours is a step too far.'

Mary-Anne stood up sharply next to Catherine Ellershaw and let rip with the words that she had been withholding out of courtesy. 'Nobody calls my daughter a bastard! It was your husband who was the bastard; he had his way with many a woman, including my mother. Bugger off and leave me and mine alone. I love your William, and, no matter what you say, I will marry him. And yes, we will have a Christmas Ball here, while you sit on your own in the gloom in the house that William provides for you. George and Grace will not be with you; they take after their useless father and are selfish and don't care for anyone but themselves. Besides, why would they want to spend Christmas with an old bag like you!' Mary-Anne glared at Catherine as Victoria sat on the sofa sobbing.

'William, how can you let this … this harlot talk to me like that?!' Catherine huffed.

'I think it is time for you to go, Mother. Go home and think about what you have said today. Just remember that you are living in a property that I own and that I could soon find another use for it if you were to keep showing your disdain for Mary-Anne. I aim to marry her no matter what and there will be a ball here, the biggest Levensthorpe has ever witnessed. You are still welcome, no matter what your views on my wife to be and her daughter – as long as you keep them to yourself.' William looked away from his mother as she stood for a second waiting for an apology that he would never give.

'Very well, if that's how you feel. I'll leave you and your whore to it. I wash my hands of you all and your threat of making me homeless does not surprise me, even if it disappoints me. I thought you realised that the words I say are only because I love you.' Catherine stood for a second before hoping that her son would beg her to stay but got no response except for a wild stare from Mary-Anne who glared at her as she left the drawing room.

'I'm sorry, Mary-Anne. She had no right to say that. Victoria, forgive her; she didn't mean what she said to you.' William put his arms around both Mary-Anne and Victoria. 'We will be a family and we will enjoy Christmas. We will not let my father's wickedness nor my mother's pride interfere with our lives. You are my family now and that is all that matters.'

*

Catherine Ellershaw sat in her small living room and looked around her. She'd walked back down the road between the hall and gatehouse, sobbing and trembling as she thought of the words said on both sides that afternoon. How could her son take sides against her? He meant everything to her, as did all her children. They had given her the strength daily to face life as she put up with her husband's decadent lifestyle. She'd always been there for them, seeing to their every need and making sure that they all had the right connections throughout their lives and that they wanted for nothing. But now they had all deserted her, not caring about her loneliness. William might have made sure she had a home but he'd not asked her to live with him at his home in the hall, not like the bitch that had at long last shown her true colours.

She made her way to her writing desk and picked up pen and paper and started to write to Grace. How she missed her daughter: the daughter who never even acknowledged her letters that she had written weekly to her. That was why Victoria had been a comfort for her, and she had enjoyed teaching her various things. Just listening to her reading a book had help to pass an hour or two out of her long, friendless days. But no matter how she tried she could never forget who Victoria was and the hurt that went with it.

She sighed and looked at the first line sprawled on the paper and thought of all the friends and family that she used to have. All had disappeared; the so-called friends were the worst. She now knew they had only been friends because they thought she was wealthy, with connections. Now, with all the scandal of Edmund's demise, the common knowledge of William's affair and the fact that she had not got a penny to her name, they had left her high and dry, lonely, and without a shoulder to cry on.

She placed her pen down and screwed the letter up. It was true what Mary-Anne had said; her children were selfish, and they did think only of themselves, even though she did not want to admit it. She should have kept quiet and not expressed her opinions. William was obviously in love with the woman and would always take her side instead of standing by his mother. And now she had lost the one person that had the time of day for her by calling her a bastard. She should not have said that to the child; she was not to blame. She sobbed and looked out of the window at the late autumn day. It was going to be a long winter. Perhaps she would be better dead in the grave; she'd be at peace then, she thought, as she wiped away a tear, gathering her thoughts quickly as her maid knocked on the living room door.

'Excuse me, ma'am, but you have a visitor.' The maid stood quietly at the door as Victoria made herself known to Catherine.

She stood trembling with tears in her eyes. 'I know why you said the words that you did. I know that it must be hard to look at me and my mother and not to think the worst of us both. But my mother loves your son, and I enjoy coming here and being with you. I'm sorry I'm who I am, but I can't help it, nor could my mother help giving birth to me. Please come back to the hall; we need you, and my mother was only defending me like you were defending your son. I don't think anyone really meant the words they said. Please try and forget what your husband did; he must have hurt you. I know you can't ever like us but if you just try to treat me and my mother civilly, I know she will in return. We are both good people, who are trying to live a good life.' Victoria trembled and hung her head. Her mother and William didn't know she was there but she had decided to make an excuse of needing some fresh air so that she could make peace with the woman that she knew probably hurt as much as she did, after all the revelations regarding her husband.

'Aye, child, you have a wise head on your young shoulders. You make this old woman look a selfish old tyrant. Forgive me. I said the words in haste; I didn't mean to hurt you.' Catherine looked at the young lass that she knew to be right. 'Now, how about we both walk back up to the hall, and I will apologise to them both. If they have got their heads set on getting married and having a Christmas Ball, we had better take part and help organise them.' Catherine put her arm around Victoria for a moment and smiled. 'I'm sorry.'

'Nor did my mother; she is too headstrong sometimes,' Victoria whispered as she watched Catherine put her shawl on.

'Well, she'll need to be if she's to marry my William. I'm sure we will have many a fall out over the next few years but perhaps that is not a bad thing. At least we will all know where we stand and that no one is sneaking around behind one another's backs. Now, let's see who we can get them to invite. Is there anybody you have in mind? A good friend perhaps?' Catherine linked her arm through Victoria's and smiled as they made their way back up to the hall.

'I liked dancing with Stephen Sanderson at the Guild Ball,' Victoria confessed. 'I hope my mother and William will ask him.'

'We will make sure that they do, as well as all the eligible young men in the district. Although you are far too young for them yet, it will not hurt for them to know what a beauty you are growing into, and with prospects once your mother and William are married.' Catherine sighed as they approached the hall; she was going to have to bury her pride just for once and apologise. After all, Victoria had forgiven her; now it was up to her to accept what she could not change and welcome the child and her mother into her family, no matter what the consequences.

Chapter 18

Eliza looked around her at the empty rooms of Aireville Mansions. It had been her pride and joy when she had first been able to buy the three-bedroom newly built house, and a wave of sadness passed over her as she wandered from room to room, making sure that all had been packed and accounted for before she closed and locked the door on her home for the last time.

She couldn't count the number of tears and the hours of self-doubt and anguish that there had been while she had lived there. Life had thrown everything at her but she had survived, no matter what. She breathed in and had one last look around the living room where she had sat for many an hour with her beloved Victoria. She smiled as she saw Victoria from behind the lace curtains; she was waiting for her patiently beside the hackney cab's horse, along with the carter with the last of their worldly goods piled high on his cart, as he waited for her instructions. It was a new life for both of them, as Victoria was soon to move into Levensthorpe, once her mother was married.

She knew she was going to miss Victoria; she had given her the fight and spirit to grab life's chances with both hands, and soon she would be living by herself; that was unless she married Tom and they perhaps had children of their own. She smiled at the thought of her sweetheart – she did love him, and he'd been working night and day to get the pit up and running, consulting her on his every move and every penny he spent. She should put him out of his misery and marry him; they would then be a true team. She sighed and walked into the hallway, looking up to where the hall mirror had always hung on the wall, but there was just an empty space there now. Holding the brass key in her hand she stepped outside, leaving the house she loved. She smiled at Victoria as she passed the sale board with sold upon it and then stopped to give the carter his instructions, the big shire horses impatient to get off on their journey as they chomped upon their bits and snorted.

Eliza watched as the heavily loaded wagon made its way down the road to her new home at Highfield. There Mary-Anne was waiting for them, no doubt organising both her maid and her own as she cleaned and spruced up her sister's new home. Bless Mary-Anne, Eliza thought before climbing into the carriage; she was always there for her, even though her head was full of the Christmas Ball, wedding dresses and William Ellershaw,

'Have you said goodbye to our home, Aunt Eliza?' Victoria sat across from Eliza and noticed her moist eyes as the horse and carriage pulled away from the home that they had both loved.

'Yes, I have. I didn't really want to sell it, but the spare money will help develop the Rose. Tom is to explore the lowest level tomorrow, so I will know the state of it by the end of the evening. I'm hoping that it will not be as costly as he's expecting and that I will be able to afford myself some small luxuries in our new home.' Eliza looked across at her niece. 'How do you feel about leaving? It must feel strange to you, too.'

'It does, I've always been happy there under your love and care, and I know that I will still be with you over the next month or two, but then I'm to live with my mother and William. It will be strange; I've never known such luxury. Do you know that there are ten bedrooms at Levensthorpe and over fifteen servants? I'm frightened that I won't know what to do and how to act.' Victoria looked out of the carriage window as they passed Woodlesford station, the smoke and the smell of coal from the train filling the air as it waited for passengers to mount. The train's whistle blew shrilly, making the horses pulling the carriage shy for a second until the carriage driver pulled on their reins and got control of them again.

'Nonsense; you will know better than your mother. You've at least been schooled in manners. You are a perfect lady, and don't you ever forget that. A perfect lady with all her life set in front of her. Make the best of it, my love. Life is too short to look back with regrets.' Eliza smiled at her niece. She'd been full of the Christmas Ball arrangements and moving into Levensthorpe, and had told her of Catherine Ellershaw's disagreement with William and Mary-Anne.

'I will, Aunt Eliza, but you must promise me that you look after yourself for once. Spoil yourself and Tom!' Victoria smiled as they pulled into the driveway of Highfield House.

'Well, here we are.' Eliza shook her head. 'I never, ever thought that one day I would be living here. It's far too posh for the likes of me!'

'Aunt! What have you just told me? Of course, it isn't. If Edmund Ellershaw was good enough, you certainly are. He had no manners or class; he definitely did not deserve what life gave him.' Victoria cringed thinking about her parentage as the carriage came to stop outside the pillared doorway of Highfield House. 'Welcome home, Aunt!'

'Oh, Lord, that sounds so strange.' Eliza gasped as she stepped down from the carriage and looked around her.

'You are here at last! Stop your gawping, get hold of a brush and help me sweep upstairs. You are not a lady yet, you know, not until you have staff under you, and talking about staff, I hope you've got more than this poor maid of yours to run the house. There's enough brass on the door fingerplates and in the kitchen to keep her cleaning every day, let alone anything else.' Mary-Anne stood with her hands on her hips at the front doorway, giving out orders to both maids who looked as if they didn't know if they were coming or going.

Eliza grinned at Victoria. 'Looks like we've been given our orders; there's no chance of ever thinking ourselves ladies of leisure while your mother has her way.'

'No, she'll always keep us both on our toes. God help William; he doesn't know what he's marrying really.' Victoria laughed as she alighted from the carriage.

'Just look at the dust coming out of that drawing-room window; have you ever seen anything like it.' Eliza walked into her new home and looked at her sister dressed in her old clothes and with a scarf around her head and a duster in her hand. 'Mary-Anne, I'm interviewing for staff tomorrow. They will soon have the place cleaned from top to bottom; there's no need to go to town on it.'

'I'm not having folk saying that you are mucky. Besides, let's get the dirt of those bastard Ellershaws cleaned out of the place. A good cleansing throughout; it will do everything and everybody good. We'll show that snooty bloody Catherine how a house should look.' Mary-Anne turned and looked around her as one of the maids dragged a carpet left by the Ellershaws out across the hall. 'Is the furniture on its way? Although you will need more than the few pieces that you have to fill this place. What are you going to do with all these bedrooms? You've even got servants' rooms at the very top. You have a study, a dining room and the kitchen is huge. It's a lot larger than my house at Speakers' Corner. You've done well for yourself, lass.' Mary-Anne looked across at the carter as he trundled the horse and cart filled with precariously balanced furniture up to the doorstep where all three women stood.

'Now, then, missus, where do you want all this stuff putting?' The carter in his shabby bowler hat and striped waistcoat got down from his cart along with his reluctant helper and started to untie the ropes that secured his load.

'You'd better not have broken anything, else you'll be paying for it!' Mary-Anne said as she watched both men start to unload the furniture.

Eliza looked at Mary-Anne and couldn't quite believe that she had put herself in control. 'Just give me a minute; I'll take my bonnet and shawl off and then I'll tell you as you enter the house.' Eliza quickly made her way into her new home and hung her bonnet and shawl up on a coat hook behind the kitchen door.

'What would you like me to do, Aunt?' Victoria looked around her at the bare rooms and at the maids that were sweeping, polishing everything in sight.

'I'll have servants in place by tomorrow evening. There was no need for Mary-Anne to do all this. A cup of tea would be appreciated by one and all, though. Could I ask you to see to that?' Eliza smiled. 'While I tell the carter where I'd like the furniture to go and try to calm my bossy sister down.'

'Yes, Aunt, of course,' Victoria said. 'As soon as our china is unpacked. That is,' she added, as Eliza looked around her sharply when she heard Mary-Anne cursing the carters as they dropped a box and made the contents clatter, 'if it is still in one piece.'

'Which bedroom are you having? Have you decided?' Eliza asked her niece as her washstand from her old home was waltzed past them, the men puffing and panting as they stood at the bottom of the stairs, awaiting their instructions.

'The bedroom at the back of the house, which overlooks the garden and stables. I'd like that one for now, if possible?' Victoria smiled; she'd picked the smallest and the warmest as the bedroom was over the kitchen, so she would benefit in the coming winter from the heat rising from underneath.

'And I'll have the large one at the front, which looks out over Woodlesford. I can't help but wonder which room Edmund, your father, died in?' Eliza hoped that she hadn't chosen his bedroom.

'Don't even talk about him,' Mary-Anne butted in, glaring at the carters as they stopped halfway up the stairs, the marble top of the washstand making their task a heavy one. 'This is your home now; it'll be clean as a whistle by tonight and any remnants of the Ellershaws will have been exorcised good and proper. Now, I'll get that tea box full of china if you give me a hand, and then Victoria can be unwrapping it in the kitchen. It's better that we perhaps break it than these two monkeys who make everything look like hard work. Besides, they have your piano, Victoria, to get off the cart next, Lord help us, it weighs a ton!'

'It will look lovely in the drawing room. I can just see us this winter, sitting in there, the fire blazing and the new thick curtains that I have already sewn hanging up at the windows. And I aim to have a Christmas tree in the hallway; it will look lovely and welcoming. I can't believe this house is mine!' Eliza exclaimed.

'Well, it is, lass; and you deserve every brick of it. Good times are here for all three of us, and it's not before time.'

Mary-Anne smiled as she walked out to the wagon for the tea box full of china, and waited for Eliza to help lift it with her. She still could not get used to being and acting like a lady, wanting to do the jobs she had always done in the past. 'This will keep you out of mischief, Victoria: unpack and find homes for all this china as well as making a drink for us all. The stove's lit in the kitchen; we saw to that as soon as we arrived. It'll not do you any harm to do a few jobs; it makes you realise how lucky you are to be in such a privileged life, unlike some.'

'I've not forgotten that I'm lucky and I don't mind getting my hands dirty,' Victoria said, as her aunt and mother carried the case of china wrapped up in the newspaper to the kitchen.

'Aye, well, another few weeks and you'll have a maid of your own; I'll see to that.' Mary-Anne grinned at Eliza, and she placed the heavy box down upon the flagged kitchen floor. 'I scrubbed this floor this morning; it looks better for a good clean but my hands are sore from using the scalding hot water and soda. Still, it keeps me grounded and reminds me who I really am.'

'Mary-Anne, you don't have to live in the past and feel guilty about how well you have done for yourself. We both deserve a good life.' Eliza hugged her sister. She'd never change, but then none of them would; their humble roots would always be there to remind them who they all were, no matter how they tried to forget.

'Right, well, I'll make a start unpacking this box and I'll put the kettle on the stove. Look, Aunt Eliza, we have a beautiful white glazed sink instead of the brown earthenware one we had back home. All your best Mason's china will look lovely on that large pine dresser and pot rail that's built into the kitchen wall over there.' Victoria smiled as she looked around the large square kitchen that was twice the size of the one at Aireville Mansions. On one side of the room there was a whitewashed pantry to store all the food in, and the Yorkshire range, with its polished lead grate filled the other side; all that was missing was a kitchen table as the one they had left behind at Aireville was too small for the room.

'Yes, it's a good kitchen,' Eliza said to Mary-Anne as Victoria started to unpack her box of china. 'Did I tell you that Madge Bailey, the Ellershaw's cook, is coming back to work for me? She stopped me in the street and asked for her job back and seeing that she was friends with our mother, I said yes, even though she is no spring chicken. I know she's a good cook; Ma used to always say that she was and she'll need the money as she never married.'

Mary-Anne shook her head in disbelief. 'You are too soft. What have you taken that old gossip on for? She'll do nothing but pry into your business and listen into your affairs. I wouldn't have touched her with a barge pole.'

'She's not that bad, and she was close to our mother at one time.' Eliza looked at Mary-Anne and both went silent as they heard the clonking of piano keys from the hallway as the two carters cursed at the weight of the piano. They both walked quickly to the hallway and watched as the mahogany piano was pushed across the tiled floor.

'In the drawing room with that, please, and the red velvet couch and matching chairs go in there as well.' Eliza said, standing with her hands on her hips as she watched one of the maids polish the mahogany handrail of the stairs clean of the carters' mucky fingermarks. It was going to be a long day but at the end of it she would have a lovely new home and tomorrow she would interview for a stable and coach-man along with another maid.

Eliza sat at her newly delivered desk and sat back and admired it. The drayman had delivered it that morning, along with a large pine table for the kitchen and two tall-backed leather chairs, also for the study. He was to return later in the day with an oak dining table and six matching chairs, ordered from an auction house. Her new home was beginning to take shape, she thought, as she ran her hand along the fine beading of the desk and opened the small drawers and looked at the built-in blotter. Outside the hall-way stood four young girls, all wanting to gain a position with her household, and two men that had applied for the groom and stableman's job. Mrs Bailey had arrived at six o'clock sharp and had set about preparing breakfast for her and Victoria, knowing exactly how the kitchen worked and what was needed in order to make the running of the house smooth. She had been no problem to interview and set to work but the people standing outside she knew noth-ing about and would find it hard to employ somebody she could trust within her own home. Eliza stood up and made her way to the door, calling the first of the men to come and join her in the study. She looked at the middle-aged man and noticed his weathered face as he sat down at the other side of the desk from her.

'Thank you for attending this morning, Mr Collins; now please tell me a little about yourself and do you have a letter of recommendation from your previous employer for me to read?' Eliza watched as the man shook his head.

'Nay, I have not,' the ruddy-faced man said. 'He wouldn't give me one. I asked him but he said if I'd anything about me I'd get a job without him having to put pen to paper. I've been working up at Rothwell Manor until they told me to pack my things and go. They blamed me for a horse dying with colic; they said I'd neglected it. I've never neglected a beast in my life, but they wouldn't listen. Then they accused me of being too fond of a drink; they were determined to get rid of me and replace me with someone younger, if you ask me.' Joe Collins cursed under his breath and looked at Eliza as she sat back and tried to get the measure of him. 'I'm good with horses and I'm always punctual; you'll not get me sleeping in on a morning.'

'Are you married, Mr Collins?' Eliza looked at him and guessed the answer; no wife would have sent her husband out looking like he did for the position of the groom.

'Nay, she left me. Ran off with the next-door neighbour and took our seven children with her. Good luck to the poor bastard that was daft enough to run off with her; she was a nag.' He shook his head and scowled.

'I see.' Eliza knew that he was not going to be the right man to look after the horse that she was yet to buy. She needed somebody she could trust, not a bitter, swearing drinker, who, by the sound of it, had been dismissed without a reference from his last employer. 'I don't think you are the right person for me, Mr Collins, but I wish you luck. ' Eliza stood up and offered him her hand.

'Oh, you lot are all the same, you toffee-nosed cow. You've got to look right and have the right reference. Well, I've got neither but I know my horses better than any man.' Joe Collins pushed his chair back and stared at Eliza before pulling a hip flask from out of his coat pocket. 'I'll make my own way out; you needn't dirty your hands on wishing me well.'

Eliza followed him as he walked out of the study, and watched him leave the house after swearing at the remaining man that had applied for the job.

'I'm sorry about that.' Eliza looked at the three young women who looked shocked at the man's attitude. 'I don't think he can handle the truth very well. Please, would you join me Mr ... err, Wilson, and then I will interview you ladies.' Eliza smiled and opened the study door for the young smartly dressed man who looked strangely familiar.

'Thank you, Miss Wild, for giving me your time; I much appreciate it.' The man took his cap off and sat across from her, only when Eliza asked him to take a seat.

'Now, have you got a letter of reference from your employer? I presume they know that you are leaving their service?' Eliza watched as he took a letter from his pocket and passed it to her. She read the letter that was headed in gilt and written on the best quality paper. 'You've been the groom and stable hand to the Wythenshawes over at Methley? They say here that they are sorry to lose you but they are moving to India, so they no longer have a position for you. They speak very highly of you.' Eliza smiled and noticed the man slightly blush. 'I'm sorry, but I can't help but feel that I know you. Perhaps I've seen you with Mrs Wythenshawe when she visited my shop in Leeds. That must be it?' Eliza looked at him and saw him blush again.

'No, Miss Wild; it's not that. You probably recognise me from when I was nobbut a child. I'm Henry, Henry Wilson, from the end house on Pit Lane; we were your neighbours. I was always playing out in the gutter with my marbles, and you and Mary-Anne used to always be teasing me.' Henry screwed his cap up in his hand remembering the poverty that they had both come from and the day that he had run like a hare to get help for the birth of Mary-Anne's baby.

'Never! I'd never have realised until you've said and now it's clear. Well, you look as if you've done well for yourself, smartly dressed and a good job with the Wythenshawes.' Eliza smiled. 'Are you married?'

'Aye, I've got two lovely bairns. They drive my Alice mad, but they are good 'uns really. If I may say, Miss Wild, you've not done so bad yourself. I couldn't believe it when I saw your advert for a groom; I was just beginning to despair and wonder how I could keep my two fed and I'm just hoping that I'm right for your needs.' Henry looked up at Eliza; she was still as bonny as the lass he had looked up to when he was but a lad.

'Well, despair no longer, Henry. You've got a good reference, I know all about you and I remember that you once helped us out all those years ago. I couldn't wish for anybody else. I'll pay a fair wage for a good day's work. Now, do you know a good horse when you see one? Because it's all right me taking on a groom but I haven't got a horse in the stable yet.' Eliza grinned.

'The Wythenshawes are about to sell their team of cobs. They are a bonny chestnut pair, good-natured too. I was fair dreading leaving them. We are used to one another; I know them and they know me. A finer pair you'd not find this side of Leeds.' Henry smiled wistfully, thinking about his horses.

'Then they are our horses. I'll write and make them an offer and tell them that I've employed their groom and would like their horses too. It makes sense.' Eliza knew she'd got a good worker in Henry. 'You could start work on Monday by riding them over from Methley, if your current employer agrees to sell me them. Now it's time to find the right person to be our parlourmaid along with Lizzie. Can you tell the first young lady to come in and join me, please, Henry?'

'Aye, I will.' Henry hesitated. 'If you don't mind me saying, Miss Wild, you could do worse by taking the young dark-haired girl that's waiting to see you outside. She's been working with me at the Wythenshawes; she's only just four-teen, and she's been there since she was twelve years old. Her father got killed down the pit and her mother was left with four bairns to raise. She's had it hard but she's a grand lass; trustworthy too.' Henry looked worried that perhaps he'd overstepped his mark.

'I see, what's her name?' Eliza looked at Henry. She could just imagine the hardship that the family was going through.

'It's Milly, Milly Towler.' Henry smiled. 'She's as bright as a button, despite all her worries.'

'Then Milly it is; you can tell the other girls on your way that I won't be seeing them today out.' Eliza noticed the shock on Henry's face.

'Oh, no, miss.' Henry shook his head. 'She'll know then that I've mentioned her; she's not one for charity and that's how she'll take it. She may not have a penny to her name but she's got her pride.'

'Then I'll interview them all, but if all goes well I'll give Milly the job after you've gone, how about that? You wish her luck and then she won't suspect a thing.'

'Yes, I'd be grateful if you could do that. You'll not regret taking neither her nor me on; we are both good workers.' Henry stood up and held his hand out for Eliza to shake.

'I'm sure I won't, Henry Wilson. Now you go and tell your wife that there's no need for her to worry any longer; you are in safe employment.'

Eliza shook his hand and smiled; she'd made the right decision, and she knew that for sure.

Chapter 19

Tom strode out across the pit yard. Things were beginning to take shape. The stable roof had been mended, hay had been stacked up ready for winter and the new stock of ponies were well looked after by a young lad he had employed. The little dark sturdy animals looked a lot fitter and healthier than anything seen before at the Rose, and that was how he was going to keep it. The coal wash area had been tidied, the giant pit wheel had been serviced and repaired, and the men he had employed seemed to be happy in their work.

Tom himself would have been happier if the pit was more productive; the first two seams that had been worked for many a year were still yielding a decent amount but it was of poor quality and was not good enough to supply the coal-guzzling factories of nearby Leeds. In order for the pit to survive, level three would have to prove to be fruitful and the water pump built and installed.

'Are you ready then?' Tom walked to the top of the pit shaft and slapped Fred Parker, his mate and number one man, on his back.

'Aye, you've put this day off long enough. Let's go and look at level three and see the exact damage that lies there.' Fred picked up his Davy lamp and walked with his boss to the pithead and the cage that was to take them down to the deep depths of level three.

'Make sure them ponies can bring us back up. I promised Eliza that I'd be with her for dinner this evening, and I don't want to be joining her in a box, not just yet,' Tom joked with the two fellas in charge of the ponies that turned the wheel that lowered the metal cage on heavy chains down to the levels required. 'They've eaten enough this last week or two; they should have the strength of oxen.'

'You'll be right boss; we'll watch you.' All four men chuckled but all four knew what Tom and Fred were about to do was not a laughing matter.

'Here, as well as our Davy lamps, I've got us two helmets with oil-wick lamps on them. I borrowed them from Stanley Arkwright – as long as there isn't any methane down there they will serve us well for light. Although you might be cursing because they smell and give off smoke.' Tom passed Fred the leather padded helmet with a small brass lamp attached to it and offered to light it for him with his vesta case before they both stood in the large square iron cage ready to be lowered to the bottom level of the pit.

'Well, here goes; we'll know soon enough if this pit is to be renamed Eliza's Folly if there's no coal down there and if the flooding has caused too much damage.' Tom smiled as the cage slowly but surely was lowered deeper and deeper underground, the winch that the ponies were pulling jolting every so often as they went further and further down, passing level one and level two, leaving the sound of the picks and shovels at work behind them.

'It looks good so far, the walls are still clear,' Tom said to Fred as he gazed around at what he could see by the light of his lamps.

'Aye, it looks sound enough. Look, we're at the bottom. There are the props leading off. Perhaps it's not as bad as we first feared,' Fred said with spirit.

'It's further on at the coal face that it floods badly. The tunnel dips and goes downward; it must hit a spring.' Tom pulled on the rope instructing the men up above to stop lowering them further as they reached the floor of the pit. At once they realised that there were six inches of water on the floor as they stepped out of the cage.

'There are enough bloody rats down here. Look at the buggers; you'd think there'd be nothing down here for them to live on.' Fred kicked one that went swimming by him and swore.

'They are worse on the other two levels; I've seen them move in packs under my feet before today.' Tom walked on, shining his helmet light ahead of him and holding his Davy lamp up to inspect the sides of the tunnel. 'It's not that bad, you know; I think I can let Stanley Arkwright down this far, and then we'll see what he uncovers as his pumps drain more water away. Are you game to walk a bit further? The level is rising now we are heading away from the mine.' Tom turned to look at Fred; the water was beginning to rise above his knee and the pit walls were running wet with seepage off the land above.

'Aye, but not that far; we both know that there is coal down here but I'm not prepared to drown for it. Let Arkwright down with his pumps first and then we can see what damage the flooding's done.' Fred didn't mind the dark but the dark and water was not a mix he liked.

'Look, the props are still strong; that's probably because they were put in before old Ellershaw was skint.' Tom pulled on one of the beams and laughed at Fred as a family of rats jumped on his shoulder after being disturbed from their nest up above him, and he thrashed about in the water. Their long tails wrapped around his face and throat as they wriggled and squeaked at the invader in their home.

'I hate these bloody things.' Fred swung his shovel out at the creatures as they jumped off him and tried to escape into the dark, but in doing so he hit one of the roof stays with an almighty crack. 'Oh, bollocks, I didn't mean to do that.' Both Tom and Fred stood in their tracks as they waited for any repercussions from the thoughtless action.

'You could have brought the roof down, you silly bugger,' Tom said as they both held their breaths and waited for what seemed to be an age. 'You go back to the cage and I'll just walk a few more yards, see how far I can get before it gets too deep for me to see what shape the place is in.'

'I don't know if I should, but water and rats are not my strongest point,' Fred said almost relieved. 'Don't go too far; once old Arkwright's pumped it out we can sort it from there. At least we know it's not in that bad a shape.'

'Aye, I'm pleasantly surprised.' Tom held his Davy lamp up and walked further along the mineshaft as Fred turned to go back to the cage, the water rising with every step. 'You are a bloody coward, Fred Parker,' he teased. 'Just wait until I tell the lads up top, frightened by a bloody rat!' Tom laughed and lost concentration on his footing, and as he did so he felt the floor below his feet give way. 'Bugger!' Tom cried out as he went down under the water into an endless deep, dark void, his Davy lamp and helmet giving him no help as their lights were extinguished and all sense of place was gone.

He thrashed about in the darkness, hoping that he was heading for the safety of the pit and that Fred had heard his cry of help. His lungs filled with water and life itself seem to pass by as he thought that his time had come. Then, when he was beginning to lose hope, he saw the glimmer of Fred's mining helmet lamp above him, shining like a celestial star in the blackness.

Fred grabbed Tom by his jacket and hauled him up through the water. 'I'll not let you drown, my old mate.'

Tom gasped for air, choking and spluttering as he fought for his life as he splayed his arms out for Fred to catch and for him to keep out of the dark depths below.

'That's it, mate, I've got you. Come on, you are nearly out, just stand up and put your arm around me.' Fred puffed and heaved as he tried to make Tom put his arm around his shoulder as he pulled him out of the seemingly bottomless well and dragged him back to the safety of lower water and the cage. 'You silly bugger, you were nearly a gonner.' Fred sat exhausted as Tom gasped for air and coughed and spluttered the black mine water out of his lungs. 'Well, you've found your spring and why it's flooding, but was it worth nearly losing your life for it?' Fred gasped. 'Let's get you back up top and then get you warmed up before you are just fit to bury.' Fred looked at his boss lying nearly helpless in the metal cage as he signalled to the cage operators that they needed to be pulled up to the surface. He'd had a close call, that was for sure; now he needed to be looked after and recover.

*

'Oh, my goodness, Tom are you all right?' Eliza exclaimed as Fred Parker and another man from the Rose helped her sweetheart into the hallway of Highfield House.

'I thought he was best being brought here, Miss Eliza. He's no one to look after him at home,' Fred said, as he looked at the shock on Eliza's face. 'The silly bugger decided he was going to drown himself ... fell down a spring in the mine. He didn't do a good enough job of it though, because he's still with us, mind.' Fred laughed as Tom tried to protest at being brought to Eliza to be looked after.

'I'm all right,' Tom gasped. 'I could have looked after myself.' Tom's clothes were dripping wet and filthy with coal dust and muck from the mine, and his face was whiter than white.

'You certainly are not. Fred did the right thing. Now let's get you upstairs and into a spare bed. I'll get Lizzie to make you up a hot water bottle and I'll send for the doctor.' Eliza followed all three up the stairs and into one of the newly furnished spare rooms, the two men supporting Tom on either side as he sat down in a chair as Eliza made ready the bed.

'I'm all right, I tell you,' Tom protested, as Fred took his jacket off from him and pulled his boots, socks, and trousers off his feet and legs. 'You'd better avert your eyes, Eliza, if you don't want to see any more of your man before he puts a ring on your finger.' Fred grinned as he took off Tom's sodden muffler, shirt and vest, just leaving him in his drawers and with Tom too weak to argue.

'Now's not the time for modesty. Besides, if you've seen one man naked you've seen them all.' Eliza blushed as Tom was stripped and then put into the comfort of a warm clean bed as Lizzie came in with a stone water bottle and some clean water to wash his face with.

'I'll do that, Lizzie. Can you send a message for Doctor Thwaite to come as soon as possible and tell him what has happened, that Mr Thackeray has nearly drowned.' Eliza looked down at Tom as he closed his eyes and moaned a soft protest. 'You stubborn man. You could die, then what would I do?'

228

'Yes, Ma'am, I'll go straight away.' Lizzie curtsied and left the room.

'Aye,' Fred said, 'now I know that he's in safe hands, we will be away too. Don't worry about the mine; I'll look after it until he gets back on his feet.' He tipped his cap and smiled. 'You behave yourself, mate; do as you're told for once.' He and his workman turned to leave.

'Fred, there's coal down there,' Tom whispered huskily, 'the seam's huge – it runs under the spring that I fell in. I saw it!'

'Never mind that now. We'll deal with that when that part's pumped out and made safe once you are back on your feet again.' Fred shook his head; how could he have seen a coal seam in the darkness amidst the confusion of drowning? It would be his brain playing tricks on him as he fought for his life.

'I did, I saw it. Tell Arkwright to make a start,' Tom whispered and then breathed in deeply before falling to sleep in exhaustion.

'Thank you, Fred; it's a good job you were there.' Eliza smiled at Tom's best friend who shook his head as he left the room.

She breathed in deeply and sat down in the chair next to her beloved Tom, reaching for the face flannel out of the dish of warm water that Lizzie had brought for him to be washed in. She wrung the flannel out and gently wiped Tom's sleeping face clean and brushed his brown hair back with her fingers. She loved him so much and the shock of nearly losing him had made her realise just how badly she did love him.

'I will marry you, Tom Thackeray,' she whispered to the sleeping Tom. 'As soon as you are well enough, we will walk down that aisle together. Money is not everything.', She kissed him gently on his brow before she got up to wait for the doctor to arrive. She glanced back at him as she closed the bedroom door; she wasn't going to let this man slip through her fingers again. She would wed him just as soon as it could be arranged, and she had kept him waiting long enough.

'Just stop complaining and stay in bed another day.' Eliza put the lunch tray down on the bed covers and sat down by Tom's side. 'The doctor says that you have to rest. Just be lucky that you are not six foot under. If it hadn't been for Fred, you would have been.' She reached for Tom's hand as he grumbled about being kept in bed for yet another day.

'I need to get up and get back to work,' Tom complained with a sigh. 'Arkwright will need to know that he can start work with the pump and pump house, and to be told where that gaping big hole is that I fell into.'

'All's in hand; Fred has dealt with it and I went up to the pit while you were asleep this morning to see Mr Arkwright and verify the plans that he's drawn up with Fred. He was a bit abrupt; I don't think he liked dealing with a woman, but he soon changed his tune when I wrote him a cheque as a deposit for his work and to show him good faith.' Eliza tucked the covers in around Tom and smiled. 'Mary-Anne's getting her way too. He says the office has to go if there's to be a pump room, so she'll be glad about that.'

'Aye, she will. You are sure the pit was all right, that Fred is coping with everything?' Tom looked down at his lunch and then decided it was futile to worry further; Eliza would not let him out of bed no matter what.

'Yes, the Rose is running smoothly. They'll manage without you for a week. Besides, Tom Thackeray, you have bigger things to worry about.' She smiled.

'Oh, what's that? What's wrong now?'

'We've a wedding to plan! I've been making you wait for me when all the time I have loved you so much. Your near-death experience has made me realise how foolish and selfish I've been. So, Tom Thackeray: yes, I will marry you. Let's make it as soon as possible and not waste any more time.' Eliza leaned forward and kissed her beloved Tom as he gasped and couldn't believe what he was hearing.

'You mean it? This time if I go to the minister and ask him to wed us, you'll not let me down?'

'Yes, go, the sooner the better. We could make it a small Christmas wedding or how about getting married on New Year's Day? A new year and a new start. My grandparents got married on New Year's Day and they loved each other so much.' Eliza grinned and nearly sobbed as she saw the excitement on Tom's face.

'Oh, Eliza, that would make me so happy. To be wed and have you forever: that's all I have ever wanted. We'll be happy, I promise, and when the mine starts making money, there's nothing that we could wish for more.' Tom held her tight, trying not to unbalance the lunch tray with his cup of tea and sandwiches on it.

'There might be something that I'd like more, Tom; perhaps the sound of tiny feet running around Highfield Hall would make our lives complete, if God is willing. I'll be losing Victoria out of my care soon and I'd like to have a child of my own.' Eliza blushed. 'If it's not too late.'

'We will have a half dozen if we can and they will all be as beautiful and as clever as their mother. Oh, my Lord, it was worth falling down that hole and nearly drowning, just for you to agree to marry me,' Tom said in excitement. 'Never mind the Rose, first port of call when I'm up is going to see the minister, and the first of January will be our wedding day, providing he agrees, and I don't think he would dare upset such a woman of standing in his community. Or, don't you want to do what your sister intends and get married in the grand Saint Mary's in Leeds? I'm taking it for granted that as we would both go to chapel in Woodlesford to tie the knot.'

'No, the chapel is perfect. It's where we first met and I don't want a big wedding; just close family … the ones we both love.' Eliza smiled; what would Mary-Anne say once she told her that she was to wed before her? She didn't want all the pomp and ceremony, unlike Mary-Anne. All she wanted was Tom by her side and for them to be happy; it was not a lot to ask for out of life.

*

Eliza sat back in her chair in Mary-Anne's kitchen and watched her sister's face as she told her the news of her and Tom's up-and-coming wedding.

'You cunning bitch! You are going to pinch my glory,' Mary-Anne shouted and then laughed aloud. 'About bloody time! Get that bloody ring on your finger and get him into bed, if you haven't done the latter already!'

Eliza blushed. 'We've had our moments of late. I didn't want to make him wait any longer, now I know just how much I love him.'

'You are no better than me, you little devil.' Mary-Anne grinned. 'How is the water rat? Recovered, I hope?'

'He is, very much so. The date for the wedding is set and he's back at work at the Rose. He's also back in his own home, now he's able to look after himself.'

'We could have a double wedding or can't you wait that long? ' Mary-Anne grinned and pointed at Eliza's belly.

'Mary-Anne! No, Tom's seen the minister and we have booked New Year's Day at the chapel in Woodlesford. I just want a quiet affair.'

'So you *are* expecting; you must be if you are to marry that quickly!' Mary-Anne grinned.

'I am not; it's just that I have kept him waiting too long, and I realised that when he nearly drowned. Besides, I'm upholding a family tradition. I remember our ma telling me that our grandparents married on New Year's Day; that's why we set that date.' Eliza pulled a face at her sister and looked at Mary-Anne as she calmed down and thought about the news.

'I'm going to be busy: there's the Christmas Ball at Levensthorpe, and various parties over Christmas that William and I have been invited to, and now there's your wedding, on top of mine, which is definitely set for April the second at Saint Mary's. I'm not a shrinking violet like you. I don't want a country wedding; I want the whole of Leeds to know that I've got my man.' Mary-Anne sat down and looked at her sister. 'You have made a start on my wedding dress and a dress for Victoria to be my bridesmaid in. Thinking about it, I could really do with a new ballgown. Do you have—'

'No, I don't have time; I agreed to make your wedding dress as a favour as it's a special day but go into Leeds and buy yourself something. Your wedding dress is in hand and I'm making myself a dress also, so I've enough on my plate.' Eliza scowled; if Mary-Anne had one ball dress she had a hundred, and some of them had never seen the light of day since her or Ma Fletcher had bought them. 'As for Victoria's bridesmaid dress, I did hers first after you chose that pink organza that she liked so much when I still had stock in my shop. It's a good job I made it when I was still at Aireville, else I just wouldn't have had the time, now that I'm still arranging my new home and with Christmas just around the corner. She's got a nice plain blue dress covered by Nottingham lace that will do for when she is a bridesmaid for me, and she wants to wear the same dress that she wore to the Guild Ball for your Christmas Ball, so Victoria is sorted.' Eliza folded her hands and looked across at her sister.

Mary-Anne shook her head. 'She can't wear the same dress twice; she's got to impress now.'

'Yes, she can. And anyway, that material for that dress cost an arm and a leg; she should get some wear out if it. It will not fit her by this spring; she is growing so fast.' Eliza sighed. 'She's growing up, Mary-Anne; it won't be long before she is married with children of her own.'

'I know; at least her prospects of getting a good man with money are a lot better than ours ever were. She won't have to plot and scheme as we did; I'm so grateful to William for taking her under his wing. Although sometimes I know he feels a bit awkward with her; after all she is really his half-sister. Things will improve when she comes to live with us once we are married. Would you like her to stay with you until that day? Or should she come and live with me once you and Tom are wed. You probably want your privacy, two little lovebirds in their newly built nest,' Mary-Anne teased and giggled.

'No, we are not as reckless as you and William.' Eliza suddenly looked worried. 'You will calm down a little once Victoria comes to live with you? She's used to a more peaceful lifestyle, with living with me all her life.'

'Eliza Wild, do you not have any faith in me as a mother? Once married we will be the most respectful couple in the district. We will definitely not be running naked around the hall as we do now when I stay there!' Mary-Anne tried to keep her face straight.

Eliza gasped. 'You don't, do you? Oh, Lord! The gossip! What do his servants say?'

'Of course, we don't.' Mary-Anne laughed. 'Your face! But that just shows what you think of me, you hypocrite. I bet you and Tom don't behave yourselves; it's just that you hide it better. Is Victoria with William's mother today? She seems to have impressed her to the point that she is even forgetting Victoria's parentage now that the air has been cleared..'

'Yes, it seems that they do get on well. I'm glad for both of them. Catherine Ellershaw needs a companion since Grace left, and Victoria will benefit from Catherine's connections and knowledge. She knows who's who and will make sure that Victoria gets introduced to the right people.' Eliza couldn't stop being Victoria's guardian, even though Mary-Anne was now there for her. 'I feel sorry for Catherine; George never visits her, and I doubt Grace will ever show her face that often. She'll be enjoying her new life in London too much. Victoria said that her mother wrote to her and asked her to come back and have Christmas with her; it'll be interesting to see if she does return.'

'Yes, even though Catherine's not been very kind to me, I can understand why. She must be hurting; all her world has fallen apart. We have got stronger and she has lost all status, through no fault of her own.' Mary-Anne sighed. 'She was, after all, used as much as me by Edmund. She's not said a bad word since we had the big fall out when we put our list for the ball together; in fact, she's been quite pleasant to us all. Perhaps she realises that we are not that bad after all and that she can't stop our marriage even if she wanted to.'

'Perhaps she does have my sympathies; she's lost everything, including the Rose. She must dislike me owning that, yet she's still fond of Victoria. I think her bark is worse than her bite. You'll be all right once you are married and living in Levensthorpe; I don't think she will be the mother-in-law from hell. Not like Tom's mother would have been if she was still alive; now she *was* an old bag.' Eliza grinned. There was such a bond between them she hoped that it would never break once they were both married. No matter what, her sister was her best friend and she always wanted it to be that way.

*

Victoria sat at the knee of Catherine Ellershaw and looked up at her as she opened the letter that had just been delivered to her. She noticed the look of sheer joy on the older woman's face as she lovingly opened the letter.

'It's from Grace; she will be replying to my letter asking her to join us all at Christmas. It will be so good to see her again. I've missed her so much. We always go Christmas shopping together and chose presents for everyone and then collapse in a tea shop with all our precious purchases around us. Oh, I do hope that she's returning home!'

Catherine looked down and read the few lines written to her and then held the letter in one hand on her knee as she tried to fight back the tears. 'She's not coming home! She says she's been invited to her new friend's – they have a country estate in Cambridge – and that she will be staying there into the new year until the college reopens.' Catherine pulled her handkerchief from out of her sleeve and blew her nose. 'It seems that her family is of no importance to her any more. That we have been replaced by these so-called new friends, who discuss politics and medicine and don't need their elders.' Catherine's head dropped as she thought about her family and their lack of care for her. 'George is no better; I've not seen him for weeks. William tells me he's making a spectacle of himself with his stupid empty-headed friends around Leeds. I really don't know what I've done to deserve all this heartache.' Catherine shook her head, then seemed to gather her thoughts after her obvious disappointment. 'Have you and your aunt settled into Highfield House? It seems that whatever I once had your family is going out of its way to possess. Although I must admit I was seldom happy at Highfield House; I thought we could have done so much better. But look at me now, living in a gatehouse and dependent on my son for any cast-offs that he sends my way, and on you for the company.'

'Aunt Eliza is happy there; she is to marry Tom Thackeray after Christmas, so it's a good job I am to move into Levensthorpe when my mother marries,' Victoria said quietly. 'They will not want me; I don't feel wanted anywhere really nowadays, although I know I'm loved by them all.'

'That makes two of us, my dear. We make a perfect pair.' Catherine smiled sadly. 'Now, how about we go Christmas shopping together? You can take the place of my Grace and we can advise one another on gifts. I suppose I will have to buy your mother something, seeing she is going to be my daughter-in-law shortly. What a mixed-up family we are! It's all Edmund's fault; I will never ever forgive him for doing the things he did. However, perhaps there was one good thing that came out of his misdeeds, and that is you, my dear. You are all things good in my eyes. And you and I must make the best of things.'

Catherine smiled at Victoria and stroked her hair.

'I am a foolish, proud old woman, but I am learning to accept what life throws at me, child. We will go shopping together but, for now, let us think about what to buy and tell me what your mother likes, because when it comes to her I have not got a clue. I also will have to bury my pride and have to ask William for an advance; I'm afraid that I am totally dependent on other people for my existence at the moment.'

'Things will get better, Mrs Ellershaw, and I'm sorry that you have been left with so much worry. You don't deserve it.' Victoria meant every word; Catherine Ellershaw was not a bad person deep down, and she just stood up for her family – the family that, by and large, seemed to have forgotten her.

'We are going to be busy this December, what with the ball on the twenty-fourth of the month and Christmas visitors at the hall on Christmas Eve and Christmas Day. And then, of course, we should all show thanks to the less fortunate than ourselves and take small presents to those who have served us through the year. Perhaps a visit to the workhouse bearing gifts would not be a bad thing. I must remind William of his obligations to the less fortunate than himself. Christmas is a time for charity, if you have the means; I've always done it in the past, even though Edmund complained at the expense.' Catherine sighed, remembering Christmases in the past with her family around her and the house a hive of activity.

'We always had a quiet Christmas, just my aunt and me, but now all that has changed. I can't wait to spend Christmas with my mother, William and Aunt Eliza at Levensthorpe, and of course to attend the ball. It will be like a fairy tale come true.' Victoria's eyes grew wide thinking of all the delights that the coming Christmas would hold for her.

'Indeed it will be for you, child, but for me, it is a time for remembrance, so perhaps not such a jolly time. So much has changed this last year, but still, life goes on. I will try and make the best of it along with trying to keep my thoughts to myself. No one wants a misery at Christmas, but I fear that's just what I will be.' Catherine looked out at the rain-clad countryside beyond her window; she would have to shed her tears in silence rather than spoil the celebrations. In her heart she could not forget or forgive Edmund for leaving her penniless. This would truly be a Christmas like no other: no husband, no family for her to love, and no money of her own!

Chapter 20

The centre of Leeds was abuzz with crowds of people busily shopping and going about their business, in readiness for Christmas. The smell of roasting chestnuts filled the air and the hurdy-gurdy man turned the handle on his barrel organ at the corner of Briggate, thanking anyone who dropped a farthing or ha'penny into his hat.

'My, it's busy, Victoria, and it's so cold. It looks like it could snow; hopefully not before we return home, though.' Catherine pulled her blue-coloured cape around her and smiled at Victoria. She was enjoying shopping with her new companion. 'Don't forget we promised William and your mother that we would bring a bunch of mistletoe back with us from off the market. Christmas would not be Christmas without a bunch of mistletoe hanging in the hallway for people to kiss underneath. Even at my age I still believe in the romantic tradition of the season.' Catherine's eyes twinkled. 'I remember when the mistletoe seller used to knock on all the great houses doors. You could hardly see the poor man;

he had a long pole over his shoulder, and on to it was tied bunches of mistletoe, but he'd usually sold it all by the end of the day. When I was a little more than your age, all the boys used to chase me with a small sprig in their hands, wanting a kiss. But you only let the ones that you fancied catch you, which was half the fun.' Catherine chuckled as she linked arms with Victoria.

Victoria removed her hand back into her fur muff as she linked her hand into Catherine's. They were both on the hunt for Christmas presents and both had ideas on what to buy as they reached the bottom of Briggate and looked across to Boar Lane where Eliza and Grace's shop used to stand.

Victoria gasped. 'Oh, look at Aunt Eliza and Grace's shop; there's nothing left of it! It used to be so busy at this time of year. I used to love going in there and seeing all the new perfumes and gifts for Christmas along with the ball gowns that were displayed there. I thought that they would at least have made a bit more headway in the building of it, but as it stands it just looks like the foundations have only been laid.'

'It's been too cold and wet. They've been impeded by the weather. By this time next year, the new shop should be open and we will be among those shopping in there, I'm sure. I must admit I miss Grace's shop. I always favoured it heavily at Christmas; the quality of goods was always to be assured; and of course Grace used to give me a discount. But alas, those days have gone; Grace is not with me any more and your aunt has been foolish enough to buy the Rose, which

I doubt will never be profitable. She would have been better sticking to what she knows best.'

'Tom says it will be profitable,' Victoria said quietly, 'once the steam pump to drain the water is fitted. He says that there's enough coal down there to keep Leeds factories going for years.'

'I've heard that one before, my dear, and look where it got me: penniless and reliant on my son who was kind enough to give me some money so that we may shop together today. So, if I was your aunt, I wouldn't hold my breath. Now, let's retrace our steps and walk through the arcades. It should not be as cold walking through them and they are full of wonders; just the right things for Christmas presents. Now, what am I to buy your aunt and mother? I thought perhaps I'd get them the same thing. Last time I walked up the County Arcade, I spotted some delightful pincushions; they were fashioned in silver with a velvet cushion – and I know your aunt and mother are both accomplished seamstresses. Would they like them, do you think? They were in the shape of animals; I think one of them was a pig, one was a hedgehog and another maybe a duck. There was also one in the form of a shoe. They looked so beautiful,' Catherine chatted as they walked back up to the entrance of the recently built set of arcades where all manner of people were strolling, protected from the winter chills by the large glass and wrought-iron ceilings that were home to a number of small businesses of the highest quality. The huge pillars that held the ceiling up were lovingly adorned with gilt leaves, and the walkway between the shops was paved in mosaic tiles, meaning that the long skirts of the women shoppers no longer got dirty and wet as they viewed the goods in every window they passed.

'These arcades are such an improvement to the slums and properties that once stood here. It's brought life to the city. One day I'm sure the centre of Leeds will be somewhere that everyone is proud of. Look, here is the shop I was telling you of; just look at the wonderful array of gifts.' Catherine stood with Victoria looking into the shop window.

'Oh, I like those gloves,' Victoria exclaimed as she spotted a pair of crimson red gloves with black fur on the cuffs. 'Mother would love those.'

'Yes, I can see your mother wearing those,' Catherine said quietly, remembering Grace telling her of Mary-Anne wearing a scarlet dress at the Guild Ball. 'Let's go in; you can buy the gloves and I'll buy two of those pincushions. They may be small but they are sweet, and hopefully they will be within my budget. I'm afraid I've never had to watch what I spent at Christmas before; it comes as quite a shock.'

Victoria opened the shop door and walked into the small deep-set shop, filled with beautiful items, embroidered handkerchiefs, gloves and parasols, small sewing sets and delicate small bottles of ladies' perfume with pictures of violets, roses and lily-of-the-valley on them to tell you the fragrance. It was an Aladdin's cave of all thing beautiful for the fairer sex at Christmas, and Victoria found herself being torn on what to get both her mother and Aunt Eliza as Catherine settled on buying two pincushions, one in the shape of a duck and the other a robin, telling the shop assistant that she would try to give both sisters similar, and not offend either of them with the gift of a pig pincushion.

Victoria watched as the smartly dressed shop assistant – dressed in a white high-necked starched blouse, set off with a silver brooch bearing her name, Eve, upon it – parcelled the two gifts up as Catherine paid.

The assistant smiled. 'Can I help you, miss?'

'Yes, I'd like the pair of red gloves from out of the window, and could you wrap them for me, please? Can I be impertinent and ask where did you get your brooch from? I'd really like one for a Christmas present for my aunt.' Victoria smiled as the assistant walked from behind the long wooden counter and opened the doors into the window space before handing her the gloves to inspect.

'Of course you may, miss. My beau gave it to me. It's real silver. I think he bought it from the Thornton Arcade next door; there's a small jewellery shop that sells brooches, hatpins and rings. It's two shops down from the top.' The assistant took the red gloves, once Victoria had looked at them, and started to wrap them in tissue paper.

'Oh, thank you. I'll go and make that my next stop,' Victoria said, as she counted the money from out of her small velvet posy bag, holding on to the neatly wrapped parcel of her mother's gloves.

'They don't cost a lot. They have everyone's names there and they look so pretty,' the assistant said. 'I was nearly dumbstruck when Charlie gave me mine; he never gives me anything.'

Victoria thanked her, and she and Catherine left the shop.

'She was talkative; I think she'd be better off without Charlie if he doesn't spend much money on her, even now before they are married. Take my advice, Victoria: find a man with money, and one that will pamper you when the time comes for you to start courting. This love business is not as grand as people make out; it only breaks your heart in the long run. Believe me, I know all too well,' Catherine lectured as they walked to the end of the Country Arcade before making their way into the Victoria Arcade upon the same row.

'I need a little time to myself, Victoria, dear; can we meet back here under the clock in about an hour's time?' Catherine looked up at the highly decorated clock depicting William Tell's shooting of an apple from off his son's head that had just been hung on the opening of the arcade, the figure of William Tell deftly making an appearance as the clock struck on the hour, the chimes ringing out down the arcade. 'I'll meet you here at one o'clock; I'm sure you have plenty more presents to buy and I have one or two that I wish to buy in secret.' Catherine smiled. She was going to walk back to the shop and buy a parasol that she had seen Victoria admiring; she only hoped that the shop would deliver it to her at home, else her present would be most obvious in shape.

'Yes, Mrs Ellershaw, I understand; I too have presents to buy and other things. I know there is a sweet shop down here somewhere and I also want to get some sugar mice and some sugar-coated flowers that Cook asked me to buy.' Victoria smiled. She was glad to have some time on her own. She too had a present in mind for her fellow shopper.

'That will be Mrs Bailey, by the sounds of it. So your aunt has kept her on? She always requested sugar-coated flowers at Christmas, to put on the fancies that she makes for Christmas Eve. Tell your aunt to keep an eye on her; she's fond of the sherry, is that one.'

'Yes, my aunt took her on when she came and pleaded for her job back. I believe she was once friends with my grandmother when they were younger. Although my aunt is not keen on her gossiping, at least she is a good cook, and Aunt Eliza also felt a little beholden to her.'

'She's an old gossip, but her heart is in the right place. She was good to me after Edmund died. She was loyal and that counts for a lot.' Catherine breathed in deeply as the clock movement finished chiming above their heads. 'I'll see you at one and then we must make haste home with our mistletoe and trimmings; we are both to help in decorating the hall tomorrow and I need to reserve my energy for the coming days. I may be officially still in mourning, but I'm sure Edmund would not have forsaken Christmas upon my death, so I'm not wasting my time skulking over him. Life is too short and I'm afraid I am beginning to agree with William: you have got to make the most of each day, no matter what. Now, one o'clock, don't be late!'

Victoria watched as Catherine Ellershaw disappeared into the crowds, leaving her wondering which shop to visit first.

She followed the shop assistant's advice and stopped to look within the window of the jeweller's shop. There was, as she had said, hatpins, brooches, belt buckles, lockets and all kinds of beautiful jewellery, some at far too large a price for Victoria's meagre purse, but she decided to enter and ask to look at the brooch that had taken her eye.

The shop was narrow and filled to the brim with all kinds of jewellery that glittered and shone in the shop's flickering gaslight. She spotted a tray on one of the shelves; it was padded with blue velvet and had an assortment of silver brooches, all beautifully patterned with a variety of names etched upon them. She looked at the price tag of a florin each; that was just the right amount of money for her to pay, and they looked so apt for her dear Aunt Eliza. She picked up a heart-shaped one with the name Eliza etched on it but put it back down as she spotted a delicate silver brooch with blue enamelling on in the shape of blue forget-me-nots and the letters Forget Me Not upon it. That was the one she was going to buy her aunt; after all, she didn't want to be forgotten by her once she had moved into the hall with her mother, although she knew in her heart that she never would be forgotten by dear Aunt Eliza.

'Could I buy this brooch, please, and could I look at the hatpin just there, the one with pheasant feathers on it?' Victoria pointed to a silver-ended hatpin with pheasant feathers of orange and brown clasped upon it.

When it was brought to her, she picked it up and looked at it; the hatpin was ideal for Catherine Ellershaw, she thought, as she added the price of the brooch and hatpin together before buying them both, thanking the assistant and stepping back out into the arcade. Next was the sweet shop, whose windows were crowded with excited children looking at all the Christmas confectionary displayed. Chocolate Father Christmases, pink and white sugar mice and pigs, boxes of chocolates with glorious bows upon them; they were all there if you had the money to spend.

The children jostled and laughed as they thought of what they would like good old Saint Nick to leave them in their Christmas stockings by their bed. Victoria went into the shop and bought the sugared mice that she had set her heart upon, and the sweet violets that earlier in the year had been picked, dipped in egg white, and then coated and dried in sugar, crystallizing them for use as decorations upon special occasion cakes and desserts.

Next, she visited the tobacconist and bought a quarter of an ounce of Kendal Twist tobacco for Tom's pipe and a fine-looking cigar for William, which she only hoped that he would like.

Shopping done, and with bags in hand, she made her way back up the arcade, and stood underneath the clock statue to wait for Catherine. She stood quietly watching all the people rushing by with presents in their hands and children pulling on their mothers' hands, wanting to gaze into the sweet and toy shops in awe of what Father Christmas would bring them.

She remembered the time when she wished so hard that she too had a mother to enjoy Christmas with; she had loved her Aunt Eliza as a mother, but had always dreamt of her own who lived in a different land appearing to her like an angel at Christmas just for her. Now, that she was here, she realised that her dreams had just been fantasies, placing her mother upon a pedestal that she could never be true to. Her mother would do as she pleased, although she knew Mary-Anne did love her dearly, and was looking forward to her living in the hall with her once she was married.

Catherine rushed up beside her and placed her bags around her feet as she drew breath. 'Have you been waiting long, my dear? I just had one or two things to do before we have some lunch and then return home. Everywhere is so busy; I'm beginning to regret that we didn't make a reservation for somewhere to eat. Do you have anywhere in mind?'

Catherine and Victoria looked around them at the crowds and pondered where to enjoy their meal. Just as they did so a terrible hullabaloo made everyone turn their heads to the top entrance to the arcade. Making their way down the arcade were three well-dressed but terribly worse-for-wear young men, singing loudly and swaying arm in arm down the arcade.

'George! Oh, my Lord, that is George! Just look at him! What a state ... he can hardly stand up. The other two are having to hold him up!' Catherine gasped and shook her head as the three of them nearly sauntered past her, only stopping when George heard his name being mentioned over the drunken chorus of 'God Rest Ye Merry, Gentlemen'.

'Mother, let me introduce you to my friends,' George slurred, and tried to stand up straight as he looked at the disdain on his mother's face. 'This is my good friend Rupert and this jolly chap is James; we've just been making merry in Whitelocks. They serve a jolly good gin in there, you know.'

The three young men grinned at Catherine Ellershaw who tutted in horror as the shoppers watched the drunken party.

'You are drunk!' Catherine snapped.

'Indeed I am, Mother dear; after all, it is Christmas. Ah, and I see that you have the sweet little Victoria with you, but she's not as sweet as my friend James here; now he's game for anything.' George blurted and squeezed the cheeks of his drunken friend as he swayed in his arms.

Victoria blushed and looked down at the floor; she was wiser now and she knew more of what George was about.

'You disgust me, George; you are worse than your father. Get yourself home and sober up. And as for you two: stop bleeding my son dry of his money, because that is all that you are after.' Catherine scowled at the three of them, and then turned her back on George, urging Victoria to join her as she stepped away from the drunken trio.

'That's it, Mother, turn your back on me,' George shouted as she kept on walking. 'It always boils down to the money with you, or the lack of it in your case.' He and his friends started singing even louder as they wended their way down the arcade.

'Come, Victoria, let us go home; I don't feel like staying for lunch now. George has quite upset me by making such a spectacle of himself. We will purchase the mistletoe from the market and then take a cab back home. I couldn't bear to speak or even see anyone else today.' Catherine blew her nose and fought back the tears. She'd enjoyed her day until seeing her son and his immoral group of friends. No doubt, once sober, he would regret his drunken display and rudeness, or so she hoped, but she knew he would never be the son that she had hoped for.

*

'Oh, William, are you staying at home today?' Mary-Anne lent back on her elbow and looked at the love of her life as he lay next to her in the bed that they shared when she stayed at Levensthorpe Hall. For appearances' sake, the servants always made sure her things were put in one of the bedrooms down the hall but everyone knew where Mary-Anne spent her nights and mornings.

'Yes, the mills can do without me today. I want to be here to watch your face when the hall is decorated in readiness for the ball tomorrow night and Christmas. I know I shouldn't say it, but I do love it when the Hall is decorated and the tree stands tall and proud in the entrance hall.' William turned and looked at Mary-Anne. 'This Christmas my home will be full of love; something that it has lacked for some years now.'

'It certainly is full of love.' Mary-Anne ran her fingers down William's chest and kissed his neck as he gazed up at the ceiling. 'I love every inch of you,' she whispered as he put his arm around her tightly.

'Do you, Mary-Anne?' he teased, as he pulled her towards him and kissed her on her lips, looking into her blue eyes to see the truth. 'Or was it my money that attracted you to me at first?'

'I have money of my own, so I'm not marrying for wealth. You should know that; I'm marrying for love, and tomorrow night we will tell the world, no matter what they think of us.' She kissed William on the neck and nestled her body next to his. 'Let the servants decorate the hall and we will stay the day in bed playing our own games,' she whispered, as she teased William, urging him to make love to her.

'You are nothing but a wanton hussy, Mary-Anne. A wanton hussy that always gets the better of me.' He grinned as he pulled the bedclothes over their heads and gave into Mary-Anne's needs. 'One hour and then we help out downstairs; I always bring the tree into the home so the staff will be expecting me. But for now,' he whispered, as he lay lovingly on top of her, 'let us celebrate Christmas our way.'

*

'No, no not there, Jenny; wrap the ivy around the bannister and then thread the red ribbon through it,' Peggy Appleby shouted at the young maid, as she struggled to thread the ivy, freshly cut from out of the grounds, around the banister. 'That's better,' Peggy shouted up and then she noticed Briggs the butler loitering idly by, listening to the chaos that erupted every year in aid of the festive period.

'I don't know what you are standing there for, there's enough to do. Go and polish your silver instead of encroaching on my part of the world. Or better still, go and get his Lordship up out of his bed. He's too busy making whoopee with that common lass that he's to marry,' Peggy Appleby said curtly. 'He, or should I say they, are holding the whole day up with their cavorting. We can't do much more until he brings the Christmas tree into the house and there's plenty still to do if we are to have the ball tomorrow night.' Peggy's face went as red as the holly berries as she saw the master standing at the top of the stairs about to come down to them to help. She averted her eyes as William stepped past young Jenny, hoping that he had not overheard her indiscretion.

'Looking good, Jenny. You are doing a fine job.' William winked at the young maid who blushed and then carried on with the task in hand. 'Morning, Mrs Appleby. Good morning, Briggs. The weather outside may not be welcoming but I can sense the spirit of Christmas has entered into our old home. Now, be a good chap, Briggs, and serve me some coffee and breakfast; Mrs Vasey will be joining me shortly and then we must tackle the tree. Did the men manage to find a big one from the far side of the estate as I told them to do? Last year was a miserable specimen, but then again, Christmas itself was not one that I enjoyed when I think back.'

William walked across the hallway and entered the dining room, which was already in the process of having the table and chairs put to one side and others added for the Christmas Eve frivolities. 'Perhaps coffee in my study, Briggs!' William shouted to his butler as he looked around at the maids and servants who wondered what to do first, now their master was demanding breakfast at such a late time in the day.

'Breakfast at midday!' Peggy Appleby whispered, shaking her head, as Briggs went off to request a late breakfast for William and his fiancée. 'Since she's come on the scene all sense has been lost.'

Mary-Anne walked down the stairs and noticed the look of displeasure on Peggy Appleby's face.

'Oh, the hall looks beautiful, Mrs Appleby. Once the tree is in position it will look like a picture on a chocolate box. You have been busy. William was just saying that he could leave everything safely in your hands because you have such good taste and he's not wrong.' She knew the housekeeper did not approve of her but had decided to be generous with compliments, just until she was wed, and then she would see that the tart-tongued woman lost her position if she didn't come round under Mary-Anne's charms.

'Aye, well, Miss ... Mrs Vasey, I try my best. It will look fine once the tree is in and the mistletoe is hung. We'll be ready for Christmas then. Although Cook says she will never be ready, that she's so much to do that she doesn't know whether she's coming or going, the poor woman.' Peggy hardly dared show her face in the kitchen as there were geese being plucked, jellies and blancmanges being set and delicious delights of all natures being created and slaved over for the entertainment that was to take place over the coming few days. She feared that a rolling pin or another piece of baking equipment would be thrown at her if she said a word out of place. Poor Briggs would already be getting a tongue lashing, she thought, given he'd been sent to order breakfast for two at this hour of the day.

'And there's William and me only just awake from our beds. We should know to set a better example. Still, I'm sure that you have everything in hand. We count on you, Mrs Appleby. Now, is William in the dining room?'

'No, he's in his study, ma'am; the dining room is being set for tomorrow night, so it's in a bit of a mess. We should, however, have a small table set for tonight's evening meal. He's ordered you some breakfast and Biggs will be bringing it shortly.' Peggy Appleby bit her tongue as Mary-Anne walked across the hallway. Cheeky bitch she thought; she'd know damn well that all the staff had been up since the early hours of the morning and there she was rubbing her nose in it by boasting that she and the master were straight out of bed. Miss Priscilla would never have done that; this one was just as common as muck! A common tart with a brat of a daughter.

*

'How lovely, William!' Mary-Anne and Victoria both looked up at the eight-foot tall Christmas tree that now dominated the large hallway at Levensthorpe. 'Now for the fun bit – to decorate it. We should be grateful that Prince Albert brought such a lovely tradition with him when he married our queen. It really does make Christmas, just to smell the fresh pine that fills the room and once it is lit with candles and decorated with baubles and such like, it will look glorious.' Mary-Anne smiled at Victoria and noticed the excitement on her daughter's face. 'And to top it all I have my family staying with us. Next year we will be truly complete, a married couple with you, dear Victoria, a part of our family. How things have changed in a year!'

'Yes, Mother, and Aunt Eliza and Tom will be married shortly, so that is good too.' Victoria gasped as William came down from off the top of the step ladder, after adding a trumpeting angel to the very top of the tree.

'There we go – an angel for my angels.' William stood back and admired his handy work. 'May she bring us joy and peace this Christmas because we all deserve it.' William kissed both Victoria and Mary-Anne on their cheeks as they gazed upon the tree while the servants added baubles and candle holders to the very top of it.

'May I please add some decorations, Mr Ellershaw?' Victoria asked with a smile.

'Yes, of course, Victoria, and do call me William. Your mother should help decorate the tree too. This is your home as much as mine, and the sooner we are all together the better.'

Chapter 21

The Christmas Eve Ball was in full swing as both sisters viewed the scene before them.

'My Lord, Mary-Anne,' Eliza whispered to her sister, as they stood together in the corner of the ballroom, which was filled to bursting with the cream of Leeds' Society, all decked in their finery, 'you've fallen on your feet good and proper. Not only have you got your own home and money, but just look at the new home you are soon to have, and all of these fine people William knows!'

'I know; I'm so lucky, but you have not done badly for yourself, girl!' Mary-Anne smiled and nodded her head in recognition of people greeting her warmly as they passed, content just to sip her champagne and chat to her sister, rather than join the throng. Carriages laden with partygoers had been coming and going all evening and now the dance floor was full. The gentleman were all dressed in their elegant black and white dinner suits, and the ladies sported the latest in fashion in a myriad of spectacular colours, most wearing elegant hair pieces and sparkling jewellery to match. 'I see Victoria has made herself a friend.' Mary-Anne nodded towards her daughter who was sitting with the daughter of one of William's guests. Both were tapping their feet as they listened to the five-piece band play the latest tunes of the day.

'Yes, she looks to be enjoying herself. Who is the girl she's sitting with? I don't recognise her.'

'She's called Miriam Walters; her father owns half the cotton mills in Manchester, seemingly. She will be a very wealthy young woman someday. Just like our Victoria. William went out of his way to invite her, knowing that she would be company for Victoria. They are of an age and she needs to mix with girls of her own age and standing. Look! See, that group of young men can't take their eyes off the two of them. They know that they both eventually will have money, never mind that they already are beautiful in looks.'

'Money that they will be able to keep to themselves, if they have any sense,' Eliza said, 'now this new bill has gone through parliament. And those young men can look all they like, but there's no need for our Victoria to be rushed into a marriage at an early age; let her play the field first.'

'You and your women's rights; you are no better than Grace Ellershaw! I thought she'd make it home for Christmas, for her mother's sake at least, but now she's gallivanting about the country with her new friends. I may not be overly fond of Catherine but I can understand why she's upset. She needs her daughter at Christmastime. Even George has not honoured us with his presence, though he was invited; he's no doubt swilling back ale with the idiots he keeps as friends. At least William's mother has got someone to talk to tonight, besides Victoria. William asked her to invite her friends – see the women she's with? William calls them the three witches because they are always gossiping about someone or other; no doubt they will be milking Catherine for every morsel of gossip they can get out of her.' Mary-Anne laughed as she looked over to where Catherine Ellershaw was sitting with two well-to-do matronly ladies of the area.

'And she them! Don't forget that she can gossip too; it's only because she's had a momentary slip from grace that she's quiet at the moment.' Eliza sipped her champagne and looked across at Catherine and her companions and smiled to herself; she might be an old tittle-tattle but she was kind to Victoria and that was all that mattered.

William came over and slipped his arm around Mary-Anne's waist. 'Now, what are you two hatching in this corner? Who are you deciding to slay with those tongues of yours? Tom and I have been socialising and doing a little business here and there while you two have stood like hawks surveying your prey. I think that it is time to dance, just to stop you two plotting. Mrs Mary-Anne Vasey, may I have the pleasure?' William bowed and took Mary-Anne's hand. 'Let us show our guests just how it is done.'

'Yes, of course, dear sir; it would be an honour.' Mary-Anne grinned at Eliza as she walked out onto the dance floor as proud as could be.

'They make a lovely couple; they were made for one another really,' Eliza said to Tom as they watched them dance the polka around the ballroom, oblivious to everyone's eyes being on them as they laughed and strutted to the lively tune. 'It's a pity both of them had to go through hell before they realised it.'

'Yes, I believe they were meant for one another. Both have minds of their own and both don't give a damn about the scandals they cause. As for us, it will soon be our wedding day and all my dreams will come true. All I need then is for us to find that coal seam and our lives will be complete.'

'Not quite complete, Tom.' Eliza blushed. 'It would be if we had a child of our own. Victoria has decided to live with Mary-Anne at Speakers' Corner after the Christmas celebrations so that she can spend some time with her before she's wed. What with her spending time with Catherine Ellershaw as well, I'm starting to feel she doesn't need me any more. So, I would like to bear at least one child of my own once we are married and if we are blessed enough.'

'How thoughtless of me. Of course we will have children; a whole nursery of them if you wish, and we are lucky enough. As long as we can support them. I've seen too many miners' children over the years ragged and shoeless because their parents have no money, and I vow ours will never be like that. Fred Parker struggles to keep his clothed and fed as well as keeping a roof over their heads.' Tom thought back to the conditions that he had found his good friend in when he had been out of work, and shook his head.

'I don't think we will ever be as bad off as that, my love,' Eliza said, 'but one child will suffice. Have you thought about what you are going to do with your house when we are wed; are you to sell it?'

'I don't know yet,' Tom said. He watched the couples twirl past him as the band struck up a different tune, this time a waltz. 'I might, but my mother loved the place so I don't really want to part with it.'

'Why don't you rent it to Fred and his family? His wife is a good woman; she'll keep it clean and tidy, and anywhere is better than where they live now. Set them up in the world; everyone needs a little help and you don't have to charge them a lot of rent.' Eliza smiled as she saw the look on Tom's face.

'That's a bloody good idea; I'll do that. Fred could do with some luck in his life. He works hard and he's a good man. It can be a thank you for him saving my life. His wife will be so relieved.' Tom grinned. 'They can even have most of my furniture because I don't need it now I've got such a wealthy fiancée on my arm.'

'Eh, not that wealthy; you'd better find that coal seam, else all might be lost after agreeing on the price of the new steam pump with Arkwright.' Eliza smiled; she knew that everything would be all right really.

'Well, enough of this talking, we are here to dance. I think I can manage a waltz like these fine gentleman. Let's show your sister how it's done. She can't hog the limelight all night.' Tom took Eliza's hand, and twirled her merrily around the dance floor. In a week's time she would be his wife and he would be the happiest person on earth, coal or no coal.

*

Victoria sat listening intently to her newfound friend, hanging on her every word, realising that the beautiful-looking young woman was just as insecure and as worried about her own background as herself.

'My father was thankful that Mr Ellershaw asked me to the ball. He knows that I do not make friends easily. Money cannot buy things like respect and social standing, and, unfortunately, my mother's life was no secret to my father's circle of friends.' Miriam sighed. 'I believe we share a similar history, and like you I have had to come to grips with how I came to be in this world. I must say it is not easy.' Miriam held her hand out to Victoria and smiled. 'Forgive me if I offend; I don't mean to hurt your feelings.'

'No, please, I'm not offended; most people here will know that I was born out of wedlock. I am the illegitimate child of Edmund Ellershaw, which makes things awkward when my mother is to marry William. He's really my half-brother and yet I will have to respect him as a father figure once they are wed.' Victoria dropped her head and remembered her Aunt Eliza and mother discussing the situation together quietly in the kitchen at home, unaware that she was listening in.

'That must be hard for you, but Mr Ellershaw – William – seems a good man and he is madly in love with your mother; everyone can see that. I'm sure he will take care of you, both as a sister and as a daughter. People in time will forget your true parentage, unlike mine. My mother was the talk of Manchester, although as I'm growing older and wiser I'm realising people are hypocrites.' Miriam held her head high and looked around the room as the music changed and a quadrille was announced. 'I bet half of these men in this room have done just what my father and your father did, but they would deny it. It is common to have another woman just for pleasure; the trouble comes when they are found out or left with a child like us two.'

'Is your mother still with us?' Victoria asked, and she noticed Miriam was close to tears as she glanced over at her father who busy talking to fellow business men at the edge of the ballroom. 'Is she not here with you tonight?'

'My mother was French; she … she was a prostitute from the backstreets of Paris. My father had visited her on a regular basis whenever he was in France on business. She'd been his mistress for years, as well as sleeping with other men, but my father, being a good man, paid for her accommodation and food. She got greedy and wanted more from him, telling him that she was with child by him and demanding that he married her. My father, being the man he is, agreed to marry her before I was born. So, he brought her back to Manchester with him and made sure she wanted for nothing until my birth. But it was then he began to have his suspicions that he was not the only love in my mother's life. The surgeon that delivered me told my father that she was suffering from syphilis and that I might be affected by it too. Thankfully I was not, else I would not be here today with you, but as my father did not have the disease, he knew that she had still been sleeping with other men. However, that did not stop him from loving me, even though I may be another man's child. He is kind and loves me dearly.' Miriam smiled and looked across at her father, who had given her everything from her birth.

'And your mother?' Victoria asked.

'My father placed her in a sanatorium and got me a nurse and then a governess. She eventually went insane and died because of her disease. She did not even recognise me as her child; all she had wanted was the money that my father could give her. So, Victoria, we are very much the same. Your father disowned you and my mother disowned me. I think perhaps we should be friends, now we know so much about one another?' Miriam smiled and held out her hand for Victoria to take.

'Yes, indeed. Let us bury our pasts though, and look to the future. We are both blessed with one good parent with enough love to make up for the one we did not know.' Victoria smiled. 'And I have my Aunt Eliza also – it was she who raised me.'

'We are both indeed fortunate. And now let's aim to have a dance.' Miriam giggled. 'Which one of those group of young men should we flutter our eyelids at? I see the dark-haired one keeps looking at you and I keep looking at the tall blond-haired one. Hopefully they will not be bashful for too long, and ask for a dance once the punch gives them Dutch courage.'

'Oh, that's Stephen Sanderson; he was sweet on me at the Guild Ball earlier this spring. The dark-haired one is his friend Terence Rowntree. Both are very well-to-do.' Victoria smiled and looked across at the group of young men who were all looking at her and Miriam. 'They'll walk over this way eventually; they just need another sip of Dutch courage, as you say.

'Then we will enjoy the night, my dear new friend, Victoria. Forget who we are and just dance the night away without a care; after all, we are young ladies of wealth and, even if I do say it myself, very pretty too.' Miriam smiled and then looked across the ballroom, nudging Victoria's elbow as Stephen and Terence Rowntree wove their way between dancers to the two girls. 'Caught! Now let us enjoy Christmas!' Miriam whispered as both girls smiled at their would-be suitors.

Both young men came and stood candidly in front of them, giving their names and asking for the next dance. Just at Miriam and Victoria accepted and stood up to take their places on the dance floor, William Ellershaw asked for the band to stop playing and, in the sudden hush, all eyes turned on him.

William looked the ever-dashing gentleman in his dapper evening dress, and he embraced the silence for a short while as he looked around him at all of his beautifully dressed guests and the ballroom decorated with Christmas garlands of holly and ivy with red ribbons threaded around the room and chandeliers glistening with sparkling light.

'My friends and family,' William began loudly, at last. 'These past few years have been very trying for my family and I, but tonight I asked you here to look to the future and celebrate life with us all at Levensthorpe Hall.' He hesitated for a moment and looked at all the faces that were turned his way. 'It's Christmas, a time to celebrate the good things in life and pay thanks to the Lord for all he has bestowed upon us, one of which I will be forever thankful for and that is my darling Mary-Anne Vasey.' William glanced at Mary-Anne, and urged her to join him by his side.

Mary-Anne picked her skirts up and for once in her life stood quietly, demure and shy.

'I'd like to announce that we are to be married this coming year on April the second, and I hope that you will now all raise your glasses and wish us well.' William hesitated as everyone reached for their glasses and waited for him to say the toast. 'To my wife to be, Mary-Anne Vasey and to my daughter-to-be, the lovely Victoria; may our lives be one of happiness together.'

William and Mary-Anne watched and listened as everyone wished them well with a chink of their glasses and then muttered in hushed voices to one another.

'I've also got another announcement, although Mary-Anne's sister will probably curse me for doing so.' William laughed as he looked at Eliza. 'My sister-in-law to be, Miss Eliza Wild, is to wed her childhood sweetheart Tom Thackery on New Year's Day; I'd like you to drink to their happiness too. To Eliza and Tom.'

William looked across at the awkward, embarrassed couple, and smiled as the room repeated the toast yet again.

'And now my friends, let us dance and celebrate; it will soon be Christmas Day, and we don't want to disturb the good bearded man delivering his presents. Carriages will await you at midnight but until then enjoy yourselves, eat, drink and make merry.'

William and Mary-Anne went and stood back next to Tom and Eliza, and smiled at the couple as they looked lovingly at one another.

'Oh William, how could you?' Eliza exclaimed. 'We were trying to keep our marriage quiet.' However, she was laughing too, secretly rather glad that their marriage had been announced.

'It's more reason to celebrate; besides, it gives my mother and her friends something else to talk about. Just look at them; she's in her element with those two old gasbags, who I knew wouldn't refuse my invite to the ball. She'll soon be back within her social circle now that there are other things to talk about than my father's fall from grace.' William took a long drink from his glass of wine and grinned at Mary-Anne. 'And Victoria is enjoying the evening with her new friend and their beaus. Just look at the four of them dance around the floor; that's just what this home needs: life and laughter.' William sighed. 'It's been lacking it for far too long.'

'I hope there will be plenty of that, William.' Mary-Anne leaned over and kissed William on the cheek.

'There will, but for now, take my hand and let us all join in the last dances. I mean to celebrate Christmas like never before, and I hope you do as well, my dears.' William squeezed Mary-Anne tight; finally his home was filled with noise and laughter, and this night could not go on long enough in his eyes.

'We will join you shortly, but there is just something that I need to do first.'

Tom gave Eliza a curious look as she led him away from the ballroom into the entrance hall, away from the partygoers.

'There ... I've got you just where I want you.' Eliza looked up to the huge ball of mistletoe suspended in the centre of the hallway, just above their heads. 'And now, Mr Thackeray, I need my Christmas kiss.'

Tom took her in his arms and held her tight as he kissed her lovingly and with passion. 'Happy Christmas, Eliza. I'll be counting the seconds until New Year's Day when you will be mine forever.'

Chapter 22

'Oh, my head! I drank far too much last night. But, what a night; I think you can definitely say it was a success.' William sat on the edge of the bed and looked back at the sleepy Mary-Anne. 'Come on, stir yourself, lazy bones. It's Christmas Day; everyone will be waiting for us. I'm glad that Eliza and Tom decided to stay with us for Christmas so that we can spend the day together. Let's go and have breakfast together, after which we can open the presents.'

Mary-Anne stretched and yawned. 'Oh, let them wait. I'm tired. Come back to bed for just one more minute.' She ran her hand lovingly beneath Williams's nightshirt in a bid to entice him back to her.

'No, it's Christmas Day, Mary-Anne; I'm going to go down to the servants quarters and give each of them a sixpence for Christmas and tell them that tomorrow they can have the afternoon off to visit parents and such like, as we will have better things to do and will be out of the hall most of the day.' William stood up and began to dress himself.

'Why, what are we to do tomorrow?' Mary-Anne stirred herself and wandered to the dressing table to brush her long auburn hair.

'It's a tradition that I give all the people that supply us with goods a small present at this time of year, and I always go to the workhouse and the orphanage to give them gifts too. Mrs Appleby has it all in hand; she sees to the list of people to whom we deliver, and what we give each household. It does not amount to a lot – it's but a trifle – however, I know it is appreciated and shows that I am concerned about others welfare as well as my own. It's usually a few sweets or some fresh fruit for the orphans and a small box of chocolates for the butcher and the rest. It just shows that I do have a heart, regardless of what some people say about me.' William came over and kissed Mary-Anne's neck as she plied her hair neatly into a bun on the top of her head.

'If I had my way I'd not be giving your Mrs Appleby a sixpence; she definitely does not like me or Victoria. Can we not replace her once we are wed? And why do you not have someone to dress you of a morning? Surely we should have our own maid and valet?' Mary-Anne held William's hand tightly.

'I've never seen the sense in having one. I like my bedroom to be private, but if you wish to have your own lady's maid, by all means, we will hire one. As for Mrs Appleby, her bark's worse than her bite; she'll get used to you and you her. She really runs the house well and I couldn't have found anyone more loyal when Priscilla was so ill. Now, let's get a move on; everyone will be wanting breakfast and then your Victoria will be eager to open her presents under the tree, I'm sure. You had better return back to your own room; we don't want the servants or our guests talking, and we have a full house this morning with my mother, and your family, not to mention Henry Walters and his daughter Miriam. I'm glad they decided to stay the night; Victoria and Miriam seemed to get on with one another so well. I had a word with Mrs Appleby, and she has managed to conjure up a present for Miriam so that she does not feel left out.' William kissed Mary-Anne once more and then left her to return to her own room while he attended to his duties down below in the servant quarters, a yearly event that he took great pleasure in.

Mary-Anne looked at her reflection in the mirror and thought of Christmases past when Eliza and she had been lucky to have had anything to eat at all, let alone a tree or presents under it. She remembered especially the Christmas when her mother had died, and Bill had walked out on them both. If it hadn't been for the charity of the Simms next door to them, there would have been no Christmas at all. Now, it was she and William who would be showing charity to one and all, by the sounds of it.

She hadn't realised that William was such a charitable man. It would be good to give something back to the poor of society. His father had never done anything for anybody, but William was definitely a different breed, she thought, as she finished dressing. She walked out of her bedroom and down to the hallway where she could already hear voices full of excitement as Victoria and Eliza gazed at the mountain of presents under the Christmas tree.

'Look, Mama, just look at all the gifts!' Victoria beamed at her mother as she joined her sister and daughter standing in awe at the boxes and parcels that were under the tree.

Mary-Anne smiled. 'Yes, we are all to be spoilt by the looks of it.'

'William has been far too generous,' Eliza exclaimed. 'You are so lucky, Mary-Anne!'

'There was me thinking that it was Father Christmas that had left them.' Mary-Anne kissed Victoria on her brow and smiled. 'It would still be nice to believe in him, no matter how old we all are. Now let's join everybody at the breakfast table and then, while we are eating, Briggs will take the presents into the drawing room for us to exchange our personal gifts.'

'I've nothing for Miriam, Mama,' Victoria whispered. 'I didn't know she was staying.'

'Don't you worry, my darling; William has made sure that she's not forgotten, and that she's got a present. Now, come let us enjoy every minute of the day in front of us – a true family Christmas with the ones we love.'

The kitchen was the busiest place in the house, a goose was roasting in the oven, potatoes were being peeled by the scullery maid, pans were filled to the brim with sauces and gravies and the breakfast was waiting to be served under silver tureens, kept warm on the top of the stove until the master of the house had given his usual Christmas address.

William stood in the centre of the busy kitchen and looked at his staff, hesitating for a moment as he looked at the flushed faces of the cook and her helpers before he thanked them all for their year's faithful service. He waited as they lined up, noticing the pots filled to the brim around them and pans boiling on the stove.

'I wish he'd blinking well hurry up,' the cook moaned quietly to the parlourmaid. 'I need to look at my plum pudding, as well as make sure breakfast is served on time.'

Briggs glared at her as William started talking and going down the line with the customary gift of a sixpence a head.

'Merry Christmas and thank you for your service to me and mine,' William said, as he shook each one's hand until he got to the end of the line, ending at Briggs the butler.

'Thank you, sir; it's been a privilege as ever.' Briggs bowed his head and then quickly looked down the line at the rest of the staff. 'Let us wish Master Ellershaw and his family a Merry Christmas,' he said and nodded for everyone to yell, 'Merry Christmas, sir', as they all waited to go back to their work with an extra sixpence in their pockets.

'Thank you, everyone, and as usual, tomorrow you may all have half the day off to visit your loved ones. I'm sure that they will be most happy to see you all, and that you will enjoy a well-deserved rest from your daily chores.' William smiled at his servants as he folded his hands behind his back and made his way back upstairs to join his own family.

'Thank God for that; I'll not moan about my sixpence but bloody hell, I'm busy enough without having to wait to shake his bloody hand,' the old cook said, as she hurriedly went about her work. 'Now, best get that bloody breakfast served to them above and then we can get on with lunch. Move, yourself, Mr Briggs, and don't you scowl at me again today, Christmas or no Christmas!'

A roaring fire took centre stage in the drawing room at Levensthorpe Hall; breakfast had been eaten, William had made sure that the servants had received their Christmas thanks, and now everyone was gathered together with their Christmas presents waiting to be given or received. William stood in front of the fire with the parcels on a table in front of him, ready to gift his guests. He looked at the excited faces gathered around him and smiled at Victoria and Miriam as they sat huddled together, both dressed in their finest dresses, with ribbons in their hair.

'For you, Mother; I hope that you approve.' William passed his mother a neatly wrapped flat parcel.

Catherine opened the present with care and gasped at the lovely embroidered shawl within it. 'You shouldn't have, my dear son; it's beautiful. Here's mine to you.' Catherine passed her present of knitted gloves to William with an apology. 'It's not much but it's the best I could do, given the circumstances.'

'They are lovely, Mother.' William tried on his gloves and smiled broadly. He set them to one side and reached for the next present. He had not a clue what was inside this particular one but it was clearly labelled. 'I do believe this package says Miriam, so this is for our very special guest.' William beamed as the young girl blushed, unable to believe that she had been thought of.

Victoria watched as her new friend unfolded the small package to reveal the most ornate hair comb, beautifully decorated with flowers and butterflies. 'Oh, it's beautiful. It will always remind me of when we became friends, Victoria.' Miriam leaned across and kissed Victoria on her cheek before thanking her host.

'Speaking of Victoria, I have something for you, my dear girl. I know it does not look much, but I hope you appreciate the thought that went into it.' William glanced across at Mary-Anne; he'd kept all his presents a secret even from his fiancée, and when he saw her looking at the thin envelope bound with a ribbon he noticed her looking at it with bemusement.

'Thank you, William; here is mine to you. I hope that I have chosen the right brand.' Victoria took the letter and pulled at the red ribbon to reveal the contents. The expression on her face changed as she read the document that William had handed her. 'Oh, how can I thank you; I only got you a cigar!'

'A cigar is quite sufficient, but if you are to be my daughter shortly, you need your own allowance and your own bank account, so I have put both in place for you. You can't touch it as of yet, but when you are old enough to do so, there will be a nice amount within it. I thought that would prove to you that I do mean to look after you and your mother. And speaking of your mother, this, my dear, is for you. I should have given it to you yesterday evening, but I've saved it for today; I only hope that it fits!' William produced a small box out of his jacket pocket and walked over to Mary-Anne. 'Happy Christmas, Mary-Anne.'

Mary-Anne could hardly hide her excitement as she opened the small box and gazed at the fabulously cut diamond ring within.

'Oh, William, you are too kind. Just look at it shine.' She pulled the precious ring out of its box and slipped it onto her finger; it fitted perfectly. She looked up at him and stood up and kissed him; he'd thought of everything. 'I love you and always will,' she said with tears in her eyes.

'I love you too, my dear,' William said with a twinkle in his eye. 'I know this: our wedding cannot come quick enough. Perhaps we should have been married on New Year's Day like these two lovebirds.' He looked across at an embarrassed Tom and Eliza. 'I'm counting the days when I can call you Mrs Ellershaw. But for now, I have something left for Eliza and Tom, and I'm sure you all need to swap your gifts before we sit down to lunch.'

*

Catherine Ellershaw looked at the nearly cleared table that William was about to ask Briggs to move; on top of it were two unopened presents. One for George and one for Grace, neither of whom had the manners or good-will to join the family at Christmas, no matter how many times they had been asked by both William and herself. She hung her head; no matter how much her eldest son had made her feel welcome, it was not the same as it had been in previous years. She was not in her own home and two of her children had abandoned her, but most of all she did not have the man she had loved all her life by her side, no matter what his foibles were. Life was going to be hard going forward; things had changed and although she knew William would make sure she wanted for noth-ing, she was no longer the fortunate woman that she had once been.

She looked down at the present that Victoria had given her, a hatpin with pheasant feathers upon it; it wasn't an expensive gift but she felt sure it was given with love. She smiled. Perhaps she had made some gains as well as losses in the last year. She would have to get used to her new family; it was all she had left now – that and the re-acquaintance of her two old friends. She'd bury her pride and get on with life.

Everyone was full and content after dining on goose and turkey and all the other delights of a Christmas dinner, the fire burned brightly and glasses of port were being drunk freely as the family and guests relaxed. Victoria and Miriam sat at the piano and played Christmas carols and everyone sang along as evening began to close in. The words of 'The

Holly and the Ivy' gave way to the haunting words of 'Silent Night', Victoria and Miriam's voices ringing out loud and clear as the family listened and contemplated the true meaning of Christmas. The past year had not been good for all but they had a lot to be thankful for, they all thought, as they looked around at the people they loved and remembered the ones not with them.

Victoria and Miriam paused for a second as Briggs came in to draw the curtains on the encroaching darkness outside and light the lamps around the room.

'Look, everybody, it's snowing!' Victoria exclaimed, as both she and Miriam peered out of the window, halting Briggs in his tracks. 'Now it really is Christmas.'

'It is Christmas now, child, Christmas as it should be.' Catherine looked into the fire, smiling through her tears as she thought of the family that was not with them.

*

It was Boxing Day at Levensthorpe and the visitors from Manchester were in a hurry to return home before any further snowfall impeded their journey.

'You will keep in touch, won't you?' Victoria kissed and hugged her newfound friend closely as her father urged their guests to get into the carriage that awaited them.

'Of course, I will; I'll write every day, and Father says you must come and stay with us as well – as soon as you are able.' Miriam hugged her friend.

'Come now, Miriam. We must be away before further snow, and these good people have business to do without us hindering.' Henry Walters shook William's hand and doffed his hat to Mary-Anne, before climbing into his carriage next to his daughter. He leaned out of the carriage's window, waved and shouted, 'You must come and stay with us shortly; you are most welcome at any time.' Then the carriage, pulled by the team of horses, made its way through the inch of snow that lay on the ground.

'Well, that's our guests gone.' William sighed. 'He's a good man, is Henry, and he idolises his daughter. I'm glad you both got on so well, Victoria.'

'Yes, I think we will soon be firm friends.' Victoria smiled and linked her arm through her mother's as they climbed up the few steps to the entrance to the hall.

'Are you two going as well?' Mary-Anne asked Tom and Eliza, as they stood in the hallway with coats and hats on, and their many presents in bags around their feet. 'Will you not stop for luncheon? I know it will be only cold meats but you are more than welcome.'

'Sorry, Mary-Anne, but we have decided to return home. You are visiting the less fortunate with William today, and we are returning to Highfield to have some time on our own.' She and Tom needed some time to themselves out of the glare of so many people; another week and they would be married and there was so much to talk about. Eliza looked at her niece. 'You will be all right, won't you, with your mother and William? Mrs Ellershaw is staying until supper time, so she will enjoy your company.'

Victoria smiled as she remembered the words her Aunt Eliza had whispered to her when she had given her the pretty little brooch for Christmas. She knew that she'd never be forgotten or cast aside by her aunt for, along with her thanks, she had told her so. 'Yes, I'm all right, thank you, Aunt Eliza; you and Tom enjoy some time to yourselves.'

Mary-Anne grinned at the two lovebirds who clearly needed some time to themselves. 'Aye, go and do what you've been wanting to do with one another the whole time you've been here. I've seen you kissing and canoodling under that mistletoe like two young things.'

'Leave them alone, Mary-Anne. We will see you shortly. Enjoy the rest of the holidays and count the days to your wedding.' William took Mary-Anne by the arm and waited for Victoria to join them after she kissed her aunt and Tom goodbye. 'Would you like to come and deliver our gifts to the poor of the parish, Victoria, or would you rather stay with my mother? It's never too early to start doing charitable work. Our father never gave anything to anybody and look how lonely and miserable he turned out to be, lying on his deathbed with only my mother by his side. I never wish to be like that.' William glanced at Victoria, and waited for an answer while she thought about her reply.

'No, I think I'll stay with Mrs Ellershaw. She too needs some kindness shown to her; I saw her looking quite sad at times yesterday. Besides, I'll be returning back home with my mother tomorrow. I want to make the most of every minute at the hall.' Victoria smiled. 'Even though I know that it will soon be my permanent home.'

'As you wish; we will just get our coats and then we will be away. Briggs has already had the carriage filled with gifts for the local tradespeople that we use and a gift of fruit and plum pudding has been already sent to the workhouse and orphanage ahead of us.' William turned and passed Mary-Anne her cape and watched as she placed her best hat, decorated with fur and feather, upon her head, admiring herself in the mirror before linking arms with him to walk to the carriage that was awaiting them at the bottom of the steps.

'Be careful, my dear, the snow is treacherous underfoot. Andrews, take care, we want no accidents on this Boxing Day morning,' William yelled at the coachman as he and Mary-Anne climbed into the carriage, both warming their feet on the box filled with hot coals on the carriage floor. 'First stop at the Green, if you will, coachman.' William sat back. 'We have about six stops with presents, this first one being at Blackett's the butcher's; he is always an obliging fellow and never lets me down with the quality of his meat. I'm leaving him a bottle of port – he's a goodly man who likes a good drink – and then we will go on to my estate manager's home. I hope Briggs has remembered that he is fond of oranges. You should have seen his face last year; you would have thought that I had given him the world.' William sat back and laughed. 'Then finally we will finish up on the outskirts of Leeds at the workhouse and orphanage. I must confess, I don't like staying at the workhouse long, even though they try to make the place look festive. It is a dark, dour place, and the poor souls are ragged and lifeless.'

William shook his head and then looked at Mary-Anne. 'Still, in some instances, it is because some are idle and prefer to be in there other than working. And the children have often been sent to the orphanage not because they have no parents but because one or both are uncaring and gin-riddled. It is truly a sad place to visit but we must show mercy at Christmas to those less fortunate than ourselves.'

Mary-Anne went quiet. She remembered when Eliza had talked her out of leaving Victoria on the very same orphanage steps when she was a baby. She would have liked to argue with William that not all mothers who left the children there were gin-soaked – they were just desperate – but she thought better of it, as they arrived at their first port of call and were greeted enthusiastically by the red-faced plump butcher, who bade them enter into his home and take a drink to celebrate Christmas.

As Mary-Anne gazed around his comfortable home, and talked to his family, she thought that if they had a drink at every stop, the likeliness of being sober once they reached the workhouse was very unlikely, and perhaps that it might be a good thing as she knew all too well the poverty and despair housed behind the walls of that institution.

Presents delivered, and a few drinks worse for wear, they finally reached the workhouse. The large grey stone walls looked even more foreboding set against the darkening snow-filled skies as William and Mary-Anne alighted down from the carriage and knocked on the large oak doors that led into the cold basic world of the workhouse and its adjoining orphanage. William turned around and smiled at Mary-Anne. 'We will stay at most half an hour, my dear, and then we will return home, our duty done.'

'Ah, Mr Ellershaw, how good it is to give us your presence this Christmas and may I thank you for your patronage of our home. Cook has got the plum pudding on the boil already and the children can't believe their eyes at having fresh apples to eat at this time of year. I've told Matron to watch them as they sit at the table, else some will be going wanting, and I know that you supplied us with just the correct amount for one each.' The manager bowed and ushered William and Mary-Anne into the hallway that led off in three directions. 'This way if you will; we are all waiting for you in the main dining hall. There is too much noise, so I have told the staff to stop everyone from talking while they have their lunch. It's because we have allowed the families we have in here to sit together, seeing that it is Christmas. You know that we separate wives from husbands and children from their mothers; we have no time for sentiment or the consequences of men and women becoming too familiar with one another, if you forgive my forthright way of talking.' The manager, who was as plump as the pudding that

William had supplied, led them down the whitewashed hall-way to the dining room.

There William looked at the scene in front of them. The rows of scrubbed pine tables with benches either side were filled with the desperate and homeless, all clothed in the grey and white uniform of the workhouse. The women and girls all wore white caps and a haunted expression, though some dared to look up at their benefactor who, for one day in the year, had brought them something decent to eat.

'All these people and they look so desperate,' Mary-Anne whispered as she looked across at a table with children as young as two and three being made to sit quietly and await the Christmas treat of pork stew and plum pudding supplied by William along with the apples for the children.

'A lot bring it on upon themselves, ma'am. They could work if they wanted. As for the children ... well, they are usually left on the steps as babies and we do what we can for them,' the manager explained. 'They are looked after here, don't you fret.'

'I don't see how – most of them look half-starved to me,' Mary-Anne replied. 'And why would you separate families, particularly at this time of year?'

'Mary-Anne, he's doing the best he can. It's better than dying on the streets and that is where most of them would be if it were not for institutions like this one.' William took her arm.' Now, if you please, sir, let them wait no longer for their dinner. Let my fiancée see that today at least they have one good meal in their bellies and that we have done some good in the world.'

'As you wish, sir.' The manager summoned the workhouse staff to start serving the pork stew, and Mary-Anne and William watched as it was ladled hot and steaming into the wooden bowls in front of each man, woman and child. But no one dared touch it until the manager walked to the head of the room and looked around him. 'Let us say grace, for each one of you is truly blessed with the Lord's riches.'

The room echoed with the mumbling of the prayer and then the clatter of wooden spoons scooping up their only decent dinner of the year, every drop of stew being licked clean from their bowls.

'I've seen enough, William; can we go home, please? I've been down and out in my lifetime but never as bad as this. We must help.' Mary-Anne looked up at her husband-to-be for assurance. 'Surely there is more we can do for the poor souls?'

'We pay for them already with our taxes and our charity, Mary-Anne. I am one of a handful of guardians that try and ease their plight, especially at Christmas. But no matter how much I give, I know there will always be more people to feed and more injustice in the world. Be thankful that we are not with these poor souls, because there, but for the grace of God, go I and you, and I for one will never ever forget it.'

Chapter 23

Fred Parker opened his front door to find his best friend Tom standing on his doorstep in the falling snow. 'Nobody in their right mind would come out on a night like this. Come on in, you idiot; what's so important that it could not wait until we are at work in the morning? Or is it a case of cold feet? You've decided that you don't want to marry Eliza, and you need me to calm your nerves?'

Tom knocked his snow-covered boots on the outside wall and shook his cap before stepping into Fred's small cottage, trying not to leave a puddle on the scrubbed flagstone floor.

'No, it's nowt like that; wild horses couldn't drive me away from marrying my lass, and I hope that you are still in agreement to be my best man. That is if we can get to the church; this snow's barely stopped since Christmas Day.' Tom walked over to the fire that was now blazing and keeping the home of Fred and his family cosy. It was a different scene this time, now Fred was earning good money to keep his family warm and fed. He warmed himself and smiled at

Betty as she looked up from darning her children's socks in the warm glow of the candlelight.

'Are you all right, Betty?' Tom asked. 'Are the children all abed?'

'Aye, they are all fast asleep and all is well, thanks to you and that pit. Can I make you a tea? Or is it a quick call just to sort out Fred's duties for Saturday? You've not long to go now, just two days then your life will change forever.' Betty smiled at Tom as he warmed his backside on the heat of the fire.

'It's nowt to do with the wedding. I've called because I didn't want the other men at the pit to hear what I'm going to say, else they'd all think they should have the first refusal.' Tom gazed around the small cottage and knew what he was going to offer them would make all the difference. 'Eliza and I have been talking. After we are wed, I'll have no more use for the house I live in at present, so I'd thought of selling it. However, she suggested that you and your family might like to rent it at a reasonable price. It's a lump bigger than this one and it's got a garden and no matter what goes wrong, I'm not about to throw you out. Not after you saved my life.' Tom looked at both their faces and waited.

'God, Tom, you don't know what that means to us. It would mean that the bairns wouldn't have to sleep head to toe and that we'd have our own bedroom and the young 'uns won't have to sleep in something like that.' Fred nodded his head towards the makeshift bed that on Tom's last visit had been full of Fred's family. 'We'd pay you a fair rent;

we don't expect charity. You've done enough for this family already; we will always be in your debt.' Fred glanced at Betty who had put her darning down and sat looking hopeful at Tom.

'You saved my life. It is me who owes you and I'd rather see the house being lived in by someone who I know will look after it. Besides, it needs a family to fill it, and Betty here to put flowers in the window and fill the kitchen with her baking. It was meant for you and I'll not charge too much rent, not like the ones old Ellershaw rented out all those years ago along Pit Lane. It's nowt to do with charity; I need good tenants and who better than yourselves.' Tom smiled again at Betty.

'We'll have it, Tom,' she said. 'You don't know what it means to me. Fred knows how I struggle with such a small house and all our family. The outside lavvy always smells foul because we share it with the neighbours – half the street use it. It's a wonder we've not gone down with something before today.' Betty beamed and then got up from her chair and gave Tom a hug and then turned to look at her husband.

Fred held his hand out to Tom and shook his firmly. 'I owe you so much; I don't know what to say. Thanks, mate; you've changed our lives once again.'

'Aye, well, I'm away now before you've got to dig me out of a snowdrift to get me home. I'll see you at work in the morning, although in two days we will be closed again for the New Year; it's hardly worth opening for this week, I always think.' Tom pulled on his cap and winked at Betty.

'You'll be happy in your new home; it's not a bad spot to bring children up in.'

'I really can't thank you enough, Tom Thackeray,' Betty said. 'I hope that you and Eliza are blessed with many years of happy marriage because you both deserve it. I'll see you at your wedding; I'll warn you, no matter what the weather my children are planning to tie the gates of the Chapel yard and they won't let you out until farthings and ha'pennies are thrown their way.' She smiled. Her children had been chattering all week about watching the wedding and profiting from the custom of holding the bride and bridegroom to ransom. 'It nearly took over as being more popular than Christmas itself, what with your wealthy brother-in-law in attendance and the thought of Ellershaw money being given away, if William puts his hand in his pocket.' Betty stood and laughed as Fred opened the door for his closest friend and revealed the wild weather outside.

'There will be plenty of brass for them to scramble and find. The more the merrier, tell your nippers. Now let me be away and tell Eliza the good news; she will be so glad that you are to accept my offer. She'll probably offer to help you move in, although at the moment her head is full of the wedding.' Tom grinned. 'I'll see you in the morning, Fred, and then Lord help me, it'll be the wedding before we both know it.'

After Tom had left, Fred sat down next to his wife and held her hand. 'He's a good man, is Tom Thackeray. I'm proud to call him my friend. I hope that they will be as happy as me and you, my old lass, because we both want for nowt now.'

*

Mary-Anne stood in her finery, wearing a rich red dress of velvet with fur trim on the collar and hem; the bodice was tight and revealing, and she held the red gloves that Victoria had given her at Christmas in her hands.

'Well, at least it has stopped snowing for you. Somebody up above must be looking over you because the weather has been fearful until today.' She viewed herself in the full-length mirror as she waited for Eliza to come out from behind the dressing screen, where her maid was helping her into her wedding dress. Mary-Anne tilted her hat to an angle to show off her auburn hair and slumped down in one of the small, delicate bedroom chairs; she gave a sigh in frustration as she waited for her sister to emerge. 'Victoria looks beautiful – she's waiting for you downstairs with a bouquet – and it was good of the Bentleys to send you some orchids. I don't think I've ever seen anything quite so beautiful,' she said, as she looked at the array of jewellery and pots of potions on Eliza's dressing table.

'Well, how do I look?' Eliza stepped from behind the screen and stood in front of her sister, with her maid beaming at the sight of such a beautiful bride-to-be.

Mary-Anne looked with her mouth agape and then managed to say a few words. 'You are beautiful, Eliza, like a princess from a fairy tale that we used to read about.'

'I know it's only plain but it's of the best quality silk and these little fake pearls took me ages to sew on but I didn't want anything too fancy. After all, I'm not exactly in the first flush of youth.' Eliza turned and looked at her reflection in the mirror and ran her hand down her waist pulling out her cream skirts about her. 'Even if I do say so myself, I don't think I could have done much finer in the time I had, what with moving in here and helping Tom with the pit. And this little veil with snowdrops embroidered upon it is so right for the time of year.'

'You look stunning, Eliza, I always thought you were the bonnier of the two of us. Tom is such a lucky man. If only our mother and father could see you now.' Mary-Anne stepped forward and hugged her sister. 'That dress is gorgeous; I only hope that I look just as good on my wedding day.'

'You will; I'll make sure of that, and William will have a beautiful bride on his arm. Now, let's brave this cold snowy day – we have a wedding to go to.' Eliza paused. 'You know, I never thought that I'd marry; yet here I am, happy as can be, in my own lovely home with my own business, and with my sister and niece by my side. And I know our mother will be looking down from above and wishing us both well when we walk down the aisle.'

'I'm sure she will, Eliza. But now let's hurry, else Tom will be worried as to where you are. William is waiting in the carriage, Victoria looks beautiful – and as for the wedding breakfast; well, Madge Bailey has everyone jumping through rings to get everything ready for our return home. The dining room looks magnificent and ready for the queen herself to dine with us, not just a few humble guests.' Mary-Anne laughed as the maid took hold of her mistress's hand to help her down the stairs.

Victoria turned her head to look at her aunt and mother as they slowly made their way down the stairs towards her. She gasped. 'You look beautiful, Aunt Eliza. Here, these are for you from the Bentleys. They are just the right colour – cream, and pink – and they match your dress beautifully.'

Eliza smiled and kissed Victoria on her cheek as she took the posy from her and smiled at the maids who were cheekily sneaking a peek of their mistress in her wedding dress as they made ready her wedding breakfast.

'Now, let me put Tom out of his misery and let's hope that the weather treats us kindly and doesn't bring any more snow while we are away.' Eliza walked through Highfield House and to the awaiting carriage where William took her hand to help her up before doing the same with Victoria and Mary-Anne.

'To my wedding then!' She smiled as the carriage made its way through the sludge and snow down the high street of Woodlesford, passing near to where their small lean-to shop used to be, where she and Mary-Anne worked so hard for next to nothing. They had come a long way from those days. They passed the tea shop that they had both dreamt about when they were living on Pit Lane, looking into the window at the ladies that took tea there.

Eventually they arrived at the chapel where she and Tom had first become sweethearts. So much had changed since those early years. Now she had more of a future in front of her, she thought, as she walked down the small chapel's aisle, her eyes focused on her beloved Tom and the preacher who was about to marry them. Victoria stood behind her looking just as pretty as a picture, and she smiled as she took her aunt's bouquet to hold while the service was conducted.

All heads turned to watch Eliza as she stood by her man in the sanctity of the chapel. There weren't many guests to witness the wedding but it was how Eliza had wanted it, quiet and intimate with those she loved the most around her. She looked up at Tom as he took her hand, his eyes filled with love as he intently followed the preacher's words through the marriage sermon. He was her Tom, the Tom she had always loved, she thought, as she repeated the same words and vowed to love Tom in sickness and in health and forsaking all others. Tom's hand trembled as he took the ring from out of Fred Parker's hand and placed it on Eliza's finger.

As the preacher declared them man and wife, he kissed her merrily and Eliza fought back the tears of joy. She was married and she held his arm tightly as they walked down the aisle, out onto the snow-filled paved path of the chapel yard.

Tom squeezed her tightly and whispered, 'You look so beautiful, Eliza. I love you so much.' As they reached the chapel gates, they stopped and smiled and laughed; the local children along with the oldest of Fred Parker's brood had tied the gates together as they had promised. The pathway and cobbles had been swept clear of all the snow in order to make it easier for the pennies to be found and the children cheered with red, frozen faces as the men of the wedding party reached into their pockets for any change that they had.

'Here you are, run for it!' William pulled his hand out of his trouser pocket and threw farthings, ha'pennies and silver threepences as far as he could, some even falling into the snow either side of the tied gates. Tom did the same and the children squealed in delight as they stumbled over one another in haste to gather as much money as possible. The wedding group laughed as all the children clambered and dug for the few pence, and Fred, knowing that they had played the game fairly, produced his pocket knife from out of his pocket and cut through the rope so that the wedding party could get to their awaiting carriages.

William, Mary-Anne, Victoria and Catherine Ellershaw climbed into one carriage, with Eliza and Tom stepping into the lead carriage on their own for the few minutes' privacy between the chapel and home. Meanwhile, Fred, Betty, and their children shared the carriage with the preacher, who was extremely glad to be leaving the old chapel behind for the warmth of Highfield House and the promise of a warming wedding breakfast.

Tom turned to look at Eliza and kissed her. 'Well, how does it feel, Mrs Thackeray, now you are a married woman? Do you think you can put up with me and my wicked ways for the rest of our days?'

'Oh, I think I can try, Mr Thackeray. I don't think that you are that wicked. Neither of us is; we will leave that part to William and Mary-Anne. We will just be the sensible couple and love one another.' Eliza kissed him back and held his hand; she was the happiest she had ever been in her life at that moment in time and nothing was going to change it.

*

Madge Bailey was giving out orders left, right and centre. There might only have been ten people and a handful of children at the wedding breakfast but she was determined to get it right. The roast beef was resting in readiness for carving and, as she looked into the large oven she was mistress of, the roast potatoes were nicely golden. The new butler to Highfield had come back and told her that the first course of game soup had been well received and that in another few minutes he would be clearing for the main course to be served.

'Bloody hell, lass, watch that pan of swede,' Madge ordered the new kitchen maid, who had barely turned thirteen, as she wiped the sweat off her brow. 'It's nearly boiled dry. Take it off the heat and give it a good mashing, and don't forget to add some butter and pepper.'

Lasses these days knew nowt, she thought to herself, as she watched the butler come back in with his silver tray piled high with soup bowls, placing them down at the huge pot sink for the scullery maid to wash and clean, along with everything else. She put the roast beef on a carving tray and covered it with a silver lid ready for him to carry into the dining room and serve but stopped for a minute as he stood beside her and started to talk.

'You know, I've worked in some of the best houses in Leeds and Wakefield, and I end up here with this family. What sort of wedding party is this? Some of them, especially that Mary-Anne, are as common as muck.' Reg Dinsdale sniffed and looked down his nose at Madge. 'She's got no manners; she and that William Ellershaw are drinking for England. I dread to think what state they will be in before the end of the day.' He picked up his tray to return to the dining room.

'Now then, Reg Dinsdale, it's a wedding day. Folk get a bit worse for wear on these occasions. What you see is what you get with this family, and there's nowt wrong with that, you snotty bugger. And if you don't like it, you don't have to stay!' Madge watched as he put his nose up in the air and walked away from her.

She dished out the potatoes and inspected the now mashed swede as the young maid stood beside her waiting for any chastisement that was to come her way. 'I've known Miss Eliza since she was a nipper,' she confided to the young lass, 'and if she doesn't deserve to enjoy this day, nobody does, and Mary-Anne come to that. They've done a lot, have them two. They've both come from nowt and now look at them, and they'll be good to work for because they've seen both sides of life. So he can just hold his tongue and you, my lass, should be glad that your first job is in such a good household, because, when it was run by Edmund Ellershaw, you'd not have been safe in your bed of a night. Randy old bugger, he was. Now Tom Thackeray is a gentleman. He'll make Eliza happy; there's no doubt about that.' Madge said nothing as Reg brought back the rest of the dirty dishes and took the platter of potatoes back with him. 'Stuck up, devil.' She grinned and winked at the young lass and then went about her business in the kitchen.

*

It was near the end of the day when Eliza and Tom finally found themselves alone in their new house. Mary-Anne had taken Victoria home with her, despite being a bit merry, and William and his mother had wished them both well and returned home for the evening, along with Fred, Betty, and an extremely tired gaggle of children.

'Listen!' Eliza whispered as they snuggled on the settee together.

'What am I listening for? I can't hear anything,' Tom said lazily and put his shoulder on Eliza's.

'That's just it,' Eliza whispered, as she gazed into the fire and cosied up to Tom, 'it's silent. For the first time today, it's silent and peaceful, and no one is demanding anything,' She yawned. 'I think it's time for bed, my husband.'

'I thought that tonight would never come: the night where we walk up those stairs as man and wife, with the rest of our lives in front of us. It's a dream come true.' Tom picked Eliza up in his arms and held her tight as she clung to him and smiled. 'And one I'm going to cherish every minute of.'

Chapter 24

'You're going to miss living with your Aunt Eliza,' Mary-Anne told her daughter, as they settled in for the evening a few days later, 'but life here on Speakers' Corner is pleasant and you have all your things here. Besides, it will give us chance to live as mother and daughter before we both go to live with William. I'm looking forward to it; you are so precious to me, Victoria. I know I haven't been much of a mother to you but I've always had your best interests at heart and we seem to see more eye to eye now.' Mary-Anne looked across at her daughter who sat next to the fire with the ageing Mr Tibbs on her knee. 'He'll appreciate your company, too, the old fleabag. I suppose he will have to come with us when we move to Levensthorpe Hall, although William dislikes cats even more than me.' Mary-Anne looked across at her daughter, and the cat she had really grown fond of, despite everything. After all, she partly had the cat to thank for her good fortunes. It was strange for her to be sharing her home with Victoria; she would no longer have the freedom to do what she liked, now Victoria had come to live with her. She realised just how much she owed Eliza; her sister had taken over her responsibilities by caring for her daughter through her formative years.

Victoria put down her embroidery on her lap and thought for a moment about what to say. 'I'm sure I'll be happy here, Mother; your house is lovely and I have everything I need and most of all it feels lovely to be with you where I belong. I'll be honest, I didn't know you at first, and even though you sent me regular letters from America, I was angry at you for leaving me. And then, on your return, you still didn't claim me, leaving me with Aunt Eliza, but I know why now. You were waiting for this day when all was in place for us both.'

'That I was, but I didn't think it would end this way. I was after revenge more than anything, and instead I found love, both from old Ma Fletcher and William. It wasn't what I had planned but I'm grateful that it happened that way, because now I can offer you so much more than just my love. You will have everything that your aunt and I never had. Eliza and I had not a penny to our names when we were your age and many were the days when we'd go to bed hungry. I never want you to have days like that. I only want the best for you, my love.'

Mary-Anne smiled at her daughter and looked out of the window. 'Just look at the snow that's falling; it's a blizzard out there. I hope William is taking care coming back from the mills. I think that he's at Kirkstall on the far side of Leeds today, so he's a long way to travel to reach home. It's not fit for a dog to be out in this, let alone a horse and rider.' Mary-Anne stood up and went to the window and looked out upon the white street scene that lay before her. The snow was being blown into drifts along the street corners, and it clung to the side of buildings and blew off the top of roofs, covering everything in a white shroud. 'Maybe he had the sense to stay at home, although I doubt it; he was eager to get his workforce back to work and to fulfil his orders, now that the festive period is at an end.'

'He'll be fine, Mother; don't you worry. I'm sure he could find somewhere to stay if he thought the weather too bad to return home.' Victoria went and stood next to her mother at the window. It truly was blowing a blizzard and she too hoped that William had taken care, and had not been foolish enough to risk his own life in the freezing conditions.

*

William dismounted his horse and pulled his muffler up around his neck before putting his head down and pulling on his horse's reins as he walked through the snow and drifts up the hill out of Leeds, on the road to Wakefield and home. He cursed under his breath as he reached the top of the deserted hill and looked back towards the city, which was obscured by the howling blizzard. There was no one else foolish enough to be on the road in this weather. His legs were tired and his horse was caked in snow and struggling with every step. He caught his breath and looked out in front of him, trying to make out the familiar outline of Rothwell pit to give him the incentive to make it home but could see nothing for the blowing snow, let alone Woodlesford and the pithead wheels. Putting his head down he faced the wind and set off yet again, only to stop a few steps further down the road as he thought he heard a noise on the wind, a sound as if somebody was in trouble.

He pulled his hat down and looked around him, shouting out. 'Hello, is anyone there, tell me where you are?' He stood still, but all was quiet. He must have imagined it, he thought, as he stepped forward through the snow. Yet there it was again: a voice, in pain, shouting faintly for help.

'Keep making a noise, I'll find you,' William shouted, following the weak noise that came from a few yards in front of him. It was then he stumbled across a body, lying half buried in the drift of the gutter, the snow around the figure was stained red with blood. William brushed the snow away from the man's face and gasped in shock. 'George! What the hell! How did you get here? Who did this to you?' William looked at his brother's battered and bruised face and tried to lift him up to his feet.

'William, thank God it's you,' George whispered as his brother put his arm around him and summoned all his strength to lay him across the horse's back. 'I thought I was going to die.'

'Don't worry; I'll get us home. We are not far now.'

George looked dishevelled and filthy, and smelled strongly of drink. William pushed and heaved his brother up over his horse's saddle. It wasn't the most gracious way to travel but he had to get George and himself home and that was all that mattered now, he thought, as he took the horse's reins and trudged further into the whiteness of the countryside, stopping every so often to spot well-known landmarks to make sure he was still on the road home and to check that George was still alive.

The sight of the gatehouse of Levensthorpe Hall had never been so welcoming a sight in his life. He thought quickly as to whether to take George to the hall but decided time was of the essence and his mother's help was closer at hand. William dropped his horse's reins and, without knocking, threw the front door open to the surprise of his mother who was sitting reading by the warmth of her fire.

'William, what's wrong?' Catherine gasped. 'What are you doing out in this?'

'Make ready your spare room. I've George on the back of my horse, and he's half dead!' William rushed back outside and dragged his brother from out of the saddle before carrying him as best as he could through the front door of the house and up the stairs into what had briefly been Grace's bedroom.

'Oh, my Lord, what's happened? He's covered in blood! What has he been doing? Nelly, light the fire in this room,' Catherine shouted to her maid, who looked dismayed as George was placed on the bed. 'Bring some hot water, and bring a warming pan for his bed. William, can you help me take his clothes off; he feels frozen. Let's get him between the sheets and warm him up.'

'Mother,' George whispered as his outer clothes were taken off, leaving him in just his overshirt as William and Catherine pulled the covers over him and the maid put a warming pan filled with hot coals into the bottom of the bed.

'Yes, George, you will be fine now. William has found you and brought you home. Hush now, save your strength.' Catherine put her hand over her youngest son's bloodied hair and shivered at how near death he looked. She couldn't lose him; she'd lost too much already in her life, and as she stood up next to William, she shed tears at the sight of one of her children looking so ill.

'I don't know what he's been up to, but presumably he was on his way here and then the blizzard got the better of him. That doesn't explain the state of his face and why he hadn't the sense to stay in Leeds until this weather cleared.' William sighed as he watched the maid get the fire blazing in the chilly room that had been unused until his unexpected arrival. 'Something must have gone wrong, else he wouldn't have been coming home at all – he never even showed his face at Christmas. I thought he'd washed his hands of us good and proper.' William took his hat and coat off, and shook the snow from it. His mother was now gently washing the pale-faced George with hot water brought in by the maid.

'His nose is broken, and he's got a big gash under his eye.' Catherine did her best to bathe his wounds and quell the blood from flowing from his broken nose. 'Oh! What have you been doing with yourself, George?' she whispered sadly.

'He's been in a fight, by the looks of it, with someone who got the better of him. Which wouldn't take a lot of doing, in George's case; he has never been handy with his fists.' William looked down at both of them and saw the love that Catherine had for her wayward son. 'I should go for a doctor but that might prove hard in this weather, and he might not want to come out on an evening like this. We will have to hope that once George has been warmed up he revives; it's too wild out there to risk a further life.'

'If you say so, William. I'll stop by his side. Hopefully, he'll be all right. The snow has to stop sometime; we will send for the doctor in the morning if he hasn't improved. His wounds aren't as bad as they first looked, now his nose has stopped bleeding and he's been cleaned up a little.' Catherine looked at the bowl full of red rags and water, and reached out to hold George's hand.

'I'll go and warm myself at home and have something hot inside me to eat. I'll send the butler over with brandy and soup for George, but I'm frozen myself and I haven't been lying in a snow drift for any length of time with my lifeblood ebbing away. I will return first thing in the morning; hopefully he'll have enough fight in him to survive the night. Send your maid if he worsens or you need me for anything.' William bent down and kissed his mother on the cheek. William tried to make his mother smile. 'He'll be all right, Mother; he has to be, to give us both something to moan about.' But she was too consumed with her son's welfare, stroking his hands in order to get life back into them.

'I hope so, because I may have cursed him for being so stupid but I do love him; he's the baby of the family, and as such I can forgive him, no matter what he gets up to. You can't be responsible for what your children do, no matter how foolish they are. And that includes you, William. As long as you are all happy, that is all I want for you.' Catherine wiped a tear away as William left her sitting by George's bedside in the dim lamplight with the fire blazing and a blizzard raging outside.

She'd sit by his side until God decided what to do with the life of her son. She only hoped that the year was not going to start with yet another death in the family. Tragedy seemed to be haunting them at the moment, and she had been party enough to the spectre of death.

'Mother!' George whispered, looking across at his mother dozing in the chair next to his bedside. 'Mother, where am I?

His mother stirred and smiled at him. 'Oh, thank the Lord, you are alive. I'd thought that I'd lost you.' Catherine breathed in and sobbed. 'Thank heavens somebody did hear my prayers, she whispered, as she kissed his forehead. 'You are at home with me, in the gatehouse. William brought you here, he found you on his way home yesterday, and we both feared you were near death.'

George closed his eyes and remembered his journey home through the snow and blizzard until he could walk no more. He had been desperate to leave Leeds as far behind him as he could, but he only had William's home at Woodlesford to go to. 'I remember now.'

'Why are you in such a state and why were you walking out on such a day? Did you not think of getting a carriage, or staying at your new home, seeing as the weather was so bad? You never joined us at Christmas. So why was it so important that you came home yesterday?' Catherine had so many questions for her son despite his weakened state.

'I'm tired, Mother, and hungry. Could you get me something to eat and then I'll sleep. I'll tell you all when I'm feeling stronger.' George turned his head away from his mother and pretended he needed to sleep; he didn't want to disclose his problems just yet.

'Yes, of course, George; I'll get Nelly to come in with some broth for you, and I'll leave you to rest. There will be plenty of time to tell me the about circumstances that led to how you were found. I'm just glad that you are home and alive.' Catherine rose from her seat and looked down at her youngest; he was back with her and that was all that mattered.

'Well, I take it he's survived the night?' William entered the gatehouse and looked at his mother who looked tired and wan after sitting up through the night with her son.

'Yes, he's awake, and talking and eating. But he's not saying why he's here and what happened to him that you found him nearly dead on the roadside. He doesn't seem to want to talk about that.'

'You look tired, Mother; go and lay down on your bed and have a sleep. I can't get to work today because of the weather, but my managers will see to my business and make sure the mills are running, so I'll go and sit in with George and try to coax what he's been doing out of him. He's been up to something, of that I'm sure.'

'I could do with a little rest; I didn't sleep much in the chair. I wanted to make sure he had someone with him, in case the worst happened. Don't question him too hard, William; he still looks so ill.' Catherine kissed her eldest son and then went to her bedroom; she was exhausted after her night's vigil.

William took his coat off and followed in his mother's footsteps upstairs to the spare bedroom where George lay, pretending to be asleep in his bed. He sat down in the chair next to his side. 'You used to do that when you were young, in order not to be sent up to your bedroom when we had guests so that you could listen into the conversation until late into the night. Our mother used to call it foxing because it was you being as cunning as a fox. So you are not fooling me. Now, what have you got yourself into, brother, to try and visit my home in such a state and nearly risk your life?' William waited for a reply. 'Someone has given you a good thrashing, that's for sure.'

George turned and looked at his brother. 'I've got you to thank that I'm alive, haven't I? Well, now that I have come to my senses, I don't feel grateful; I wish that you had not found me ... I wish I was dead.'

'I could have left you there if I'd have known that was what you wanted, but then I would have had to live with the consequences for the rest of my life. Anyway, you were shouting for help when I found you; you wanted to live then. I couldn't have left you. So tell me, what is so bad that you wish yourself dead this morning?' William looked at the surly face in front of him and pondered what had gone on in Leeds to make the normally arrogant George feel so low.

'Oh my God, William, I've been a fool. I've lost it. I've lost everything. I've not a penny to my name because I've gambled my fortune away over Christmas and the New Year. I was foolish enough to get into a card game in a room above the Scarborough Taps, and I was taken like the fool that I am, for every last penny of my inheritance. Then, to make things worse, when I'd run out of money, I put my home up as a bond, in the vain attempt to win it all back. I was certain that I'd won! I was just one deal away from having a royal flush, but I lost it all on the turn of a card. And now I've not even a roof over my head.' George broke down and cried. 'But that's not all ... when I lost, I accused Mathew Ketteridge of cheating. He followed me into the privy and gave me a beating – he called me a faggot and said I deserved all that I got. I can't show my face to any of my friends in Leeds,' George wailed. 'I can't let anyone know that I'm penniless all because of drink and cards.'

'Oh, George, you are an idiot. How can you have lost all of your inheritance? Mathew Ketteridge, as I'm sure you are aware now, if not before, is a blaggard and a cheat; he's known to have made his money by his deft hand in cards. As for your so-called friends in Leeds, if they wouldn't help you in your time of need, they're fair-weather friends indeed – leeches, in fact. I suppose they too have bled you dry?' William stared at his younger brother, and could not believe just how naive he had been. He shook his head. 'All that money, George; it should have made you comfortably off for the rest of your life, and now you haven't a penny.'

'When it comes to my friends, I was just glad of their company and friendship. I didn't mind paying for our nights of revelry. But I can't forgive myself for being plied with drink and encouragement by Mathew Ketteridge and his friend, while I recklessly lost everything because of my pride.' George put his hands in his head and sobbed.

'At least our father kept his money for a while longer than you. I've never known anyone to lose such a large amount in such a small time. You've been an idiot. An idiot that we are going to have to now look after. Now, what are we to do? Mathew Ketteridge is not an understanding soul; even if I go and talk to him and reason with him, he will not give you your money back. After all, if you were fool enough to gamble it away, it's your fault. You've got to face up to your sins and admit that you have lost it all.'

'Don't, William, don't be so harsh. I can't bear to think about it. You'll not tell Mother, will you? She's already displeased by my actions of late – she'll probably disown me if she hears of my foolishness. And I know that I've wronged her but she doesn't deserve any more grief in her life.' George hung his head in shame.

'No, I'll not say anything to Mother; she's had enough pain and heartache this year. But we are going to have to cover your losses, and explain why you have appeared at my home in such a state.' William, for once in his life, felt sorry for his younger brother. He'd obviously been taken advantage of by those a lot more worldly wise than himself. 'I'll tell you what, I'll give you a job as one of my managers. The mill at Wakefield is in need of one. You'd be away from the bad company in Leeds over there. Under my guidance, you'd learn the trade fast enough and earn your keep. There's a decent house that goes with the position, so you can be your own man.' William looked at his brother as he took in his suggestion. 'It's that or you face up to the music, and you make your own way in the world. It's time you grew up, George; you can't always get what you want, no matter how fine your clothes!' William sat back.

'Oh God, me a manger of a mill!' George said, aghast. 'But I've no option, have I? I can't live off thin air. As for my cuts and bruises, I'll say I fell when I was drunk and was foolish enough in my stupor to think that I could walk to see Mother after not visiting her at Christmas. Mother saw me in town with my so-called friends before Christmas when I was worse for wear so she'll accept that as an explanation. I promise, William, I'll try and learn quickly at the mill, and I am grateful for the position you are offering me, even if I don't seem it … and I don't deserve it.' George looked at William and knew that without his help, he'd truly have nowhere to go, and nobody would want him. He'd no choice but to earn his living from now on like any other common man.

'It's a hard lesson that you've had to learn, George, but look at this way: perhaps it has taught you that money has to be respected, not taken for granted. It can make you or break you. Now you will just have to make the best of your life and pray that you find someone of wealth to perhaps marry whether you love her or not.'

'I think I would rather end it all here and now if I have to do that. No, I'll pick myself up and make my way in the world another way. Married life is not for me and well you know it.'

Chapter 25

It was breakfast time at Highfield House, and Eliza and Tom were discussing how things were progressing at the Rose Pit and the problems that the bitter month of January had brought and how they would navigate around them.

'I'm glad I agreed with Stanley Arkwright that he could use the office for the pump house; it's not held him up with the weather being like it is and with not having to build a new building for his machinery. It's made his life a bit awkward as well as mine but it's paying off now. Besides, it has saved us money, and I know I will not always be running the pit from the dark den of the storeroom. A few weeks of hardship is nothing to see the pit eventually show what it is exactly worth. You should come up and see the new machine, Eliza; it's a beast. It even snorts steam like a dragon, all shining in brass and copper. Once it starts pumping out the water, it will be magnificent; I'm sure it will pay for itself within a few months.' Tom smiled across at his new wife and watched as she patted her mouth with her napkin.

'I'm still sorting the house, Tom, but I will come once the pumps are up and running; besides, it is pouring down outside today. February is just as wet as January was snowy. I will be so glad when spring eventually arrives; I hate these winter months. Plus I can't bear to think about how much that pump is costing us; I keep looking at the bills and just hope that all this money being spent is going to be worth it.'

'If you are worrying that the pump is costing money, then don't. I tell you there is coal down there, more coal than there has ever been mined before in the Rose. I've even spoken to William about supplying him with some and his friends with coal for their mills, because I have that much faith in the venture.' Tom rose from his chair and went and put his arm around the most precious thing in his life, and bent down and kissed her gently. 'I know that in truth you are missing Victoria, aren't you? Why don't you go in the carriage and see them both? Go and listen to the gossip, or perhaps have a walk down the arcades; that way you'll keep dry. The house can wait. Besides, to me it looks perfect already; there's nothing more that's needed and the staff are looking after everything.'

'Oh, Tom, in truth, I'm not used to being a lady of leisure. I've nearly finished Mary-Anne's wedding dress, and Victoria's bridesmaid dress is ready for the big day, and after that, I don't know what I'll do to occupy myself. And I do miss Victoria; she's left a gaping hole, which can't be filled.' Eliza admitted. 'I've had enough of sewing, embroidery and compiling scrapbooks with pretty pictures. There must be more to life!'

'All the more reason for you to go out for the day. Go and have tea or something. Come on, share my carriage; you can call in at the pit and then go on and see Mary-Anne and Victoria.'

Tom smiled. The last few weeks had been the happiest of his life; he'd seen good progress happening at the Rose. The pit was working well, despite the disruption from the steam pump being fitted, but more importantly he was enjoying life as a married man. He relished coming home to his loving Eliza and a warm, welcoming household with meals served to him and the fires lit; it was everything a man could wish for.

'I suppose I could; I've been leaving them alone so that they get used to living together as mother and daughter. I bet Mary-Anne is enjoying having Victoria living with her, but she will be finding that she isn't as free as she used to be. It will be doing her good to have responsibilities for once. I'll stop by the Rose for a minute or two and look at this marvellous machine and see what you are all up to.' Eliza looked across at her maid. 'Could you tell Mrs Bailey that I'm not here for lunch today and that this evening's menu looks ideal to me.' Eliza got up from the table and followed Tom into the hallway, both of them taking their coats and umbrellas as they dashed out in the pouring rain to climb into the waiting carriage to take them to the Rose Pit.

'Maybe I should have stayed at home,' Eliza moaned, as the carriage turned the corner into the yard. 'Just look at the rain that's falling. The pit yard will be awash; my skirts will be filthy. '

'I think, my dear, that you will find one or two changes that you might like.' Tom grinned as he opened the carriage door.

Eliza gasped as she stepped out of the carriage into the still pouring rain. 'Oh my Lord, what a difference to the last time I came here before Christmas. The yard is no longer rough soil, you've covered it with stones and the ponies have proper stables at long last, and just look what's happened to the office and pithead.'

'Quick, let us run into the pump shed and look at the engine; you'll be even more impressed. Even I'm surprised at the speed that Arkwright and his team have got on with things.' Tom pulled on Eliza's hand and ran into what used to be the pit's offices, but now it was filled with a monster of a water pump, smelling of oil and gleaming with metal with a full team of Arkwright's men attending to it, tightening and adjusting the new machinery.

'Now then, Tom, Mrs Thackeray; it is good that you both have come to view this beauty.' Stanley Arkwright patted the machine. 'She'll soon be up and running and then you'll wonder how you managed without her when all the levels are drier than ever before and level three has disclosed the seam that both you and I know is there.'

'I hope that you are both right, Mr Arkwright. I can't help but doubt if my investment is perhaps a foolish one,' Eliza replied to the red-faced, down-to-earth man.

'Nay, don't you worry, Mrs Thackeray. Ellershaw also knew there was coal down there, but hadn't the brass nor the means to get at it. Besides, your man here said he saw it when he nearly drowned himself, so it's there all right. Once we've laid the outlet and drainage pipes, we'll set this old lass in motion and then it will only be a matter of a week before we have drained most of the water out and everybody can see for themselves what's down there.' Stanley grinned. 'The weather's not been our best friend at the moment, but it's only rain. It's like water off a duck's back to us, as that's what we deal with. It's a lot better than the snow and frost that was making everything such hard work.'

'Have faith, my love; we will find the coal seam and this machine will be nothing but a boon to us.' Tom squeezed Eliza's hand as she looked worriedly at the pump engine and the pipes leading down to the mine.

'I'm sure it will. It's just I know nothing about water pumps and the likes; I'm more at home with dressmaking and the fineries of life, but at the same time, I hate not to be in control of a situation. This, I fear, is engineer's work, so I will leave it with you and look forward to hearing of our success in the near future.' Eliza walked to the doorway and looked out at the rain that was still pouring. 'I don't think that I'll go into Leeds shopping, but I will visit Mary-Anne and Victoria. It will be good to see them and catch up with affairs. I'll see you tonight, Tom; I'll give your love to them both.' Eliza left both men to go about their work and lifted her skirts up as the groom gave her his hand to help her climb into the carriage.

She looked out around the pithead. A lot of her money had been spent on putting things right already; she only hoped that both Tom and Stanley Arkwright were going to be proved correct and that the steam pump would soon pay for itself and the money already spent.

*

'Am I glad to see you … I was just saying to Victoria that this weather is dismal. First it was snow, and now it doesn't know when to stop raining. I've not bothered to show my face in Leeds for days,' Mary-Anne groaned. 'Plus William is busy; he's been foolish enough to take on George as a manager at his mill over in Wakefield, and all he's doing is moaning about him.'

'George? As a manager?' Eliza exclaimed, as she doffed her coat and hat and sat down next to the fire between Mary-Anne and Victoria. 'I thought that he was too busy living life to the full as a gentleman of leisure to be bothered about a little thing called work!'

'He's lost every penny that he had, but we are not supposed to know,' Victoria butted in, while Mary-Anne gave her a warning glance to be quiet.

'He's what?' Eliza looked at both Mary-Anne and Victoria.

'He's gambled it all away – every ha'penny,' Victoria explained with a sad smile, 'and now he's left with nothing.'

'Shush, Victoria,' Mary-Anne said, gently chastising Victoria, 'we are not supposed to tell anyone, and God help him if his mother ever finds out; she will surely disown him. But at present, she is blissfully ignorant of the fact and is just glad to get her son back into the fold.'

'Oh! That poor woman,' Eliza said, 'and yes, I do genuinely mean it. She might not exactly love you and me, Mary-Anne, but she has had her fair share of tragedy in her life, and still she keeps herself graceful and serene. Are you still going to see her regularly at the gatehouse, Victoria? It must be nice for her to have your company with Grace gone.'

'Yes, I'm going when the weather permits; she's kindness itself to me. Although I have a feeling she sometimes struggles to forget how I came about in this world when she has one of her dark days, as she calls them. Then I just try to be kind and be quiet, and not stay long with her. Though I'm thankful George has gone to live at a house that William has given him in Wakefield, despite his mother's demands that he stay with her. He used to be so charming but now he just seems to feel sorry for himself, despite his advantages in life!' Victoria shook her head and thought about how flattered she had been, receiving George's earlier attention when younger but now realising that she had just been a cover for his weaknesses.

'Listen to you; you'd think that you were as old as us two. You are only a spring chicken yet.' Eliza laughed and looked at her sister. 'Are you enjoying staying with your mother or is she driving you to distraction yet?'

'Eh! Careful, little sister; I was always there for you and looked after you well. I'm doing the same with Victoria and we are both counting the days to my wedding and when we can both live at Levensthorpe.'

'I'm enjoying my time with Mother, but I also miss you, Aunt Eliza. I hope you and Tom are happy together?' Victoria looked across at her aunt, whose care she missed so much. Her mother tried to do her best but her Aunt Eliza seemed to know instinctively what she was thinking and needing without being told.

'Yes, very, but you know you can visit us at any time, don't you?' Eliza felt her heart ache; Victoria had always been more her daughter than Mary-Anne's, and she missed her.

'Yes, I know, and I will; it's just been such bad weather and William sends a carriage at last twice a week for me to see his mother, just to keep her company.' Victoria held back the tears; she wished she was still living with Eliza.

'Your dress for your mother's wedding is finished and I've just a few adjustments to yours, Mary-Anne, and then it will be done too. Both of you are going to look the most beautiful ladies in the district.' Eliza grinned. 'It will be the talk of all the society pages; I can just see it now.'

'Yes, Mama says I can get some ear drops and have my ears pierced for the occasion, now that I am nearly grown.' Victoria looked excited at the prospect of being able to wear ear drops that would shine and sparkle along with her dress.

'Oh, no, Victoria. Ladies do not have their ears pierced; that is not for the like of you. If you want to be part of society,

321

it is better to not look gaudy and common with ear drops in your ears. Mary-Anne, I'm surprised at you even agreeing to the idea; Victoria is to be brought up as a lady.'

'Oh, Eliza, she will still be a lady with or without ear drops. Besides some of the most respectable people in New York society wear ear drops and earrings; she will suit them.' Mary-Anne smiled across at her daughter and noticed the disappointment on her face.

'That's in America, where it seems to me that anything goes. Here men prefer their women to be more demure.' Eliza sighed, her influence over Victoria was not as strong now, but she still felt she had to guide her older sister in Victoria's upbringing. 'They're for common people, Mary-Anne – common people and gypsies!'

'Well, we'll see. It's not worth arguing over now, is it? Perhaps if we wait until you are a little older, Victoria, then you can make your own mind up on the subject, without either mine or your aunt's influence. I'm sure that they will become respectable in time, no matter what your thoughts are, Eliza.' Mary-Anne noted the disappointment on Victoria's face but didn't want to upset her or Eliza. 'We will have plenty of time in the future for ear drops and other things that come and go into fashion. Now, let's have some tea; I'll ring for the maid, and I think a plate of crumpets might not go amiss on a miserable day like today.' She rang the bell for her maid to come and see to their needs, and noted the look of satisfaction on Eliza's face, knowing that she could still influence Mary-Anne on Victoria's upbringing. Eliza needed a child of her own, to give her love and attention to and so she would leave Victoria in her sole care; she was, after all, her daughter.

*

The month was nearly at an end and Tom was anxious that the new pump had so far not extracted a single pint of water out of the pit, let alone the promised gallons. However, Stanley Arkwright had told him that today was the day when the pump would show its worth and that by the end of the day the drainage pipes would be full of the black pit water being drained off into the River Aire a few hundred yards away.

'Right, lad, do you want your lovely wife to be here when we put her into action?' Stanley Arkwright patted his steam pump and looked across at Tom, knowing the next few days of excavations would either make or break him. 'She's ready now for pumping out; we'll see how she copes with that, and then we will rig her up to bring the cage up and down to all levels. If you and I are right, that cage will be up and down like a tart's nightdress if we find this famous seam.' Stanley laughed and then noticed the worry on Tom's face. 'It'll be all right, lad; I've never known it not work before. In a year there will be that much coal stacked up in this yard, you'll not be able to get rid of it fast enough. Have faith in me, lad, I know these parts. Once the water's been drained away, you'll have your coal.'

'I'm sure you will be right, but no, let's start the pump working without Eliza. Once I know for sure what's down there and the strength of the seam, then I'll bring her to see the pump in action. She's spent sleepless nights over this and she'll expect results straight away, if I know her.' Tom watched as Stanley nodded to his right-hand man to start the pump up, the noise of it echoing around the red-brick room it stood in.

'Listen to it purring like a kitten. Now let's go and look. What it's pumping out? I bet there are gallons of water, especially after this month's weather; it's never stopped raining or snowing. Though you might not even need to use it over the summer months once you have got on top of the excess water and found where the spring is that is flooding that bottom level.' Stanley opened the pump room door and stepped out into the pit yard, followed by Tom. The whoops of the miners could be heard all over the yard as the pump started to do its work, the miners gathered around the pithead listening to the water travelling along the pipes being carried out of the mine and into the river.

'It's working, Tom! Bloody hell, it's working!' Fred slapped his best mate on the back and grinned as he stood in awe of the new pumping machine.

'Aye, it seems that it is. Come and walk with us to see what it's pumping out. It should be gushing gallons of water into the Aire if Stanley here is right.' Tom grinned as they set off following the drainage pipes across the yard and out across the scrub land between the pit and the river's bank.

'Lord, just look at that all that water, mucky and black as hell, but at least it's out of the pit. It's fair gushing out; the water level must have dropped already.'

'That's nowt, lad, give it a week and then go down and look for your coal; it'll be the driest and most profitable pit, not to say the safest, in the whole of West Yorkshire.' Stanley slapped Tom on the back as all three men stood on the river's bank and watched as the water from the depths of the pit entered into its swell. The machine age had made its mark on the Rose Pit; there would be no looking back now, especially if there was coal down there for the taking.

*

'Oh, Tom, what is it that can't wait? I need to just add the finishing touches to Mary-Anne's wedding dress today. I've also to write to Aunt Patsy and see if she can attend Mary-Anne's wedding; nobody thought of her for ours, but it's time she was reunited with us both if the address I have is still where they live. There are so many things to do. The wedding is nearly upon us. I can't believe that it has come around so quick. I thought I had ages to finish it off, which I had, so I just don't know what I've been doing with my time. I've been spending too much of it worrying over Victoria, who seems to be growing more like her mother every day – and that blasted steam pump, which you don't seem to have mentioned of late. And did I tell you that, despite me advising against it, she's only gone and had her ears pierced and is now displaying the gaudiest pair of ruby ear drops that I have ever seen. I'm afraid Mary-Anne is a bad influence upon her.'

'It's good that she takes after her mother, and I'm sure a pair of ear drops aren't going to be the end of her; after all, she is soon to become one of the most eligible young ladies in the district. Besides, didn't I notice at Christmas that her newfound friend from Manchester was wearing them, so she's just keeping up with her.' Tom smiled. 'Now, come on; finish your breakfast and come with me to the pit. I've something I need your advice on; it's a bit of a problem and I need your sensible head to sort it for me.' Tom smiled at his worrying wife and watched as she shook her head and looked at him darkly.

'It's that pump, isn't it? It's not working correctly. We are going to be left without a penny to our names, and be a laughing stock in our community. I just knew that things couldn't continue as good as they were.'

Tom smiled. 'Stop fretting, Eliza; it's nothing like that.'

'I don't know what you are about Tom Thackeray.' Eliza scowled as she pushed away her unfinished breakfast plate and went to follow him out to the carriage, pausing only at the hallstand to pick up her hat and shawl that she wore most days.

'No, today put this hat on my dear, and this cape; it's colder than it looks.'

Tom passed Eliza her favourite blue bonnet and her blue plaid cape, and smiled as she put them on, looking at him with questioning eyes.

'You are up to something, Tom Thackeray. What is it?' she quizzed.

'Nothing to worry about, I can assure you. It's just Stanley Arkwright would like to see you for your advice as well, and you need to look your best,' Tom said, as he guided Eliza into the waiting carriage. He'd kept his secret long enough and now it was time to stop his darling wife from worrying. She'd looked a little pale of late and had lost her appetite of a morning through her worry.

The pit miners and their families were all lined up at the pithead of the Rose. Despite the weather, they wanted to show their appreciation to the woman that had given them jobs, saving them from having to depend on charity or worse. The pithead wheel and cage no longer needed to be powered by the pit ponies, steam power replacing the poor hardworking creatures from turning the wheel as they had done for centuries. This was to be the first day that the cage was to be powered by the steam pump as it lowered the men down to their work and, unbeknown to Eliza, she was going to be the first one to push the handle in order for them to do so. But more importantly, the yard was filled with newly hewn coal found from the seam on level three that was now virtually free of water and contained one of the best coal seams that Tom had ever seen. His hunch had paid out, more than he could have ever dreamt of, and now he wanted to celebrate with his wife who had done nothing but worry since he had first suggested that they upgrade the pit that no one else had any faith in.

'What's all this? Why are there so many people at the pit-head, and where did all that coal come from?' Eliza looked around at the women and children and their husbands waiting for her to step out of the carriage.

'They are waiting for you, my love; you are to send the first men down the pit today by use of the steam engine … and the coal, well, that is the first hewing from level three and believe me there is a lot more coal down there than we will ever be able to mine. Our dream has come true, Eliza: the pit is going to be more profitable than we ever dreamt of and it's all ours, my love. It's the safest mine in the district, all thanks to you and your investment.'

'You mean, the pump is now working? I thought when you were coming home looking so tired that there were problems with it and I daren't ask as you seemed not to want to talk about it. While all the time you were having me on. Oh, Tom! Thank heavens for that. I've been worried sick of late.'

She looked out of the carriage and opened the carriage door herself before climbing out and smiling at all the colliers and their wives. 'He didn't tell me why I had to come; I'd no idea that the pump was working. Look at all this coal!' Eliza said aloud.

'God bless you, ma'am,' one of the miner's wives said loudly, and everybody cheered.

'Aye, God bless you,' one of the older pit workers said, as he shook Eliza's hand. 'We'll not let you down. Mr Thackeray is a good boss and you both deserve our support.

The days of Ellershaw's rule have well and truly been put to bed, and now it is time to move forward.'

'Thank you. I know that you depend on the Rose for your livelihoods, just like my family did. I'll try not to ever let you down.' Eliza felt tearful as she looked at the goodwill all around her.

'Now then, don't you cry on me! Come and send this first shift down the shaft in the new cage driven by the steam-powered winch and then, as I said when we set off, Stanley is waiting for you in the pump room. He wants to seek your advice.' Tom grinned at the workforce as they nattered and nudged one another; they knew what was to be revealed to her.

'I have a spare bed if you need it, Tom!' Fred shouted teasingly from the edge of the crowd.

'What does Fred mean by that?' Eliza turned and asked Tom.

'Nothing, nothing … take no notice,' Tom replied with a grin.

'Ah, the mistress and owner of the Rose,' Stanley said. 'Good day, my dear. Now, we thought it was only right that you be the one to send the first shift down in the cage, and your husband here also insisted that I give my old lass here a name.' He caressed the brass boiler. 'She's as good as any wife. So I have done just that and named her. Please do remove this cloth from above this lever to reveal what she is called before you send the men down to their work.'

Stanley smiled as Eliza looked at the pump that was now busy working, making constant noise and doing its job of clearing the bottom level, as well as being able to send and bring men to their work.

Eliza hesitated for a second and then lifted the coal-covered piece of cloth to reveal a shining brass plaque with the inscription *To the memory of Sarah Wild* written on it, in a delicate script. She smiled and then wiped away a tear. 'Thank you. Now people will always remember why this pit had to be fought for, and why people should be treated with respect no matter what their circumstances. My mother would have liked that.'

'Aye, I thought as much. Now, let's get these men to work. Push this lever here, lass, and let's see that pithead wheel turn, and make us all some brass.'

Chapter 26

'I still can't help but worry that you are to marry Mary-Anne; although I have grown to accept her, I can't forget where she comes from, William. Plus, it's so soon after you losing Priscilla, and while I know you love her, she is not right for a man of your status.' Catherine Ellershaw looked at her oldest son dressed in his wedding suit and shook her head. 'Your father was bewitched by her good looks too, and it seems that you are the same. I suspect that this marriage will end in tears, given time.'

'Breathe Mother, she won my heart over many years ago and I should have had the strength of character to admit it, and not have made Priscilla's life hell with my treatment of her. It was always Mary-Anne I loved, but I needed the money and position that marrying Priscilla gave me. Mama, you are not going to convince me to change my mind, no matter how you whinge.' William played with his cufflinks and straightened his cravat while looking in the mirror in the hall, as his mother gave him her final thoughts upon the day's wedding.

'Well, you needn't have made such a big fuss about it; a quiet wedding would have been better all round. You have both been married before, just look at the household staff running around like busy bees getting ready for your wedding breakfast and arriving guests; it must be costing a fortune.' Catherine shook her head as the servants laid the dining-room table with their best silver and crystal, and a maid ran in with a vase full of flowers.

'For the first time I'm spending money on myself; Lord knows everybody else bleeds me dry. And for your information, Mary-Anne has never been married before.'

Catherine stopped in her tracks. 'I thought she had been previously married and that she was called Mary-Anne Vasey because of that.'

'No, she just took John Vasey's name. She let it slip one night when she was the worse for wear, and I chose to forget it, and have never questioned her about it. After all, it is irrelevant; the man is out of her life. I am to be her first husband; that is if we get to the church on time and you stop lecturing me.' William turned around and asked for his mother's arm as he prepared himself to step outside into the carriage to take them to Saint Mary's, the largest church in Leeds.

'I suppose the dig that people are bleeding you dry is aimed at me. Well, I'm sorry, William, but you are my son; you have got a responsibility to look after me, and I can't undo what your father did. Else believe me I would. As for Mary-Anne, I should have known that she never married that man she'd lived with; he would not have had enough money for her. The only good thing about her is her child, Victoria; I find her quite gentle and good company.' Catherine took William's arm and looked up at him. 'I love you – that's why I complain – but I see your mind is set and I'll say no more on the subject. In fact, I'll give you my blessing now and I only hope you are doing what will make you happy now and in the future.' Catherine turned and kissed her son on his cheek.

'Thank you, Mother, that means a great deal to me. I'll always be there for you, so don't you worry that Mary-Anne will get in the way of my duty to you.' William smiled, the day was going to be one of the happiest in his life and this time around he knew he would have no regrets.

*

'Breath in, nearly there.' Eliza pulled on the laces of Mary-Anne's corset and tied them quickly. 'Are you sure you won't faint with them tied that tight? Just look at your waistline. You are not Victoria's age, you know; you can have a more fuller figure now that we are both ladies of certain years.' Eliza stood back and watched as her sister controlled her breathing and got used to the restraint of her new corset.

'I want to look my best. All those people will be looking at me; I don't want them to think that William is marrying a fat pig. Besides, I like my corset this tight; as long as I can bend and sit I'll survive the day.' Mary-Anne cast a critical eye over her reflection in the full-length mirror in the guest bedroom of Highfield Hall. 'I still think I look fat. Just look at my hair; the curls are all in the wrong places, and I'm sure I have a spot coming on my chin.'

'Just be quiet. You are worse than Victoria. The maid is helping her get dressed in her old bedroom, and I can't hear *her* whining. You will look beautiful when you've got this dress on, not that you don't already. Now, put your hands up, or do you want to step into it?' Eliza folded the decadent bridal dress over her arm. The delicate white lace shone with the silver threads of embroidery as they were caught in the early spring light.

'I'll step into it; knowing me I'll only get my arms stuck and tear it if I wriggle into it – pulling it up over my hips is a lot safer.' Mary-Anne watched as her sister laid the dress at her feet so that she could pull it up and slip her hands into the long, lace, scalloped-edge sleeves without any problems. She looked at herself and couldn't quite believe the transformation as Eliza buttoned the delicate cloth-covered buttons all the way up to the top of the high-standing collar.

'I tell you what: William's not going to have any time for undoing all these buttons tonight. I doubt my handiwork will get in the way of his passions.' Eliza smiled over Mary-Anne shoulder at her beautiful sister's reflection. 'You look stunning, Mary-Anne; you are fit to walk on any king's arm, never mind William Ellershaw's.'

'I wish our mother was here to see us both and Victoria; she would have been so proud. Despite William being an

Ellershaw, she'd have grown to like him. He's not like his father in any way, really.' Mary-Anne turned and looked at Eliza. 'Thank you, Eliza; you have done more for me than I could have ever have expected from my little sister. I'll always be in your debt.' She hugged Eliza close and swept a tear away from her cheek as they stood in one another's arms.

'We have both got what we dreamt about all those years back, but we should never forget the pain and anguish that we went through to get here. I hope that you will be happy with William and that you'll take care of Victoria, and make sure that she wants for nothing.' Eliza hugged her sister. 'She is like a daughter to me and I will always be there for her.'

Mary-Anne looked at her sister. 'I hope that you and Tom will soon have a family of your own, my dear Eliza; it's not too late for you both, you know.' Mary-Anne noticed a twinkle in her eye and a wry smile upon Eliza's face, and realised that her words were already ringing true. 'You're not …? Have you been keeping a secret from me?' Mary-Anne grinned and watched as Eliza blushed.

'I have! Tom doesn't even know yet, but I am with child. The doctor confirmed it last week; it's a good job we got married in January as the doctor says the baby's due in August.' Eliza grinned and watched as Mary-Anne laughed.

'So you're not as innocent as you seem, you hussy, you. You've got to tell him soon. Tell him today and then we can both celebrate. I can't believe I'm going to be an aunt. That is the best wedding present you could have possibly given me.' Mary-Anne hugged her sister. 'You don't have to worry about Victoria; William is talking of adopting her, and making her his heir. He visited the solicitor the other day and secured her future. I'm also keeping the house on at Speakers' Corner, so when she is older, if she needs a home of her own, it can be hers. Ma Fletcher would have wanted it that way.'

'Do you think William and you will have children?' Eliza asked with a worried look on her face. 'He's bound to favour his own over Victoria if you do.'

'Perhaps, but to me it doesn't matter so much. I have Victoria and, you know me; I can't bear demanding crying babies. I wouldn't know what to do with them. Don't you worry your head about Victoria; she will always be our priority, even if I do find myself with child.' Mary-Anne held back a tear and then smiled. 'It will be how life falls, and who can see into the future?'

'Oh! Mary-Anne, we have been through so much and now look at us both.' Eliza took Mary-Anne's hand and smiled at the reflection of them both in the mirror. 'What would our mother and father say, do you think? Knowing that we both have everything we ever dreamt of and more besides.'

'They wouldn't believe it, would they? Two lasses from Pit Lane, one the owner and saviour of the Rose, and the other one about to marry William Ellershaw, owner of numerous mills in Yorkshire. We've come a long way, my little sister. We should be proud. So, enough of these reminiscences; today we are going to celebrate. It is my wedding day, and I can't keep the guests waiting. Let's put on my veil and then walk out to the carriages with Victoria and Tom. I'm so glad that he agreed to give me away. He's a good man, is your Tom – a bit steady but just right for you.'

Eliza picked up the delicate Nottingham lace veil and placed it upon Mary-Anne's head, securing it with a band of white silk roses. 'There; you make the perfect bride.' Eliza gasped as Mary-Anne stepped away from behind the mirror and stood in the centre of the bedroom. 'I don't think that I have ever seen one so beautiful.'

'Nor I a bridesmaid. Just look at our Victoria; now she is truly a beauty.' Both sisters' eyes turned to Victoria as she entered the room dressed in her bridesmaid dress of light pink taffeta, which was embroidered with delicate rosebuds and a sprig of soft pink silk rosebuds in her hair.

'We are not a bad trio, are we? Three girls who came from rags, and are now three of the wealthiest ladies of the area.' Mary-Anne smiled. 'My precious daughter and my equally precious sister, let us enjoy this day and look forward to the future. William, I know, will be waiting and I can't wait to meet and greet the guests who have come to celebrate our wedding.'

The bells of Saint Mary's rang out across Leeds, telling everybody of the importance of the wedding taking place within its walls. William stood with George, his best man, at the front of the church, and smiled at the vicar as he checked the time and looked nervous, hoping that the bride was not going to keep him waiting too long. The packed church full of friends and well-wishers whispered to one another as they all waited for Mary-Anne to appear.

Catherine Ellershaw gasped as she saw the woman walking down the aisle towards her. It was no other than her daughter Grace, her beloved Grace.

'It's so good to see you, Grace,' Catherine whispered, and wiped a tear away, once Grace had paid her respects to God. 'I'm glad that you have come to your brother's wedding. I've missed you so much.'

'I couldn't miss William's wedding, now, could I? I'll be staying a few days, if that is all right, Mother? We can catch up with one another after this day is over. I've missed you so much – I'm sorry I didn't make it home for Christmas.' Grace smiled at her mother; she looked tired and older, she should have kept more in touch with her she thought as they both listened to the church organist play with fervour awaiting the appearance of the bride.

'You are here now and that's all that matters. I've missed you too; no matter how many miles are between us, I'm always thinking of you.' As the organist changed tune, the congregation rose, and Mary-Anne and her attendants entered the church, Catherine Ellershaw squeezed her daughter's hand.

William turned around and looked up the aisle at his beautiful bride and held his hand out. He smiled as Mary-Anne walked demurely to his side and took his arm. Passing her bouquet of white roses to Victoria, she concentrated on the man she was about to marry.

'Now, isn't that a bonny sight and hasn't Victoria grown into a beauty,' Aunt Patsy whispered to Eliza. 'I feel under-dressed for such a posh do like this. I should have known it would be a posh affair when we got the invite. I had to work on Mick to persuade him to come, but I had to see one of you married.' She blushed.

'I'm just happy that you are here, Aunt Patsy, and I'm sure Mary-Anne will be equally as pleased. I'm sorry you missed my wedding but I was so glad that I was able to track you down for Mary-Anne's. You are family and fam-ily is important. More important than any pomp or cere-mony,' Eliza whispered. 'And your dress is fine; don't you worry.'

The whole church watched as Mary-Anne and William took their vows, with William gently taking Mary-Anne's hand and placing the plain ring of gold on her delicate finger and kissing her tenderly as the vicar proclaimed them man and wife.

Mary-Anne kissed William back and for once in her life showed her true love in a demure and tender fashion as they walked down the aisle together. She had got her man at long last and it was no longer about money or revenge; it was about love and commitment.

'Aye, doesn't she look like the cat who's got the cream,' Tom whispered to Eliza as he watched his sister-in-law walk out of the ancient church.

'She's every right to; she's got her man and she's won the heart of Victoria.' Eliza wiped her eyes clear of the tears that were falling. 'She might be full of bluff and bluster, but when she sets her heart on something she usually gets it.'

'Now don't you get upset. You've always known that she would see fit to do as she pleased. And, as for Victoria, you should be glad that she's back with her mother; it's where she belongs.' Tom slipped his arm around Eliza and kissed her on her head, seeing that she was in tears. 'We've plenty to do to keep us occupied in the future; we will soon have the busiest pit in Yorkshire and we'll be able to rival William and his wealth.' Tom smiled down at his wife.

'That's not the only thing we are going to be busy with Tom.' Eliza smiled and wiped away her tears. 'We are going to be blessed with a child of our own shortly. A baby to love and nurture of our own, just like I did for Victoria when she was little.'

'Oh, Eliza, that's wonderful news; I'm going to be a father! This fancy do means nowt to me, but the words you have just said mean everything. What more could we ask for? A thriving pit; a good roof over our heads; and now a child of our own.' He grinned around him at the guests following the wedding party out of the church, and then couldn't stop himself from shouting his good news to everyone. 'I'm going to be a father! She's just told me; we are to expect a baby!' He stood in the aisle and beamed as men slapped him on the back with congratulations and their womenfolk smiled at the blushing Eliza.

Hearing Tom's yells, Mary-Anne and William stopped at the church doorway. Mary-Anne turned back and smiled at her sister and shouted to her over the top of the crowd, 'All good things come to those who wait.' She smiled as she took the hands of her new husband and daughter, her eyes shining with tears, before leaving the churchyard.

Eliza lifted her head and looked up to the heavens and whispered, 'Yes, I'm the happiest person alive. I've come from rags to riches and want for nothing more in my life.'

Read more gritty and heartwarming sagas from Gracie Hart

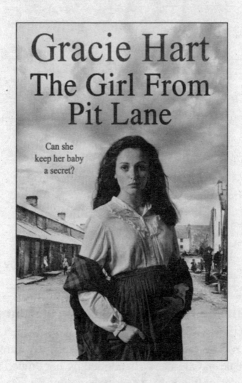

Can two young, coal-miner's daughters survive on their own?

When their mother tragically dies, Mary-Anne and Eliza are left under the care of their drunken step-father. Unable to rely on him, they are determined to stick together. But things are complicated when Mary-Anne, the eldest, falls pregnant with the child of a married mine-owner. Scared and unsure what to do, the sisters try to hide Mary-Anne's pregnancy. But such things cannot stay secret for long …

Can she find somewhere to call home?

Victoria Wild is only four years old but already knows about
heartbreak, having been abandoned by her unwed mother
when she was only a baby. Luckily her Aunt Eliza was there to
take her in but times are still hard on Pit Lane and while Eliza
does her best to make sure there is always food on the table,
Victoria bears the stigma of her illegitimacy. Her aunt also
fears the day when Victoria will start to ask about her father ...

But even when Eliza is offered a chance to make a better life
for herself and her niece, there are sacrifices to be made. And
more trouble is around the corner – in the form of Victoria's
mother, Mary-Anne Wild, who is finally coming home, not to
be a proper mother to her daughter, but to exact her revenge on
the man who ruined her life ...